THE PARROTS

FILIPPO BOLOGNA

THE
PARROTS

Translated from the Italian by
Howard Curtis

PUSHKIN PRESS
LONDON

Pushkin Press
71–75 Shelton Street
London WC2H 9JQ

The Parrots first published in Italian as *I Pappagalli*

This edition first published by Pushkin Press in 2013

ISBN 978 1 908968 19 7

Set in 10 on 13.5 Monotype Baskerville
by Tetragon, London
Printed in Great Britain on Munken Premium Cream 90 gsm
by TJ International Ltd, Padstow, Cornwall

www.pushkinpress.com

CONTENTS

THE PARROTS

He saw all kinds of birds,
among them one that had no arse.

Antonio Pigafetta
Report on the First Voyage around the World

For Arianna,
who flies higher

PART ONE

(Three months to The Ceremony)

I F ONLY MEN looked up at the sky, they would see different things. Not the things they usually see: the blackened asphalt, the yellow leaves, the puddles, the dogshit, the used chewing gum, the unmatched earrings, the coins that only the luckiest can spot.

No, they would see different things.

They would see the cockpits of planes glittering in the sun, clouds frolicking like dolphins in love, treetops swaying in the wind, the sky changing colour, the horizon curving with the turning of the seasons, they would see the first star of the evening and the last of the morning, the lights going on and off on the top floors of the apartment buildings, they would see flower-filled terraces, roofs bristling with antennae, sheets hung out to dry on washing lines.

They would also see a young man standing in pants and T-shirt on the terrace of a small loft on the top floor of a Fascist-era apartment building that had once been working class and was now much coveted by property companies.

He is leaning on the handrail of the terrace and looking down, towards the still-illuminated signs of the petrol stations and the scooters stalking the overcrowded morning buses. If he looked up instead of down, the young man would see a dark unidentified object slowly but inexorably approaching.

Behind him, beyond the large glass door wide open on the dawn, her long black hair spread over the white pillow, his girlfriend is lying asleep on a small, uncomfortable but hypoallergenic double mattress, and inside his girlfriend, someone else is asleep—as it's early days yet, it might be better to say "something" rather than "someone"—something is asleep, something the young man doesn't yet know but will get to know in three months' time.

Hard to say why he's woken up so early: maybe a bad dream, or maybe he's just feeling nervous because it's not long now till The Prize Ceremony.

Don't be deceived by the fact that he's in his pants and T-shirt on a terrace in Rome on this bright spring day. The young man is a writer, a writer at the beginning of his career, so he won't be offended if we call him The Beginner (it's what everyone calls him anyway). That's what he is, because he's written and published just one novel, but one that hit the bullseye. You don't actually have to have read it to know that it's one of those books that will last, one of those once-in-a-lifetime novels, the work of a young man who already seems mature, as the critics have been at pains to point out.

On the other side of the city, almost in open country, some twenty kilometres as the crow flies from the terrace on which we have just left The Beginner, in the house of the caretaker of Prince —'s estate, a full bladder drew the attention of the owner of the body in which it was imprisoned. This owner was a thin, white-haired man who loved—indeed, insisted on—being called The Master, and as we have no objection, that is what we shall call him.

The Master grunted beneath the blankets and groped on the bedside table for the lamp switch. This clumsy gesture only suc-ceeded in causing a tottering pile of books on a little table to fall. The Master finally managed to locate the switch, but the lamp did not come on: the fuse had blown again. One time it had been the alarm clock, another time the hairdryer, another time the electric shaver… When he won The Prize, he would have those dammed kilowatts per hour increased from two to at least six. In fact, if the book did as well as he said it would, with the advance on the next one he would even ask to be connected to the industrial three-phase. And then tumble-driers, air-conditioners, record players, cassette decks, television sets, video recorders, refrigerators, washing machines and dishwashers would all start together, simultaneously, like the elements in a mighty orchestra of domestic appliances playing the last movement of a symphony. But at the moment, with the tiny advance granted by The Small Publisher who brought out his books, all that was as remote as it was unlikely.

What's more, if they had The Master's CAT scan on their desks, no publisher would ever give him a single euro as an advance, regardless of the quality of the book. But all in good time. The priority now is to let a bit of light into the room and allow The Master to pee, because he can't hold it in much longer.

The Master threw his tired legs over the edge of the bed and searched under the bed with his foot, but succeeded only in shifting a few balls of dust. He was looking for his flannel slippers, which always got stuck in the most absurd places, as if they took advantage of the night to walk home, calmly doing without his feet. Unable to find his slippers, The Master placed his cold feet on the floor. He grabbed a dark heap lying on the armchair that had been pushed up against the bed in the hope that it was his dressing gown (it was), put it on (inside out) and stood up. That was what the second of the three finalists for The Prize did.

"Damn and blast!" We can assume that this was the oath uttered by The Master who, in his clumsy move to the arched window, had knocked over the chessboard precariously balanced on the desk.

The Master threw open the blinds and a weak light penetrated his den. That's a bit better now, he thought.

In a manner of speaking. The morning light was dim but there was enough of it for him to contemplate the mess: the chessboard on the floor, the pieces scattered around the room. To the not easily quantifiable intellectual damage—very difficult, if not impossible, to remember the positions in that thrilling endgame—had to be added other possible damage, the alabaster pieces being quite hazardous to his bare feet. The Master's oath was not entirely ascribable to the disaster of the chess pieces. It was also and above all related to the stab of pain at the level of the perineum which this movement had caused him: even though they had taken out the stitches more than a month ago and the scar was now completely healed, it still hurt.

As he went back towards the bed, tacking amid the disorder of his room, The Master tried as best he could to co-ordinate his movements in order to cross a space as yet barely illuminated by the first light of day: crumpled clothes on the armchair, books covering every surface and creating unsafe architectural structures, overflowing ashtrays balanced on the shelves of the bookcase, a pair of chipped Chinese vases, a portrait resting on the floor with the frame gilded and the content so dark and greasy as to make the subject impossible to distinguish, the small electric heater with only one bar working, and the (constantly slow) wall clock marking six something... Wherever he turned his gaze, The Master found something that reminded him that his life up until now—and it was already quite a long life—had not gone as he had expected. Although he was now of an age when he could no longer even remember how he had expected it to go, which actually made him feel him a little better. What he did know was that his discontent encompassed more or less everything. It needs to be said in all honesty: The Master was really disappointed by life. But given what was to happen later, life could have said the same of him.

In the meantime, The Master headed for the bathroom to satisfy the urge that had roused him from his bed, and all at once realized, or recalled—at The Master's age they amounted to pretty much the same thing—that the flushing of the toilet the day before had let him down. He looked disconsolately at the chain hanging uselessly like a bell pull for calling the servants in a house belonging to aristocrats who have been guillotined. He had vowed to call a plumber the next day, which unbeknownst to him had already become today, but in the meantime he needed to find a solution. And fast.

He thought of doing it in the bidet or the sink, then had qualms and told himself that these weren't things a Master did. Fortunately he now saw his slippers, his old flannel slippers as nibbled as a donkey's ears, in a corner of the bathroom, next to the shower, and put them on. Then he pulled his dressing gown around him and went out into the cool of the morning.

Prince —'s estate was bathed in a cold, transparent light. Tall grass besieged the pigeon house: the base for his squadron of homing pigeons—now decimated by illness and by a beech marten that had found a hole in the wire netting—which needed a good clean inside and a coat of paint outside. But not today: afterwards, afterwards.

After The Prize. After the victory. After the glory. When it was all over. Then, a bit of manual work would actually be… relaxing, thought The Master.

He lowered the slack elastic of his pyjamas and at last, in the meadow damp with dew, at the foot of a centuries-old pine, in the bright morning of what had once been open country in Lazio and was now a green island surrounded by concrete, he gave himself up to the sweet relief of urination. The operation lasted an indeterminate length of time, but long enough for The Master to become intoxicated with the alcoholic scent of resin, to feel the morning breeze caress his face sandpapered with beard, and to contemplate the majesty of the age-old pines and oaks that populated Prince —'s estate. Those trees, shrouded in morning birdsong and hidden by the dawn mist, seemed to him magnificent. One in particular filled him with pride, the one he had chosen as the target of his foaming jet. Being a man of letters and not of the jungle, The Master was not to know, first of all that the pine was a cedar, a Lebanese cedar to be precise, and that, to the detriment of its power, it was sick and would soon collapse onto the roof causing considerable damage to the house of the caretaker of Prince —'s estate.

Millions of greenflies, little parasites as big as lice behind the rough bark, were patiently emptying the trunk from inside, reducing it to a sickening mush not unlike sawdust.

By a cruel, subterranean analogy, the same thing was happening in The Master's exhausted body, inside which millions of tumorous cells lurking tenaciously in the prostate—removed, though belatedly—were proliferating in his organism, joining forces in metastases that would soon attack his old bones and reduce them like the cedar on which he was peeing, although rather more quickly.

In any case, that was of no concern to him right now, because the fall of the cedar would happen well after the end of this novel, and unfortunately, well after the end of The Master himself. And this in spite of the encouraging opinion which a well-known urologist would soon be expressing during his check-up—marked down, in his secretary's diary, for that very morning.

Elsewhere, while The Beginner was sweeping the terrace of what remained of his glass door (an event closely related to the dark unidentified object approaching slowly but inexorably) and The Master, unaware that he was entitled to an over-70s card allowing him to travel free on public transport, was punching his ticket on a bus heading to the central area where the well-known urologist had his clinic, a beautiful young woman closed behind her the door of a house in a residential neighbourhood.

Ever since the young woman, who had recently become The Second Wife in front of witnesses and a minister of the Lord after the annulment of The First Marriage by a church tribunal, had resumed work after her pregnancy, that precise moment—ratified by the liberating slam of the reinforced door, the click of heels on the gravel drive and the hum of the twin-cylinder engine of the Fiat 500 as it started up—represented for the man universally referred to in the captions to his photographs as The Writer the most beautiful moment of the day.

Most beautiful because The Writer, the third and last finalist for The Prize, could only write in the morning. Not, however, before observing a whole series of what could be seen either as procedures or as rituals, depending on whether they were viewed from a secular or a religious standpoint.

First of all, then, The Writer went into the bathroom, evacuated his intestines with great satisfaction, then showered and shaved, as he did every day, in order to remain close to an ideal (a fragile one) of (his own) youth. Still in his bathrobe, he went to the big bedroom windows, drew back the curtains and looked out. A radiant spring morning in Rome. The clear sky, the newly pruned hedge—although here and there troublesome clumps broke its evenness—the sonorous noise of tennis balls that reached him as if from the far end of the neighbourhood—who on earth was winning? The Writer sighed, closed the window and drew the curtains in order not to fall into temptation.

After which he got dressed in the kitchen left untouched by The Filipino (who at the moment was not here), emptied into the sink the lukewarm coffee that The Second Wife had left for him with instructions to heat it in the microwave, and prepared a prodigious pot of coffee with all the meticulousness of a bomb disposal expert defusing a device. As he waited for the coffee to rise with a gurgle, The Writer looked through the sheaf of newspapers The Filipino had placed on the kitchen table before disappearing (what on earth had become of him?).

To say that he read them would be an exaggeration. What he did was leaf through them. An oblique, distracted, summary glance at the headlines, then straight to the sports page, and only then to the arts page. He checked if any colleague or journalist had written anything about him or about his latest book, the one which was up for The Prize—they had—and thought about whether he should let it go or reply, thus contravening the first principle that had made him a beloved, successful writer: Never respond. To anybody. Whatever they said. Because the only sure way to hurt a person isn't to talk ill of them (what naïvety!) but not to talk about them at all. If you don't talk about something, it means it never happened. Silence equals death.

From a jug, The Writer poured himself a little orange juice, already oxidized, took a bite of the now cold toast The Filipino had prepared for him (he ought to be dismissed without mercy) and looked at the page, forcing himself to be as detached as possible. In the dead centre of an imaginary triptych which he formed with the other two, there was an old photograph of him, with the copyright of a well-known agency. There he was, near the bottom of the page, younger and bolder than he was now, equipped with an invincible smile, worn jeans and creased shirt, challenging the photographers against the background of a dazzling park: "Well? Is that all you want to know?" he seemed to be saying to the ravenous lenses of the digital cameras. Beneath it, a caption: *Forty-six years old, Writer*. His photograph was mounted between the two others, in a forced iconic cohabitation, which gave him an unpleasant feeling, the kind of discomfort we feel when we are hemmed in by a crowd. The other two photographs captured an old man with unkempt hair and a mean-looking face, and a young man with a ridiculous goatee and an expression of impunity (or was it stupidity?) typical of youth. Even though he knew both of them, the sight of those faces made him nauseous.

That was why The Writer immediately went on to read the article. The author of the piece commented on the "trio"—as the shortlist of finalists was known in the profession—vaguely summarized the three books in contention, and finally speculated wildly on the likely winner of The Prize. The commentator considered the old man, whom in a couple of passages he also called "The Master" (though not without a streak of irony, thought The Writer), to be out of the running, and The Writer to be the favourite. The Writer instinctively put a hand just under the belt of his bathrobe, and took another bite of his cold toast. Like a condor (*Vultur gryphus*) circling over a plateau in search of a moving prey, The Writer skimmed over the rest of the piece, which was just idle chatter, and went straight for the prey, the last sentence, extracting from it a juicy morsel: *"Even though victory seems within reach, the game is far from over: to win The Prize, The Writer will have to watch out for The Beginner..."*

But if The Writer had to watch out for The Beginner, who did The Beginner have to watch out for? That was something the newspaper did not say.

And yet on the terrace of his loft, The Beginner would have had convincing reasons to watch out. Starting with that dark object approaching, an object The Beginner could not see because he was looking down, or at best in front of him.

As he was staring at the digger on the subway construction site, motionless in the brown morning air, his mind was elsewhere. He was thinking about The Prize, about what he would say at the event due to be held in a famous theatre that afternoon, and about other small details, the result of his insecurity and his incurable desire to please. Nevertheless, beyond the galaxy of The Prize, there was something on the ground that captured his attention.

On the crane on the building site, towering over the digger, there sat a large flock of seagulls (*Larus michahellis*), rubbing their wings, creasing their feathers and jamming their gullets between their tail feathers. The Beginner had re-emerged from his thoughts and was now watching them, his curiosity aroused: they seemed to have fallen in line, as if waiting to swear an oath. There must be some kind of logic in their arrangement, but what was it? The biggest and strongest had secured the best places along the arm of the crane, the most sheltered places and the closest to the tower. Those on the end of the arm, on the other hand, the most exposed to the wind, were trying to regain ground, to move up the line, only to be forced back with a lot of pecking as soon as the attempt became more insistent. Until, exasperated and phlegmatic, they would launch themselves into the air, circling around the crane, and after one complete turn find that their places were gone, having been immediately occupied by other seagulls. And so they hung suspended in the air, beating their wings against an imaginary mirror, before again roosting in the few free centimetres at the extremity of the arm. And this merry-go-round went on uninterruptedly, like an impossible quadrille in which the dancers step on each other's feet because the platform is too narrow.

All at once, a shudder ran down the line of seagulls, spreading along the crane's metallic conductor. Their feathers stood upright, their wings opened and the line broke. The seagulls rose in flight and circled the arm, unsure whether to come to rest or leave. Then they flew away, scattering nervously, as if something had disturbed them.

The Beginner felt a shudder at his back. Maybe it's the brisk air of the morning on my bare neck, he thought. Maybe I shouldn't go out on the terrace in my pants, he thought. Maybe I'm getting a fever, he thought.

But no, it was none of these things. It was as if he felt himself being watched by the menacing eyes of a stranger. He sensed a looming presence, the atavistic but indemonstrable certainty that he was not alone on that terrace. A sensation which lately he had already felt at least once.

He inspected the terrace: the rack of dormant jasmine, the stone vases in which lizards took shelter on hot summer nights, the rubber hose coiled in a corner. A slow pan of the buildings surrounding the terrace offered nothing better: closed windows, lowered blinds.

He leant over the railing: the small, faded pedestrian crossing beneath the pines, the pines themselves climbing vertiginously, their tops challenging the roofs of the buildings, not a single passer-by in that measly stretch of street, only a Carabinieri car returning in resignation from a night patrol.

Even though the sensation had become even more distinct and intolerable, The Beginner did not yield to the instinct to turn: there wasn't anybody on the terrace because there couldn't be anybody. So he decided to go back inside.

The question is: as he closed behind him the massive glass door that slid obediently to the end of the runner, and especially as he drew the heavy curtain to stop the light from flooding the room so early, could The Beginner imagine the fearful crash which, in a fraction of a second, would shatter the window into a thousand pieces? No, he couldn't. You can bet on it.

With the house at last empty and silent, The Second Wife trapped in the Fiat 500 as she drove alongside the river, The Baby fast asleep in her room and The Ukrainian Nanny ironing in the linen cupboard beside the screen of the baby monitor so firmly imposed by The Second Wife and equally firmly challenged by him (only two months old and already on video—how can we complain if they end up on Big Brother?), The Writer only had one thing left to do. Something shameful, unforgivable and irrevocable: to write.

The Writer sat down on the ergonomic stool The Second Wife had given him for his birthday (sceptical at first, he had had to think again: it did wonders for his backache), switched on the computer, waited for the smiling face of a baby, which he had chosen as a screensaver, to appear, looked for a particular file with the suffix *.doc* to which every additional word added a nerve-wracking amount of time waiting for the word processor to launch, and double-clicked on it. During that interminable moment it took the application to load the file, so slowly as to make him regret having opened it, the telephone rang at the far end of the living room.

Someone answer it, thought The Writer. Damn, just when the file had opened and he had glimpsed—maybe—a clause to be moved to the next paragraph.

"Someone answer it!" This time the words, which he had previously only thought, emerged from his mouth. But the telephone kept ringing, and nobody had responded to its call.

Anyway, seeing that The Filipino wasn't there and that not even the author of a novel can guarantee that every character will be available at all times, and given that nobody in the whole house was lifting a finger to answer the telephone, which was still ringing, The Writer had no choice but to get up from his desk.

A pity, just when the sentence was on the verge of coming together, first in his brain and a moment later on the keyboard. The telephone rang again, and The Writer approached it. Against the light, the corridor was shiny with wax polish, the surface of the floor looking like asphalt after a nocturnal shower. The telephone rang, and The Writer walked, without speeding up or slowing down, taking care not to slip on the polished floor, as a painful domestic experience had taught him. The telephone rang, and The Writer reached it. The telephone rang, and The Writer lifted the receiver.

"Hello?"

"It's me."

There was only one person in the world who could call and say "it's me" without being The Second Wife. Let alone The First.

"This is your prostate."

"What is?"

To hear this line, you would have to be in the centre of Rome, in the prestigious clinic of an even more prestigious Roman urologist. The Master had answered mechanically. His attention had come to rest on a poster hanging on the wall, just behind The Urologist's armchair.

He couldn't take his eyes off the image, which was surrounded by a plethora of diplomas and testimonials to victorious campaigns around the world. Where had he seen that painting?

"This."

The Urologist pointed with the tip of his pen to a darker area floating in the grey sea of the scan. A kind of lunar crater shaped like a chestnut, a pyramid built on the moon by an alien civilization and recorded by a space probe: his prostate as shown by the ultrasound.

Those eyes, once bright and now watery, had become small and sharp over time after perusing thousands of close-packed lines in cheap editions in the gloom of furnished rooms, but still managed to establish a familiarity with that picture.

It was a reproduction of a painting. At the bottom there was a small semicircular bay, a cove imprisoned between an inlet and a bare, twisted tree. In the centre, a man standing on a rock, his trunk tilted forward, leaning towards the water. Behind him, an elemental horizon and a flake-white sky. From every part of the picture, hundreds of creatures, fish, birds, reptiles, were converging on him, like lines towards the vanishing point in a study on Renaissance perspective. Turtles, crabs, lobsters, a seal or a sea lion—The Master couldn't tell which—even a shark and a hippopotamus, as well as seaweed and plants, all seemed attracted by the man's magnetic force. The animals had come from the depths of the sea, the expanses of land above sea level and the boundless skies to hear his words.

"And this dark patch…"

In the Wien Museum in Karlsplatz. That was where he had seen it. *Vogelpredigt des Hl. Franziskus*: in his mind that caption echoed like the chorus of a song. As a young man, The Master had studied German for a while, not enough to master the might of Germanic philosophy as he had hoped, but sufficient to remember the name of that little painting.

"…is the tumour."

"But didn't you take it out?"

"Of course we took it out. Why else would we have done the operation?"

The Urologist laughed, The Master didn't.

"This is the image of the prostate we removed, and this is the area affected by the carcinoma, do you see?"

The Master could not see. The professor traced a kind of half-moon, making a mark with the cap of the biro on the surface of the image. "In your case a radical prostatectomy was the only solution. The result of the biopsy on the lymph node was negative, which means the tumour probably wasn't invasive. In any case, I'm convinced we caught it in time!"

In time, maybe. But we need to see where we caught it, thought The Master.

"The picture seems reassuring."

"Which picture?"

"What do you mean, which picture? The clinical picture, what else?"

The one The Master was looking at, that was what else. The Master abandoned his prostate, sunk there in the murky backdrop of the scan, and took shelter again in the intense contemplation of that image.

It was a painting by Oskar Laske, a pupil of Otto Wagner, *St Francis Preaching to the Birds*. How envious he felt. Not so much of the painter, who wasn't even all that gifted—too graphic for his taste—but of the saint.

The Master would have liked to read his poems and stories to men and animals, and have them listen admiringly, docile and grateful. Basically, St Francis's sermons were readings *ante litteram*. The birds were the readers, and the wolves the critics. And the cruel wolf of Gubbio that St Francis had single-handedly tamed and made as playful and tail-wagging as a puppy was that critic (the only one) who spoke well of him only because every time one of his books came out The Master wrote to him expressing respect and admiration for his latest literary effort.

"Anyway, look, a cancer of the prostate at your age isn't a rare occurrence, you're not the first and you won't be the last, and there's very effective chemotherapy now which is less stressful for the organism…"

Hypnotized by the painting, The Master felt as if the spaceship of his youth were abducting him in a cone of light and carrying him back in time.

Now the spaceship had taken him to Vienna, a crash landing in the Resselpark, the prostate still in its place, ready to produce all the quantity of seminal liquid that the hypothalamus had requested, with a raging snowstorm beating down on the city, and on his young shoulders.

The snowflakes were whirling about him with such fury that he had felt as if he were being attacked by a swarm of frozen wasps. Floundering in the storm, he had headed straight for the massive building at the far end of the park. Beyond the curtain of snow a light could be glimpsed inside the building. Without knowing what the building was, he had pushed open the door and gone in.

Wooden floors and warmth. Light and silence. A refuge for wayfarers sheltering from the cold? More than anything else, a museum. A deserted museum. Nobody to greet him at the ticket office, nobody in the cloakroom. Hesitant at first, The Master had taken this as a sign of charitable welcome, and pushed on inside, starting to walk through the warm, desolate rooms, still half numbed by the cold, until he had noticed a human presence at the far end of one of the rooms. He had taken off his steamed-up glasses and approached. The human figure had turned out to be a girl, standing motionless in front of a painting. The Master had come up behind her to get a better look at both the girl and the painting.

The painting was *St Francis Preaching to the Birds* by Oskar Laske. The girl was very beautiful. She was staring at the painting as if it were a window wide open on a dream, and she was crying: her cheeks were streaked with big tears.

"…by a study carried out on a number of Asian and African men who had died of other causes, more than 30 per cent of fifty-year-olds given post mortems present signs of a carcinoma in the prostate…"

The Master ignored this bothersome interference and re-established radio contact with the spaceship of memories.

Without a second thought, he had asked her in his laboured German, "Why are you crying?"

"Because St Francis was good," the girl had replied.

"…in eighty-year-olds the figure reaches 70 per cent. In any case, from now on you'll have to undergo regular PSA tests, but I feel moderately optimistic in your case."

When they left the museum, it was still snowing, although less hard. She had put her arm through his as if afraid of getting lost. They had taken shelter in a café near the Naschmarkt, where they had laughed, drunk hot tea and eaten Sachertorte.

"…without a prostate you will encounter a number of small inconveniences…"

Then they had ended up in a pension behind the opera house and made love all night, while outside it had snowed without respite.

"Such as impotence…"

Where did that memory come from? Did the prostate have a memory and was this one of its reminiscences? Why had he never thought of it again until today? Were they his memories or his organ's memories? The Master wondered.

"Are you listening to me?"

The Master left the girl sleeping in the unmade bed in the pension, and nodded at The Urologist.

"I was saying that without a prostate you will encounter a number of inconveniences, such as impotence. But at your age certain appetites are probably…"

The Urologist said this as if he were a priest hearing the dying confession of a whoremonger. The Master looked at him sternly.

"Impotence, and incontinence."

"Am I going to piss in my pants?"

"You see, since the demolition phase of the prostatectomy, the bladder, the distal urethra and the periurethral and perineal muscles have remained intact. Except that we had to reconstruct your urinary tract, establishing communication between the bladder and the remaining urethral segment. This will cause you problems with urination."

The Master got off the spaceship. "Are you saying I'll have to wear incontinence pads?"

"You'll have to undergo rehabilitative treatment to strengthen the muscle fibres and the perineal region."

"Doctor, I'm in the running for a very important prize. There's a strong possibility I'll win it. I can't risk pissing myself onstage."

"It's just a matter of doing some very simple exercises, for instance, interrupting the flow of urine."

"…"

"When you feel the urge, go to the toilet and try to interrupt the flow suddenly… then start again… then interrupt it again, on and off, on and off… like a tap… Treat it like a game."

"…"

"Another very useful exercise worth repeating is this."

The Urologist stood up, walked solemnly to the middle of the room and planted his feet firmly on the floor.

"Back straight, legs open…"

The professor threw his weight onto his thighs, bent his knees and slowly crouched, down, down, down, as if intending to shit on the carpet.

"Then pull yourself up by contracting the perineum."

The Urologist got back into a standing position, although not without a certain effort. A bead of sweat glistened on his tanned forehead. Then he straightened his coat and sat down again.

"Another exercise, which also involves contracting the perineum, is to contract it as much as possible and then…" The Urologist coughed twice, sharply. "Or else blow your nose. All these exercises involve the abdominal muscles. The important thing is to keep up the contraction. Is that clear?"

"Almost. How do I contract the perineum?"

"Clench your buttocks, damn it! Now we really should end there. Oh! Perhaps before you go you'd be so kind as to inscribe something… for my wife, you know, she has all your books."

The fact that she had all of them didn't mean she'd read them, but The Master kept this thought to himself.

The Urologist opened a drawer and took out a book still in its cellophane wrapper, which he proceeded to tear off without any embarrassment.

The book, thought The Master, was like one of those whales that die choked by plastic bags. On the cover was an erotic scene, a detail from a Greek vase. It looked less like a book than a brochure for a guided tour of an Etruscan tomb. And then they complain my books don't sell, thought The Master. Angrily, he grabbed the pen.

"To?"

"I'm sorry?"

"What's your wife's name?"

"Oh, Sara. But, well, actually… it isn't for my wife… Write 'to Alessia', or rather, no, 'to Alessia' sounds wrong, write 'for Alessia'."

So now as well as teaching me how to pee, he also has to teach me how to write, thought The Master.

Behind the trendy glasses, The Urologist's eyes oozed self-satisfaction.

The biro traced a nervous inscription on the title page. As he autographed the copy with a grimace, he was already trying to contract his perineum—or at least to clench his buttocks…

"My secretary will give you an information leaflet summarizing the exercises, along with a measuring cup and a urination diary."

"A measuring cup? And what the hell is a urination diary?"

"It's a diary in which you note down the frequency with which you urinate, and the volume of urine you expel. It's a very useful tool. Please keep it with you at all times and write everything down, symptoms, sensations and so on… Anyway," said The Urologist, "don't worry, you have in front of you… I won't say a bright future, but at least a future. Which isn't to be sniffed at."

He turned a dazzling smile on The Master and held out his hand. The Master shook it without vigour. As he left the consulting room, his steps made no noise on the carpet. It was as if he were floating. Could a man without a prostate actually be lighter? How much did a prostate weigh?

The Master's questions remained unanswered. He paid the secretary for the consultation: two more like this and the advance from The Small Publishing Company would be gone. The secretary handed over the urination diary—a little notebook with a dark cover—and an anonymous-looking plastic measuring cup. Of the two things, he couldn't have said which was the more demeaning. The secretary came to his aid.

"Don't worry, it comes in a bag," she said, inserting the measuring cup into the top of the bag and immediately extracting it again, as if the bag could bite. Suddenly The Master had an idea. Instead of heading for the exit, he turned on his heels. The secretary watched him anxiously, unsure whether or not to intervene. Without knocking, he walked back into the consulting room. The Urologist, who was on the phone, instinctively looked up and covered the receiver with one hand.

"Excuse me for a moment... What is it?"

"Could you give me the scan?"

"What's the matter, missing your prostate?"

There was a fearful thud, and glass showered the room like dew. The Beginner felt tiny fragments of glass frost his bare legs, and a weak current of air filled the room, made the curtains billow and lifted the corners of the tablecloth. Glass everywhere, on the carpet, on the cupboards, in the kitchen sink.

"Darling, where are you?"

The crash had woken The Girlfriend.

"Here."

He gently moved the curtain, then drew it right back.

"Are you all right?"

"Yes."

"What happened?"

He walked barefoot, a fragment of glass lodged in his right foot. He brought the foot up to the height of his left knee, twisting the sole inwards, and extracted the splinter. A small amount of blood came out. He didn't feel any pain, although he probably would later. But first of all, before anything else, there was that dark patch in the middle of the terrace. Whatever it was.

He advanced towards the dark—or rather, black—patch—or rather, mass—in a corner—or rather, in the middle—of the terrace, two metres—or rather, one metre from him, and two from what remained of the pane of glass.

"What was it?"

"…"

A huge black bird lay lifeless on the terrace, its half-open beak looking like a congealed streak of lava, its eyes a cobalt blue, its stiff legs pointing skywards, its wings outspread as if crucified.

"That's disgusting… What is it?"

Standing in the doorway, her breasts pushing against her nightdress, The Girlfriend looked on in horror as The Beginner walked towards the bird. He was silent for a while.

"A parrot."

The police helicopter flew over the ring road around Rome, bestowing its blessing from the sky on a sesquipedalian traffic jam between the Cassia Bis and Flaminia exits. From above, the tailback looked like a steel lizard sleeping in the sun. Among the vehicles caught in the bottleneck, there were two which deserve closer attention.

Neither of the two drivers was in a position to know the reason for the tailback. It was in fact due to a rather delicate operation: the removal by the fire brigade of a nest of white storks (*Ciconia*

ciconia) from a speed camera. The presence of the winged couple had interfered with the sophisticated equipment, which explained why it had recently been malfunctioning, resulting in a large number of fines and an equally large number of appeals.

Now although the drivers of the two cars worthy of closer attention were as unaware of each other as they were of the storks, there was a relationship between them, one that was both coincidental and elective. Not so much because the two of them were listening to the same song on the same radio station, which can happen, but because they were two of the three finalists for the same Prize.

The Writer looked at the woman on the seat beside him. The woman was silent. The Writer raised the volume of the radio:

...y me pintaba las manos y la cara de azul...

...pienso che un sueño parecido no volverá mas...

The Beginner lowered the volume of the radio and looked at the cardboard box on the seat beside him. In the mysterious darkness of the box, something was about to happen.

All this was going in inside these two cars caught up in the traffic jam. The Writer was on his way somewhere, The Beginner was coming back from somewhere. But where?

"To the sea?"

"To the lake."

He had never liked lakes. They had always made him feel really sad, like empty restaurants, cover bands, fifty-year-olds on motorbikes and inflatable swimming pools in gardens. He had only said it for fear of meeting someone who might know him, which would have been quite likely if he had headed for Fregene or Circeo on a fine day like today.

She was passing through the city, or so she had said, and had hired a car.

"Would you like to drive?"

"You drive on the way there. I'll drive on the way back."

She had agreed to this pointless arrangement with a touch of amusement, as if it were one of the games they had played when they were younger. The Writer had wanted her to drive so that he could get a better look at her. If only she'd take off those sunglasses! Then The Writer could read her intentions in her eyes.

How many years had passed since he had last seen those eyes, sometimes as calm and clear as an Alpine lake, sometimes green and sparkling like a beetle's wings?

They had taken the Via Cassia, heading north. As she drove, she occasionally pushed back the blonde hair that kept falling over her face and nervously touched the frames of the big Bakelite glasses that only a diva could have worn with the same nonchalance.

He would have liked to talk, to tell her everything that had happened between the last time they had seen each other and now, but he couldn't concentrate enough to find the words (which may seem strange for a writer, but there it is). And not only because of the inhibition her beauty had always exerted on him, and not even because he did not really know where to start—but rather because something was interfering with his thoughts. And that something was the feeling that he had forgotten something important, as if he had not switched the gas off before leaving home, or had left his car with the headlights on. The food for The Baby? No, that wasn't really a problem, The Filipino would pick it up (talking of whom, was he back yet?).

As they got farther from the city and the landscape became less oppressive, the unpleasant sensation also began to abandon him, as if the origin of the sensation were the city itself, or something undefined but now too distant to harm him. Warehouses gave way to cultivated fields, vineyards and vegetable gardens, villages with curious names, cut in two by the road like watermelons split on market stalls, old men on benches in squares or at the tables of bars looking impassively at the passing lorries.

The car with The Writer and the mystery woman on board was rolling down the Via Cassia on a journey without direction and without time.

This may be the moment to reveal the identity of the mystery woman: she was the great love of The Writer's youth, and for the purposes of her fleeting appearance in this story we shall call her The Old Flame, not so much because she's old, no, that wouldn't be very tactful, but because it's an old story, an affair that once flamed passionately and is now like a lamp with its wick dry.

We can talk freely about her, given that The Second Wife is in her office and can't hear us. She is sitting at her desk, replying to the mountain of e-mails that have accumulated during the night and the early hours of the morning.

Some time later, just before The Second Wife stepped away from her desk for her lunch break, The Writer and The Old Flame were walking beside the lake, which was streaked with silvery light.

They were walking unhurriedly, already drawn into the tranquil lakeside rhythm. They sat down first at the tables of a café, then moved to those of a restaurant, one of the many which, with the somewhat homespun optimism so common in the provinces, had already put tables outside.

They drank house white and ate seafood salad (even though they were at the lake) and fish (even though they were still at the lake) with potatoes.

At last she took off her glasses, and he saw her eyes. They were girlish eyes, just as he remembered them, still bright, but obscured somehow by an invisible veil of sadness, like a pale sun behind a cloud of ash.

"I read your last book," she said. "It was very moving." Then she added, "There's something I have to know."

"Go on."

"I'm the main female character, aren't I?"

The Writer smiled without replying. At the beginning of his

literary career, every time someone close to him saw themselves in one or other of his characters and demanded an explanation, he would give a reply of an aesthetic and literary nature, to the effect that *novels are works of fiction, it's all a process of casting a critical eye on reality, even in an autobiography the narrator doesn't exactly correspond to the author, you always start with a real event and transfigure it through your imagination...* and so on.

Then, as time had passed, he had given up. Not so much because he didn't find such replies satisfactory (although that was part of it, of course), as because the others found them unsatisfactory. The only thing, the ultimate thing that you could do when someone asked a question like that was to say, "Yes. It's you."

Even though this could provoke a quarrel or bring a friendship to an end, it was the only possible reply. The only one capable of satisfying that morbid curiosity, that sordid voyeurism, the only truth that people really wanted to hear. For some unknown but human reason, recognizing themselves in a character in a novel made it possible for them to recognize themselves as individuals in the real world. It was like a literary Eucharist that signified their rebirth, their transition to a new life.

Once, a friend who had recognized himself in a character had phoned him to say he was very angry with him. The Writer had listened patiently to his friend's hasty conclusions and then, instead of rebutting them point by point, had said, "You ought to thank me. Thanks to me you've discovered you exist."

"Well? Is she me or not?"

"Yes. She's you."

"What's that smell?"

"We've got a gorilla under the knife."

"A gorilla?"

"Yes, a gorilla from the zoo. Extraction of a wisdom tooth."

We are now inside a veterinary clinic just outside Rome, where The Beginner knew a young vet who had once come to see The Girlfriend's cat and diagnosed toxoplasmosis.

"I don't have much time, I have to go back into theatre in a while."

"Are you operating?"

"I'm not operating, but I'd like to assist because it's a procedure that doesn't crop up every day."

"I can imagine."

"What did you want to show me?"

The Beginner handed over a huge cardboard box, which had once held a pair of boots The Girlfriend had bought from a shop in the Via Condotti.

The Vet opened the box. "What is it?"

"I was hoping *you'd* tell *me*. That's why I came."

Holding the black parrot by one wing, The Vet took it from the box. The stiff body, the tilted head, the unfolded wing sticking out at an angle of forty-five degrees: in that pose the black parrot looked like a diligent seminarian raising his hand to ask a question. The Vet placed the bird on a metal surface, lit a powerful lamp with a telescopic arm and began to examine it.

"I don't understand… Where did you find this?"

"On my terrace."

"That's impossible. These birds don't live in the wild. It must have escaped from a cage."

"Certainly not mine."

"And how did it die?"

"Forget the post-mortem. What I want to know is, what is it?"

"A parrot."

"Even I can see that. I mean, what kind?"

"I'm no expert on parrots. It could be a macaw or an Amazon, but the colour's really strange, and the size… It may be a genetic anomaly. You should talk to an ornithologist, I have a friend at the Natural History Museum, if you like I can——"

"There's no need, it's not that important."

"Listen, let's do something. Leave it with me. I'll photograph it and e-mail the photos to my friend. Then we'll get rid of it."

"Get rid of what?"

"The body."

"No, no. I'll take it back."

"You know you can't just throw animals in the dustbin."

"I'm not planning to throw it anywhere."

"Oh? What are you planning to do with it, then?"

"Bye."

He was planning to stuff it.

The Master stopped on the pavement and looked up at the apartment block, heedless of the sun and the usual early afternoon traffic. With its faded façade, cracked plaster and chipped window sills, the building exuded an air of listlessness, of exhaustion, as if it were asking only to be demolished, or at the very least abandoned. But The Master did not notice all these details, shielded as he was by the Polaroid lenses of his magnificent glasses, which were held together with adhesive tape. The halls of Roman apartment blocks always smell of fried eggs, rubber and polished brass. Often, as in this case, the lifts are out of order. The Master looked at the stairwell spiralling up into the air like the thread of a bolt. He knew those stairs well, from having so often climbed them, driven on by the promise of victory, and just as often descended them again, dragged down by the gravity of defeat.

And he knew equally well that, if it had not collapsed yet—and this could be said both of him and of the building—this really was his final opportunity to climb to the top floor and win this last prize. Which would actually be the first.

Even though there were not many people in the restaurant, and nobody was paying too much attention to them, even the most distracted of the waiters would have immediately dismissed the hypothesis that The Writer and The Old Flame were husband and wife. The theatrical way she arched her back, the gesture with which she moved her hair away from her forehead, her shrill, childish voice, and the way he kept both filling her glass with white wine and filling the silence with his words were all signs of an invisible grammar that said more than his words ever could.

The Writer nodded distractedly at The Old Flame's account of the failures disguised as successes with which she had dug the grave of all those years during which they had lost touch with one another. A trench filled with the corpses of lovers executed with a karate chop to the back of the neck, wounded friendships and the carcasses of projects left in the rain to rust. The years that separated him from her, as she went on with her stories, now seemed to him like a pontoon bridge about to be swept away by the current of a swollen river.

The Writer looked at The Old Flame: her face, spared the botox that had already devoured half her contemporaries (one, though not the only, reason he had left The First Wife for The Second) was still beautiful, although there was only a trace left of the almost indecent beauty of her youth, like a mark seen through a sheet of paper.

Park in front of a plastic surgery clinic, and take a book to read. Sooner or later you'll see what remains of the woman who drove you mad go in (or come out). That was the Zen concept of revenge The Writer applied to the female body. Whereas he became more interesting the older he got: "mature" according to his young female admirers, "youthful" as his older lovers said.

After lunch The Old Flame wanted to get an ice cream. The Writer, who was more tempted by the thought of taking her to a cheap hotel—partly because he couldn't believe he had come all these kilometres for an ice cream—acceded to her wishes. With ill-concealed annoyance, but he acceded to her wishes. And then what also put paid to The Writer's erection (not even an erection, for now only a kind of intoxicating tingling of the bladder) was the lemon that smelt of detergent and the cone-shaped wrapper, which was why his ice cream ended up in a bin, while The Old Flame finished hers, even saying how good it was, which The Writer found excessive or at the very least irritating, and which put him on guard against the dangers of this woman who had re-emerged from out of the past.

In order not to think about the waste of that morning, The Writer looked at the sheet of water in front of him, shining like the bottom of a steel pot left to dry in the sun. Suddenly, he recalled Latin translations he had done at school. Texts that recounted how, one day thousands of years ago, after a back-breaking journey, two immense armies had confronted one another by that same lake, strangers who had come to fight and die on those tranquil shores.

"Why did you go to Africa?"

"Because I wanted to do something good for people."

"You could have done something good for me. There was no need to go so far."

A pair of herons (*Ardea cinerea*) landed in the middle of a cane thicket like two inexperienced parachutists, stirring The Writer's dark thoughts.

After the ice cream, The Old Flame had suggested with touching candour (or was it deceit?) that they take the little boat that did a circuit of the lake and moored at one of the two small islands. The Writer had agreed, partly because of that half-hearted intention that had crept into his mind—and his pants—and partly out of weakness. And partly, too, because the thought, watered by the wine and fermented by the first sunshine of spring, that he had forgotten something was maturing in the dark cask of his consciousness, and was turning into the clear, bitter feeling that he had left the nest unattended and was now somewhere he shouldn't be, in the company of someone he shouldn't be with.

These thoughts abandoned The Writer when The Old Flame smiled at him and took his arm as the boat left the landing stage, glided smoothly onto the waters, and set sail for a possible adventure.

"Why did you leave me?" said The Writer when The Old Flame placed her head on his shoulder, but he said it so softly that the noise of the propellers and the wind covered his words.

Years before, when The Old Flame had still haunted his heated fantasies, when she had appeared at the most inappropriate moments of the day in the form of an auroral ghost, when her white face had sunk in the deep waters of his dreams like a mermaid, The Writer would have taken advantage of a moment like this to throw her in the lake.

The boat was empty apart from an elderly couple who were sitting in the stern, although inside the cabin for fear of catching cold, but they had got on a lot earlier than The Writer and The Old Flame and didn't seem the slightest bit interested in them.

It would only take a push, the noise would cover the screams, and the temperature of the water would do the rest. Of course, there would be witnesses (waiters and barmen), but he could always counter with his version for the police and the press: we parted after lunch, and that was the last I saw of her. Unfortunately, that version would be sunk by the ticket they had bought at the landing stage: a stupid stub in the bundle of a sleepy ticket-seller would land him in it. It's incredible sometimes how the obtuseness of objects can threaten the most intelligent of minds.

Anyway, alibi apart, there would never be a better moment. Courage certainly wasn't lacking, quite the contrary. What had diminished in all this time, thought The Writer, wasn't his courage, but the motive: so weak now, he couldn't even remember it.

That day The Old Flame had entered the little rented room where he lived, where they made love and studied for their exams and dreamt of growing old together, and, instead of undressing in the most natural way and getting under the blankets, had informed him with disarming candour of her sudden pitiless intention to dump him, The Writer had immediately thought of killing her.

Strangling her, then and there. Throwing himself on her and choking her with his bare hands, pressing his mouth to hers, his lips on hers, squeezing her throat until those big eyes rolled backwards in their sockets like a tortoise on its back. Obviously he hadn't done it. He had merely begged to see her again, lain in wait for her, rung her bell at night and talked to her through the entryphone. But the thought of killing her, as a final clarification, a miracle cure for that incurable pain, had never completely abandoned him.

The only thing that had lightened the nights of sobbing on those pillows still imbued with the smell of her hair, beneath the same sheets that had wrapped her scented body, was to think about the various ways in which he could kill her. Because he could not accept the idea that others apart from him could enjoy her—he was aware that it was a childish thought, and for that very reason an innocent one—which had initiated him into a kind of dionysiac priesthood of bodies.

Among the various ways in which he had imagined her dead after she had so inexplicably abandoned him, some images had imposed themselves more strongly than others.

In the dead of night, The Writer, eyes wide open, flew up through the worm-eaten beams of his room, took the roof off her building and flew into her bedroom, where he found The Old

Flame's corpse waiting: someone had already done his dirty work for him. Then he imagined wrapping her naked and still-warm body in a soft Persian rug he saw displayed every day in a shop window on the way from his house to the faculty. As if obeying an ancient ritual, he would wash her in a tub of hot water with a bar of herbal soap, the expensive kind she liked so much, which smelt of sandalwood, musk or cypress, then he would dry her, brush her hair, put a flower behind her ear and give her a last kiss on her cold lips, before wrapping her in a shroud. Only then, like an unscrupulous antiquarian or a seasoned grave-robber on a rainy winter night, would he would load her in the boot of his car and, driving carefully and smoothly, take her to paradise, because that was where she deserved to be, seeing that she had died so young and beautiful.

At other times, he had only managed to get to sleep at dawn, exhausted, cradled by another terrible image: The Old Flame's saponified corpse floating just under the surface of the water, her hair spread like golden seaweed, the Botticellian features of the face, her mouth open in a smile of benediction—deep down, she forgave him—and her eyes, those wonderful eyes staring up at the sky, as if waiting to commence her ascension into heaven.

But now that The Old Flame had come back to him, having passed through all those years and all those feelings unscathed, wrapped in a beauty too tragic to still be convincing, now that she was squeezing his arm in a nervous grip in the stern of this flat-bottomed boat and tilting her head as a sign of forgiveness, now that he had the strength and clear-headedness to bring that long-imagined plan to fruition, The Writer became aware of something really tragic: he no longer felt anything for The Old Flame.

There had been a time when he had experienced that story in a heroic way, like a stylite stuck up on the high column of pain, indifferent to time, exposed to the rain and wind of love. But now?

Everything had changed. He did not love her, nor did he hate her. He did not even want her, as he had at the beginning of that strange morning. What was she to him, now? A fragile legend, a decapitated Venus. That was what she was. An elegant way to say that she had become—simply, odiously and irredeemably—of no more interest to him than the rest of the human race.

In Rome strange things happen that can only be explained by the fact that they are strange and happen in Rome.

Among the many, some had struck the imagination of The Beginner as soon as he arrived in the capital.

The flower-sellers for example. An excessive number of flower-sellers. Flower-sellers in the streets, in the squares, at traffic junctions, on street corners, flower-sellers outside schools, barracks and hospitals. Every damned day, at all hours of the day, in all weathers and all seasons, with their plastic buckets beneath the spouts of the fountains, the flower-sellers were there.

One flower-seller for every person in love in the city, The Beginner had thought the first time he had noticed that unusual presence.

There are flowers for leaving people and flowers for winning their hearts, flowers for seduction and flowers for betrayal, flowers for lying and flowers for swearing, flowers for birth and flowers for death. There are flowers, and above all flower-sellers, for every state of mind of every inhabitant of Rome. Every Roman has his own personal flower-seller, ready to rescue him at those moments in life when he finds himself powerless to deal with the amazing meaninglessness of existence, stunned, dazed, without ideas or words, his head as empty as a vase, which can only be filled with equally stupid and senseless flowers. Pointless, wonderful, scented tributes to human frailty.

But the strangest of all the things that happened in Rome was something else: moped chains without mopeds. Sheathed in coloured rubber tubes, tied to posts, to traffic lights, to bus shelters, to traffic islands, bolted to the bars of gates or basements, with the links intact and the padlocks closed, in defiance of the laws of theft. Every time The Beginner saw one, he couldn't help wondering *how it had ended up there*, imagining the events that had led up to its being there, events of which the chain represented nothing other than the obscure seal. Maybe the thief had opened the chain without forcing the padlock. But how? With a hairpin like you see in spy films? Or with one of those tools that only thieves and panel-beaters use? Or maybe, more simply, he had the keys. But if so, how did he get hold of them? What if it was the actual owner of the moped who had stolen it? But did it make any sense to steal your own moped? And besides, even if you could get past these logical obstacles, you had to assume that after opening the padlock and stealing the moped the thief had taken care to turn back and lock everything up again. All of which implied a great deal of time at his disposal, combined with a remarkable degree of self-control and a fanatical love of order that was positively anal.

So much for the chains. Then there were the mopeds themselves. Abandoned at the sides of the street, and gradually cannibalized, as if invisible mice or mechanical bacteria picked the bodywork clean at night, starting with the softest parts, first the saddles with their foam-rubber fillings, the plastic chain guards, the rubbery wire casings, then the more difficult Plexiglas windscreens, the tough indicator fairings, the indigestible Bakelite rear-view mirrors, until the mopeds had been reduced to sinister skeleton-like frames.

Something else apparently inexplicable, which also happened in Rome, and at that precise moment, was that the shoe box on the seat beside the driver's seat of The Beginner's car was moving.

Or rather, that something inside it was moving, and as we know that what was inside was the corpse of a black parrot, that could only mean two things: one, that the parrot wasn't dead, and two, that it was alive.

When the box jumped, The Beginner, who had been planning to consult the Yellow Pages in search of a good taxidermist as soon as he got home, took fright, skidded, got back on the carriageway—provoking in a motorcyclist a fervent and moving invocation of the dead people in his family—pulled over and cautiously opened the box. From under the lid, electric eyes were staring at him with a look of hatred.

The Beginner came out of the shower and stared at his own naked body in the mirror. The down that climbed like ivy up his abdomen from his pubes and sprouted on his chest, the swollen belly, like that of a drowned man or of Christ being taken down from the cross, or like the ascitic fluid that accumulates in the abdomen in the sick or the cirrhotic: he wasn't looking well. Lately, because of The Prize and the official duties it involved, he had had to put up with an exhausting number of events and presentations which, when they were over and everyone could relax, always ended in cocktails. Almost a month had passed like that, a whole month during which The Beginner had eaten out almost every night, a month during which he had never gone down to the supermarket to do his shopping. He would return home with aching feet, his head heavy with chatter and wine, ears humming with the rumble of stupid questions and the clinking of glasses and plates. He would take off his shoes, unbutton his shirt and instinctively go to the fridge, open the door in search of a drink to cure (or feed) his headache and contemplate that illuminated space: half a lemon floating in a sidereal void, as if part of a conceptual art installation. Before closing the door, attracted by that moist emptiness, he would stand there for seconds on end listening to the hypnotic hum of the refrigerant in the coils of the machine. This—he was almost convinced—must be the closest thing to the noise of an intelligence at work. If there had ever been such a thing as the sound of writing, an inner, metaphysical sound, it absolutely had to be just like the sound of his refrigerator, so different from the vulgar pounding of a keyboard.

For reasons that could not easily be verbalized, he felt that his fridge had strong analogies with a cool kind of writing currently fashionable, especially among young authors. When he was a bit clearer about the concept, he would write a nice essay about it and send it to one of those literary blogs where all the losers who can't get their books onto bookshelves badmouth each other and which are the equivalent of a soya beefsteak for a carnivore forced to subsist on a vegetarian diet.

It was especially in the mirrors of fitting rooms, the photographs on documents, and in shop windows that he saw how old he had grown. There were even a few white hairs in his beard, although at the moment they were confined to the chin and sideburns.

And yet The Beginner, in spite of that swollen belly, and those timid white hairs in his beard, in spite of the fact that even The Girlfriend had reprimanded him in a recent quarrel ("You've changed"), didn't feel as if he had changed. Since the publication of his book, something had certainly happened to him, and not just to his physical appearance. But he wouldn't call it a change—no, more like an evolution. That was it, he felt a better man, a reptile about to slough off its skin: soon he would be free of his old skin and its hindrance, and would be equipped with a bright, shiny shell of certainties, harder and tougher new scales that would protect him from even the most fearsome predators.

The Beginner came out of the bathroom in his dressing gown and looked at the parrot in his cage in the middle of the room.

On the way back home, having overcome his fright at that unexpected resurrection, The Beginner had seriously considered the idea—an idea he had not yet entirely ruled out—of throwing the box in a dustbin.

But something had held him back from doing so, and it wasn't so much public-spiritedness or sensitivity about recycling as a kind of respect for the dead, or rather, a solidarity with the risen: it must be extremely tedious to go back to hell. So he had decided to stop at a pet shop he knew from having once looked for new toys for The Girlfriend's cat there, before the moggy had found an effective antidote to boredom beneath the tyres of a speeding vehicle.

An assistant had hastened to satisfy the customer and his extravagant requests.

"What's your parrot like?"

"It isn't mine."

"All right but… I mean, what kind of parrot is it? Big, small…"

"Big."

"Is it a cockatoo? An Amazon? A grey? A macaw? A parakeet?"

"Maybe."

"Maybe what? Which of those?"

"I don't know. All of them. Give me the most expensive cage you have."

He had chosen a big cage, the biggest they had in the shop. The assistant had even gone down to the basement storeroom to fetch it, and had re-emerged with a huge cage, almost an aviary: it had taken the two of them to load it on the roof rack of the car. The Beginner had also bought a perch, an expensive manual on the raising and care of parrots, and two food troughs. Now he had to figure out what to put in the food troughs.

"Mostly they eat seeds, but there are species that also eat vegetables. If you were just able to tell me more precisely what kind of parrot it is…"

"Seeds and vegetables. Mine eats everything."

He had bought a basic feed, thinking that he could easily

supplement the parrot's diet with fruit and vegetables (The Girlfriend was a vegetarian, and there was never any lack of greens in their apartment).

So that was why the same cage that had crossed the centre of Rome on the roof of The Beginner's car now hung in the middle of the room, abnormal in comparison with the dimensions of the little apartment.

Cautiously, The Beginner approached the cage. The bird was no longer looking at him with hatred, but had assumed a tough-guy look, like a terrorist ready to blow himself up with everyone in the building rather than reveal where he has planted the bomb.

The seeds in the food trough and the water in the bowl were untouched. The bird seemed stiff and distant, as if stuffed. The Beginner distinctly heard the creaking of the old lift and recognized The Girlfriend's energetic steps on the final flight of stairs. The key turned in the lock. The door opened.

"…"

"Hi, darling."

"What is this? A joke?"

"No, a present."

According to an unwritten code, those competing for The Prize were not supposed to put in an appearance at The Academy before The Ceremony, a simple hygienic measure designed to guarantee the transparency of the voting and let the machinery of The Prize proceed calmly and correctly. The Master was perfectly well aware of this. But he was also aware that he wouldn't get another chance.

He rang, and as soon as someone came to open up he crossed the threshold of The Academy with his head down, like those who enter an underground train without waiting for the others to get off. The intern who was working there stammered something, but was pushed back by the weight of this old dehorned bull. The Master was at home, he knew the labyrinthine layout of the apartment by heart. The corridors lined with books, the drawing rooms wallpapered with books, the bedrooms covered with books, even the toilet was tiled with books: every hallway, every chapel of this dilapidated apartment which was now the offices of The Academy was filled with books, which had accumulated over the years like files in the basement of a Roman courthouse.

The ladies who every year dragged themselves up to the top floor didn't know. The critics didn't know. The journalists didn't know. The writers didn't know. Even The Master, who had lived long enough to know—or to think that he knew—everything there was to know, didn't know. Know, that is, how many books could still be crammed in.

It depends on the materials and the construction techniques, but generally the average weight a floor is able to bear is about 200 kilograms per square metre, which is calculated by gradually filling water mattresses or by using hydraulic jacks. What weight were the floors of The Academy able to bear? What was the maximum load per square metre? Hard to say.

How many plates can a waiter carry without dropping them? How many betrayals can a wife take before she walks out? How many kilometres can a car engine go before it gives up the ghost? How do you recognize the snowflake that will cause the branch to snap?

And what is the title—and how many pages does it have—of the book that will make the floors of The Academy collapse?

"Are you writing?"

This is the only question never to ask a writer. Even though the question may seem relevant, his activity is private and not public. Which is why the answer will inevitably have to be evasive, like the answer to such indiscreet questions as: Do you pay your taxes? Or: Are you faithful? Besides, the question is partly tautological and partly voyeuristic, analogous in a way to asking an adolescent if he masturbates. If on the one hand it's quite likely that he does, on the other it's difficult to obtain an explicit confession, and even if you were able to obtain it, would it be sincere? You would have to know if he does it frequently, how satisfied he feels, or how guilty.

"Are you writing?"

This question, uttered for the second time without receiving an answer, had come from the attentive and delightfully flighty young woman who was handling publicity for The Beginner's book. The Beginner replied with a vague tilt of the head and puffed again at his cigarette while waiting for the event to begin.

It is generally believed that nicotine helps concentration and relaxes nerves and muscles. That is why restless young men smoke as they wait to become men while their wives are in the delivery room, why tormented students flush away their cigarette butts in the university toilets before they sit down in front of the examining board, why unhappy women smoke after making love with married men. So was it for one of these reasons that The Beginner was smoking before going up on stage? No. It was for another reason. He was smoking to think, or rather, to remember. Apparently nicotine helps the memory. Apparently.

The Beginner was trying to remember something situated a little way back along the straight line of his life, something that had happened when the Italian Cultural Institute had invited him to London to present his book, which had recently, and perhaps undeservedly, been published in Great Britain.

Among the first memories he recovered was one of himself on the plane, sitting in economy class, watching the stewardess mime that idiotic procedure about emergency exits—as if at the crucial moment you were really in a fit state to keep a steady nerve and follow the instructions. But that wasn't the memory he was trying to focus on. At last the smoke of memory dissipated and he saw himself out in the street, a street in London.

It was when he was in that street, doing something he shouldn't have been doing, that he had felt that unpleasant sensation for the first time, that sense that he was being followed, spied on, as if someone were scrutinizing him through a periscope sticking up from a manhole or in an enemy satellite in orbit above his head. It was the same damned sensation he had felt on the terrace before the aerial attack from the parrot.

How does it feel to be successful? Not an easy question. The Beginner signing copies couldn't have said, and The Master cursing the defective boiler or waiting in the rain for the 246 bus that was late arriving might have been able to say how it felt *not* to be successful.

If you're looking for the right man to answer your question, there he is, wrapped in his raincoat, which is swelling in the breeze like a fish's gills in a current. Without giving any explanation, he has just left the car in the forecourt of the car hire company with the keys in the instrument panel, crossed the parking area with long strides, walked for a while by the side of the road and hailed a passing taxi with a confident, relaxed gesture, which only ever happens in American films. But not in Rome. Where taxis never stop. Never.

"There's Rome for you," the taxi driver had said, indicating a car that was trying to go the wrong way down a busy street in order to avoid the electronic traffic surveillance system that guards the historic centre. And he had said it only to draw the passenger into the spider's web of a conversation riddled with deadly clichés. But The Writer had immediately understood what kind of taxi driver he was dealing with: the kind who transforms a ride around the block into a political rally. That was why he had remained taciturn, resolute in his silence: he had sensed the trap and had no intention of falling into it. All the driver could do was weigh him up—anyone who doesn't speak always instils fear—with suspicious glances in the rear-view mirror.

And it wasn't clear from those glances whether or not the taxi driver had recognized The Writer. He might have, given that The Writer was one of the few writers whose countenance was well known even to those normally unversed in such matters, perhaps because he was constantly being talked about in the newspapers, or more likely because of that successful TV programme he had presented years earlier, when he was still surfing the foamy crest of his world-beating debut. The driver was still staring at him, unsure whether or not the buttocks of a famous person were resting on the back seat of his Zara 6. Once he had won The Prize, such confusion would be a thing of the past. Taxi drivers would open their doors to him with a smile and shake his hand before letting him out, honoured to have had him in their cabs.

But for the moment, it wasn't so much a famous man as a pensive man who was framed in the narrow concave surface of the little mirror as he looked distractedly out of the window. He was looking at the traffic police taking away a car, Japanese girls laden with designer bags, barmen in black aprons coming out of bars, double-parked delivery vans, but only looking. What he was thinking about was what he had done to The Old Flame. He had not thrown her in the treacherous waters of the lake, or pushed her between the jaws of the propellers while the roofs and bell towers on the coast shrank as far as the eye could see. He had not kissed her, he had not raped her (there had been a moment in which he had thought about that), and he had not slapped her and left the mark of his five fingers on those innocent cheeks. He had done worse. To return for a moment to the fatal question,

58

if our hypothetical journalist trying to retrace their extramural excursion had ended his report by asking, "How does it feel to be successful?" The Writer would have been able to reply with an example. He would have paused for a long time, then explained solemnly that, for example, owning a private island might be something that would approximate fairly closely to the concept of being successful. Actually, he would gloss, owning a private island surrounded by sea means being successful, while owing a private island surrounded by a lake means being successful but not quite so much, a local, circumscribed success. Besides, not all Italian authors were as successful as he was in having their books available on the foreign market.

But to go back to the islands of the lake, we have said that one of the two was private, the other not. Which is why, the private one not being The Writer's—successful as he was, he wasn't quite that successful yet—it's worth focusing on the other one and on what happened there.

On that island, there was a Renaissance villa that was open to visitors. Once they had landed, The Old Flame considered this a romantic and inevitable destination. The Writer had consented: even though he already knew things would end badly, he still wanted to know how.

"Come on, let's go up!"

The Old Flame insisted on wanting to go up and visit the villa. So her childlike enthusiasm had not abandoned her, that generalized, irritating awe at things. She could go into ecstasies over a pebble in a river, a mediocre romantic comedy or a flock of sheep beyond the guard rail on the motorway. Her enthusiasm, in short, was always on the hunt for pretexts to manifest itself.

And The Writer hated that because, deep down, he rather envied her, being someone who never got enthusiastic about anything. He had tried, but he just couldn't. And as if that wasn't enough, apart from enthusiasm, he had also lost interest, wonder, indignation. He wasn't interested in the decay of political life, didn't become embittered about the widespread corruption, wasn't offended by the vulgarity of public taste or the morbidity of crime reporting, any more than he was offended by the duplicity of friends or the predictability of lovers. Not because there weren't things around that were worthy of admiration or disgust. The things were all there, in their place. It was he who wasn't in his. As time had passed, it was if he had become blind to the world. He was aware of noises, he sensed movements, variations of light and colour: something was definitely happening behind that plasterboard wall that separated him from reality. Saying what it was, though, was difficult, because whatever it was, it was something that didn't concern him. The Writer was *inside*, immersed in a liquid, shadowy sleep, the kind in which he imagined people in comas floated, as if wrapped in an enormous placenta through which he was vaguely aware of the unknowable territory *outside*. And yet, at the end of that dark tunnel, there was something. A golden glare, a silvery shimmer, a burst of blue flame that illuminated the cave of his existence for a moment: winning The Prize. That victory was light for his dull eyes, oxygen for the blocked pores of his skin. He half closed his eyes and saw the plaque and the cheque being handed to him, heard the thunderous applause, the popping of corks, the clink of glasses, buried his nose in the inky pages of the reprint, carefully ran his finger along the sharp edge of the wrap-around band, looked at the newspaper headlines and shielded himself from the grapeshot of the photographers' flashes...

But these glorious thoughts crumbled like snow in the palm of a hot hand, and his bad humour grew on the glacier of his consciousness like an avalanche, became heavy and massive and rolled downhill threateningly.

"Shall we go up?"

The Old Flame had stopped outside the entrance to the

Renaissance villa, which had once been used as a shooting lodge by an old local family.

So now you want to go up. Why didn't you want to go up that day twenty-five years ago? Old as it was, that humiliation still stung, as if The Writer had rubbed his face with an excessively alcoholic aftershave.

"It's best if you don't go up."

With these words, so many years earlier, The Old Flame had stopped him from going up to her apartment to meet her parents. The Writer had prepared well, had gone over in his mind the words he would say, had tried out the best smile in his arsenal and suppressed his own embarrassment: the woman meant too much to him, and so did this meeting. But just outside the front door she had suddenly changed her mind. He had insisted, but she had been so cold and resolute as to brook no argument. Putting off that encounter could mean only two things: either she didn't think he was ready, or she didn't consider theirs an important enough relationship to involve the families. But if that was how things were, why had she come to his parents'? To create a diabolical asymmetry, to gain a moral credit with which to keep him in check for ever?

The Writer had emerged devastated. In a few seconds, he had been crushed beneath the weight of imaginary, immovable guilt feelings, and a resurgent sense of inadequacy had taken possession of him. The Old Flame had noticed it, and in order to compensate him had taken him down to the cellar. She had taken him by the hand like an air hostess guiding a lost child in a terminal, and had led him down to a typical city cellar, a claustrophobic space lit by fluorescent lights, into which not even a serial killer would gladly descend. Once there, as if they were staging the reconstruction of a rape for a drama documentary, surrounded by the smell of deflated tyres, yellowed paper and kerosene, she had dropped her jeans down to her calves and had let him take

61

her standing up against the wall of the room. At the height of her orgasm, he had put a hand over her mouth to prevent the sound of her pleasure spreading through the unreal emptiness of that icy cellar.

Letting him have sex with her had been much less of a bother than taking him up to her apartment and introducing him to her parents.

It's too late to go up, The Writer had thought. From now on, the only way is down.

From the moment they had met in a bar, and he had thought he had caught in her a naturalness that betrayed nervousness, to a few moments later, at the car hire company, when she had fiddled with her handbag, looking for her licence, feigning an abnormal nonchalance, because it was neither normal, nor appropriate, to be with him in a car hire office at that hour of the morning, especially after so many years of silence and mutual incomprehension, The Writer had realized that he had been wrong to accept her invitation. And he had also realized that his day—looking at it optimistically—or his life—looking at it pessimistically—would somehow be ruined. And it wasn't just the excessive expenditure of ill humour that the extramural excursion with The Old Flame had already cost him, there was also the interest to be added: the unease that had been with him ever since he had closed his house door behind him, the unpleasant feeling that he had forgotten something, something important, not crucial, but important. And putting his hands in the pockets of his raincoat to pay the taxi driver and feeling how light and empty his pockets were, he at last realized what it was: his mobile.

"The President isn't here…"

"He's busy!"

The intern, urged on by a secretary with a hooked nose, had tried to repel The Master's attack on the heart of The Academy: The President's office. But with the determination and consummate cunning of a veteran, The Master had faked a retreat to his right, but then suddenly changed trajectory, charging straight down the centre of the room towards the door of The President's office. By the time the intern and the secretary had thrown themselves at him and tried to tackle him, it was too late: The Master was already inside.

The President looked at him as you might look at a neighbour who comes down late at night in his pyjamas to complain about the racket you're making in your apartment, where you're having a party. Then he cast a glance pregnant with reproach at the secretary and the intern, and with a nod of his head indicated to them that they could leave him alone with the old goat: he had known him for ages, in one way or another, he would manage. The door closed behind them.

"What do you want? You shouldn't be here!"

The Master dropped his threadbare shoulder bag on the chair.

"Did you meet anyone on your way here?"

The Master shook his battered head.

"You know competitors aren't supposed to come to The Academy."

The Master did not pay too much attention to what The President—an old comrade from avant-garde days evicted from the tables of taverns and welcomed as President in drawing rooms—was saying. He was too busy to search in his leather bag, so he simply tipped out the contents on The President's desk. In order: a bunch of keys, a gas bill, a slip to pick up a jacket from the dry cleaner's, the urination diary, a poetry booklet that had arrived by post, a bill from Glauco's restaurant, a diary from the previous year, a not very original postcard with a view of Nice and the words "Greetings from Nice" (without signature), and finally, what he was looking for.

"What's that?"

The Master waved the accused object in front of The President's nose. "Look."

The President looked, but saw only a faded black-and-white image that could have been a frame taken from stock footage of the moon landings.

"What is it?"

"A scan."

"Male or female?"

"It's a tumour of the prostate."

The Master violently tore the scan from his hand.

"I'm sorry."

"Is that all you can say?"

"What am I supposed to say?"

"You really don't understand, do you?"

"What's there to understand about a tumour?"

"There won't be any more prizes for me."

"Don't say that."

"This year is the last."

"Maybe they can operate."

"They already have."

"But with chemo today—"

"Two months, three maximum. They've told me it's incurable."

The Master put the fingerprint-smeared scan back in the pocket of his wallet, rested his chin on his chest and started crying.

"Come on, don't get too down."

The President stood up and put a hand on his shoulder, more for good luck than out of compassion, as we do when we catch ourselves touching coffins at a wake.

"If there's anything I can do... I know everyone in Rome, if you need a bed in a clinic."

"No, no, forget about clinics. But there is something you could do for me."

"…?"

"Listen, I deserve it."

"No, not that. You can't ask me that."

"Oh, yes, I can. If there's one person in this country who deserves to win this Prize it's me."

"What do you mean?"

"I was with the avant-garde when everyone was with tradition, I came back to tradition when everyone was with the avant-garde. I've always turned my back on the big publishers, even though they all wanted me!"

"Don't raise your voice!"

"I'm in all the anthologies, the critics have written pages and pages about me, I was a finalist for the *Non expedit* internazionale prize…"

"I told you not to raise your voice!"

"Third place in the Marchesa Maironi Memorial, an onyx vase for my last collection… a silver arrow for best Latin composition…"

"Calm down!"

"I've deserved goblets, plaques, cheques, reissues…"

"You should be grateful you're a finalist, considering what an awful book you wrote."

"How dare you? *My last book is a masterpiece!* Do you even read the books or do you just give them prizes? Did you read last year's winner? You handed over the prize in your fat hands, did you actually read it?"

"Get out!"

The sun had gone down but the light still hung over the city like a promise of eternal life. The Writer rode up to the gate of the residential neighbourhood where he lived. The interior of the porter's lodge was soiled by the purple light from the TV set. The porter took his gaze away from the set, saw The Writer, pressed a button to open the automatic gate, gave him a distracted wave and went back to his programme.

Although it was late, and although he was devoured with anguish at having left his mobile at home, The Writer, like a repentant peeping Tom drawn back to his old vice despite himself, could not help stopping outside the window of the lodge. The porter did not notice his presence: he was too absorbed in the TV programme. He was watching a Lombrosian quiz in which contestants had to guess people's professions from their physical appearance and from a few clues supplied by the presenter. As the director lingered over some of the faces—the audience, the presenter, the contestant, the person with the mystery profession—they all struck The Writer as anonymous faces, as neutral as bars of soap, ordinary people he might have met in the underground or the supermarket. But The Writer did not take the underground or shop in supermarkets, which was why those faces seemed to him somehow exotic, wild and curious: were they the faces of his readers?

The superimposed captions suggested a few possible professions to match to the person: "*Owns a news stand*", said the first caption, "*Works as a train guard*" the second, "*Manufactures souvenirs*" the third, and so on... "*Makes sanitary towels*", "*Teaches in primary school*", "*Sells coffins*", "*Was voted the handsomest father in Italy*"...

And what if it were him on that quiz? What would the contestants say about him? The thought took shape and became a vision. He saw himself on that shabby little stage, blinded by light, surrounded by a curtain of applause, while the presenter flashed his teeth at the audience and introduced the day's contestant. And the contestant was his porter.

His porter, yes, the smallest, least useful element of the neighbourhood where he resided, the last link in the chain, who lived on tips and gossip, always the bearer of unpleasant news or inappropriate comments, a basic existence spent in the unhealthy, confined atmosphere of the porter's lodge, saturated with cigarette smoke and cathode rays, a Soyuz drifting in the sidereal space of ignorance—yes, could his porter, who had never read a book of his (could anyone actually live without his books?), or anybody else's (of course they could!), but had become servile only after seeing him on TV, have guessed The Writer's profession just from his appearance?

"*Invented an espresso coffee dispenser*", said one of the captions superimposed over the image of The Writer, who, as expected, was making an effort to maintain a detached and inscrutable expression. "*Has been studying the Inuit people for years*", the captions continued, "*Has patented a genetically modified maize*", "*Trains fighting dogs*", "*Sells underwear in the United Arab Emirates*", "*Writes novels*" …

What did he look like? In other words, what did other people think he looked like? If the porter asked him to show him his hands—which the contestants were allowed to do—he would immediately rule out the option "*Trains fighting dogs*". His stern, charismatic look might have supported the idea, but it was difficult to believe that a trainer of fighting dogs had never met a dog which, not wanting to be trained, had left teeth marks on the trainer's hands.

Logic would also lead one to rule out the Inuit expert. The icy wind and harsh temperatures of those inhospitable regions would certainly have left their mark on the virile but still-boyish features of The Writer: people who have lived for a long time in the cold usually have luxuriant eyebrows, thick beards, broken capillaries and scratched skin, and such was not the case with him. His discreet but sensual gaze might have been suited to the underwear salesman, but such people don't usually look too virile and move in a guarded way, in order not to alarm male buyers or embarrass women, and that certainly didn't apply to him... You could say anything you liked about him, but not that he didn't look virile... The Writer smiled to himself, surprised by that flippant thought. There remained the man who had patented genetically modified maize, the inventor of the espresso coffee dispenser and... The porter was staring at him.

The Writer smiled reassuringly and raised his eyes to heaven, pretending to be making an effort to remember something. Then he clicked his fingers, pretending to have suddenly remembered what he had just pretended to have forgotten, smiled at the bewildered astronaut through the porthole of his space capsule and headed for the avenue where his house was situated.

The sprinklers hummed obediently, lights indicated the way like those leading to the emergency exit on a plane, bicycles stood side by side in the rack, everything seemed to be in exactly the same pointless order in which he had left it when he had gone out to meet The Old Flame. Even the SUV with the smoked windows and hundreds of horsepower sleeping beneath the bonnet was neatly parked in the space allowed in the condominium's rules: a car and two scooters, or else a car and a motorbike, or an SUV and a Fiat 500, like The Second Wife's... except that it wasn't there. It wasn't there? No, it wasn't there. Although it should have been there at this hour, the Fiat 500 wasn't there.

As the sky grew dark and the light faded, wiping out the infinite illusion of day, The Writer was overcome with remorse, which had diabolically waited right until those last few metres separating him from his house door to punch him in the back. He put on speed, guided by the age-old certainty that drives heroes on their way home, which was that something pernicious had happened in his absence.

In the last metres that separated him from the front door he thought again about the empty rooms of the Renaissance villa, smelling of wood, where he had wiped out his own traces, shaking off the guide, the visiting party of tourists and—above all—The Old Flame.

As he searched the pockets of his raincoat for the keys, which were cold to the touch, he thought again about the peasant he had found hoeing the vegetable garden, to whom he had given a handful of banknotes to get him back to terra firma.

As he found the keys, he heard the whirr of the little outboard motor and felt the precariousness of the plastic hull slicing through the low waters of the lake, saw again the logo of a firm making animal feed on the peak of the peasant's cap, felt the wind striking his forehead and saw the island disappearing into the distance.

As he took out the keys, but illogically decided it was better to ring the bell, he saw himself sitting aggressively behind the wheel, pushing the engine of the hire car to its limits, leaving behind him—this time for ever—the blondness of The Old Flame, the dampness of the little island and the sadness of the lake.

The door opened. The Filipino (so he was there!) looked him up and down with a disapproving expression. The Writer entered, avoiding him, and hung his raincoat on the rack.

"The Signora?" he asked as he walked towards the dark kitchen across the living room, which was being guarded by The Ukrainian Nanny as she rocked the pushchair with one hand and with the other aimed the remote control at the TV set: the same quiz the porter had been watching was on here, too.

"Signora hospital," The Filipino said before The Writer had time, in his neurotic inspection of the house, to enter the bedroom and bathroom in a futile search for The Second Wife.

The Writer stopped and turned abruptly. "Is she ill?"

"Mother ill."

"Mother of Signora?" said The Writer, who regressed linguistically without even realizing it whenever he talked to The Filipino.

"No, *your* mother"—and this time The Filipino pointed his index finger unequivocally at The Writer.

It was then that The Writer remembered, painfully and intensely, for the second time, that he had not had his mobile with him since the morning.

He rushed into his study and found his smartphone exactly where he had left it (had he doubted it?). The display showed twenty-six missed calls and eight messages. Was this the revenge of the gods for having disconnected himself from the world for a few hours? At that moment, the phone vibrated (if you're famous, or if you have something to hide, vibration is always preferable to ringing), walking a few centimetres across the desk as if it were a primitive life form, a ciliate or flagellate protozoan. The Writer pressed the *answer* button.

"Where on earth have you been?"

It wasn't The Second Wife at the other end, but The President of The Academy in person.

"They've been looking for you all day, your press officer has been getting hysterical, they're all here waiting for you, you're the only one missing!"

So he hadn't only forgotten the phone, he had also forgotten the unmissable joint presentation with the other authors organized by The Academy, one of the crucial stages in the lead-up to The Ceremony.

"My mother hasn't been well."

"…"

"She's in hospital."

"Oh… I'm sorry… Would you like us to postpone?"

"No, no, send a taxi. I'll be right there."

If we bombard a very thin sheet of gold with alpha particles, 90 per cent of them will go right through the material without undergoing any deviation in their trajectory. Only 10 per cent will turn back as if they have hit an obstacle. From this, Rutherford drew the conclusion that matter must be largely composed of a vacuum, a vacuum gathered around a heavy nucleus. The Master, who had been aroused from his afternoon nap by the sound of a car horn, would have drawn a different conclusion. This time, too, his slippers had let him down: instead of awaiting him at the foot of the bedside table, where he was convinced he had left them, they had wandered God knows where. The car horn was insistent, but who could it be? The Master got out of bed, barefoot, intending to go to the window and satisfy his curiosity.

Largely composed of a vacuum as it might have been, the black alabaster bishop hurt a lot as he stepped on it with his bare sole. Once he had handed the fugitive bishop back to the authority of the chessboard, there remained somewhere in the room, by default, two final dangerous objects: a white pawn, easier to spot because of the colour, and a black knight (when he found them, he'd be able to resume his long-distance game).

But to the intense pain spreading from his foot was added another sensory complication: the bishop was wet. And not only the bishop. The bedside rug was damp, too. There was a yellowish patch on the floor. How was it possible?

The Master's measuring jug, empty and overturned, demonstrated that it was possible.

But there was no time to think, or to repair the damage, seeing that the car horn was still baying outside, and amid all that untidiness his slippers were at least as invisible as his last book in the shops. That was why The Master decided stoically to wade across the space that separated him from the window. And as barefoot as a worm, with his foot still hurting from its collision with the black bishop, putting only his heels down, he waded through that lake of urine and looked out.

The Director of The Small Publishing Company had got out

of his clapped-out old van and was waiting outside the closed gate of Prince —'s estate.

"Aren't you dressed yet?"

"What time is it? I didn't hear the alarm."

"Come on, we'll be late!"

"I'll be right down!" said The Master, who had completely lost track of time. And he disappeared inside the window as if he were the mechanical device of a cuckoo clock.

"When are you going to make up your mind to put in an automatic gate?" cried The Director of The Small Publishing Company.

Cuckoo: The Master looked out of the window again.

"After I win The Prize."

In the persistent silence of the empty apartment The Beginner stared at the big charred block which was nothing other than his parrot shut up in its cage.

It had lost that tough-guy look and seemed resigned to the cage, as if its fate were no longer of any interest to it.

Neither the seeds nor the fresh fruit in the feeding trough had been touched, nor did the level of the water in the measuring jug seem to have fallen. Maybe it was a question of mistrust, of adaptation. Sooner or later The Beginner would make that feathered terrorist change sides, he was sure of it.

The Beginner approached the cage to get a better look at the parrot. From close-up, he seemed to detect in the bird's eyes something like a stern judgement, a tacit accusation that made him shudder.

The Beginner turned away to avoid that gaze. But as he turned his bare back to the bird to look for a clean shirt in the wardrobe, he felt as if he were being watched: exactly the same distressing sensation he had felt in London, when, in the middle of the street outside his hotel, he had failed in his loyalty to The Girlfriend by sticking his tongue into the mouth of the translator of his novel.

Unfortunately, there was no time to indulge in that transgressive memory: he had to change and rush to the event. A theatre full of people was waiting for him, and The Beginner, if he wanted to win, knew he had to be on time.

One day, when he was a great writer, he thought as he put on his jacket on the stairs, he'd be able to grant himself the most tyrannical of privileges: that of being late.

For anyone entering only now, the man in the middle of the stage is The Writer. He has strong hands, a sailor's rather than a typist's, which he rotates in the air as he speaks, so gracefully that sometimes, as now, he makes it look as if he is untying complicated knots rather than underlining his own words. The same hands then close again like a mother-of-pearl cigarette holder, revealing his pale knuckles, at the end of the propositions he maintains with the persuasive vigour of his gestures. He has a voice as tight as a cross in a football match, which vibrates over the heads of the spectators and crackles against the walls of the theatre, spreading respect and confidence. He wears his hair tousled like a boy's, and he's elegant, but with a kind of scruffy elegance. He wears brightly coloured shirts which he buys in a shop that only he knows—or thinks that only he knows, because The Beginner also recently discovered it—and which he keeps unbuttoned, even in winter, revealing his heroic chest and an Adam's apple like a peach stone under his skin, an anatomical detail that makes him manly and fascinating even when he's silent and swallowing a glass of water to recover from his own torrential speech, which would leave even a llama without saliva. His eloquence knows no bounds, his dialectic is prodigious, no rhetorician would be able to compete: The Writer is capable of talking about any subject for a sufficiently long time to convince the others that he knows so much about that subject that, if he wanted, even when the conversation comes to an end, he could still talk about it for hours. In other words, ask him a question, any question, and he will answer you. Even if you don't ask him.

Mainly, at presentations, on the back covers of his novels or on the covers of women's magazines, he appears in jeans and ankle boots (or tennis shoes), which he will still be able to wear for a few years more before it starts to look ridiculous. But when that moment comes, he won't realize it and will continue to wear the same shoes and the same shirt because, being a writer, by definition he has no sense of the ridiculous.

"Where do you get the ideas for your novels?"

The man who has just addressed this question to The Writer is someone we have already met: The President, the de facto host of all The Academy's events and round tables. Stiff and elegant in his regulation jacket, he looks rather like a high-class wine waiter who has climbed up through the ranks, tasted everything and has now become teetotal and judges the wine only in thought.

"Where do you get the ideas for your novels?"

The question was still vibrating in the air. A little cloud of anxiety shadowed The Writer's face slightly, but the wind of self-control blew the cloud away, and once again he gave a radiant smile.

"It's the ideas that get me." (Smiles in the auditorium). "You see, a writer enjoys limited freedom, it's the responsibility for what he writes that's unlimited."

The President of The Academy nodded serenely. But then what else could he do? He could only trust that answer. He certainly couldn't know where The Writer really got his ideas. And what else could the audience do, their heads lolling on the velvet seats filled with mites? Nobody can really know where a writer gets the ideas for his novels, not even the writer himself. Except ours. He knew.

While The Beginner was trying to shield himself from the bright lights and a dull, perfunctory introduction in praise of the sponsor of The Prize, thanks to whom all this was possible, in the small bathroom of a one-room apartment a tampon previously soaked in urine was turning blue, thus indicating the unmistakable presence (unmistakable except in the case of a false alarm) of the hormone Beta-HCG, a hormone absent in women who were not in what is called an "interesting" state. What was really interesting was that the urine was The Girlfriend's.

At the moment, however, The Beginner had no way of knowing this fact, or the related implications it would have for his future life. Because some women, out of an instinct for self-preservation, keep some pieces of news to themselves, ready to use them like deadly weapons at the most appropriate moments.

Talking of moments, The Beginner's had now arrived.

"How and when did you first become interested in writing?"

"I always thought of being a writer, even before I actually started writing."

"Thank you. And now let's come to you…"

The President had turned to The Master. Who had eyes like swimming pools filled with rainwater and could not see from here to there (even though somewhere in the infinite depths of his pockets he must have his glasses). All he could do was float amid outlines and shadows, but thanks to the thermal imaging camera of his experience he was able to reconstruct a three-dimensional image of the theatre: firemen bored to death at the back of the hall, bejewelled ladies in the front rows, slumbering husbands in the boxes, restless schoolkids torn by force from their afternoons on Facebook and transported to the gallery, adolescents laughing beneath their incipient moustaches, their teachers' stern looks, The President's dandyish tie, The Writer's poker-faced smile, The Beginner's innocent (but no less lethal) shyness.

The Master wasn't born yesterday, he had been involved in other prizes—he hadn't won them, of course, but he knew how to behave.

The Master at last found his glasses in an inside pocket. At least that was something. He put them on his gibbous nose and found that, despite the greasy, opaque halo of his lenses, everything was exactly the way he had imagined it.

"Earlier," The President went on, "in presenting your book, I said that its poetic origins are evident in many of its pages. Yours is a very special book, almost a kind of prose poem, with an epigrammatic, fragmentary quality that somehow magically recreates unity. So I wanted to ask you, as far as your style is concerned—"

"Here I have to stop you," said The Master. "Style doesn't exist. It may have existed once, but now it's the dear departed, a completely outdated concept. Style is what we do without knowing how we do it."

"This definition of yours"—said The President, turning to the audience—"really deserves underlining."

The Master made a gesture, flinging out the palm of his hand but keeping his arm still, like a cat that only wants to play harmlessly: he was about to say "Let's drop it."

"You know that, according to the rules, the authors cannot read their own works. However, if your colleagues won't be upset with me…"

The Beginner shook his head—why deny the poor old man his moment of glory?—and The Writer shrugged his shoulders: it is in the mercy he extends to the defeated that a victor's greatness lies.

"…I don't think I'll be accused of favouritism if I take advantage of this opportunity to ask you to read for us, not the prose from your book (which, as I've said, is forbidden by the rules), but some verse: I know you have some unpublished poems…"

The Master nodded smugly.

"Please…" The President indicated the lectern from which, at the beginning of the evening, a fading actress had read extracts from the three competing works in a manner that made it clear she understood nothing.

The Master temporized.

"Take mine," said The President, like a literary butler, passing him the microphone as if it were a torchbearer's beacon.

The Master stood up somewhat clumsily from the armchair in which his buttocks had been grounded. In his crumpled jacket, his swollen feet moving unsteadily in his cork sandals (poets are allowed to dress badly), he walked towards his pulpit. The lights dimmed until all that remained on the stage was a Caravaggesque face, a head topped with unkempt white hair and suffused with light in the midst of darkness. Silence fell over the auditorium. The Master dug his glasses out of his pocket again. He cleaned them on his shirt tail, which was sticking out of his trousers, and put them on. He searched in his jacket pocket and took out his notebook.

He opened it.

He closed it.

He opened it again.

He closed it again.

The differences that exist between a conventional imitation moleskine notebook and a urination diary would not have escaped a trained eye, from the format—the notebook being smaller and more compact, the diary larger—to the cover—the former stiff with elastic, the latter pliable. Not to mention the paper—slightly yellowish for the notebook, strictly white for the dairy—and the layout—simple horizontal lines for the notebook, a preprinted grid complete with headings (*volume of urine in the measuring cup, time, voluntary urination, involuntary episode, intensity and urgency of the stimulus, notes, etc.*) for the diary.

Even though the differences are so marked, it would be unfair to ignore the slight analogies presented by the two objects. Let's see: both have dark covers and… well, that's it really. There aren't actually any others.

But to weak eyes looking for an object in a dark room, such fragile similarities can become fatal. Eyes deceived rather than supported by the other senses. Like a hasty touch, which trusts the first object within reach, even though positioned, it should be said, deceptively close to the second object.

That's why it is hardly surprising if, leaving home in a mad rush, because of the delay, in the absence of electricity (the fuse box had blown again), in the dark and without glasses, with The Director of The Small Publishing Company continuing to sound his horn implacably to hurry him up, The Master had committed a fatal and perhaps even unforgivable error.

The Master now stood at the lectern in front of the packed auditorium with his urination diary in his hand. Time flowed like liquid, emptying the space of his consciousness and filling the space of the theatre, as he cleared his throat and read in a steady voice:

Time: 5:30
Volume: 340 ml.
Urination: voluntary
Intensity: moderate
Urgency: pressing
Notes: farted

The Master stared with his little eyes into the auditorium: all he saw was a kind of human vineyard, rows and rows of heads turned towards him.

The theatre was silent for a moment, holding back from delivering its verdict. The first to break the stalemate was The President, who started clapping, in a somewhat lukewarm manner at first, but eventually triggering a thunderous round of applause from the audience.

"You've really surpassed yourself. In the concision of these lines, worthy of the greatest Hermetic poets, we see a painful attempt to convey the tragic nature of existence, in a classical form invigorated by postmodernism, which recovers and recycles heterogeneous material…"

The Master was a poet.

Everything looks better from above. Even Rome. The great roads choked with traffic, the sick old snake of the walls, the flying saucer of the Pantheon taking off over the oblivious ruins, the empty streets and the arenas orphaned of champions, the elusive aqueducts and decapitated columns, the arches sinking beneath the weight of their own beauty, the silent temples and dazzling squares and glittering fountains, the steps flooded with light, the motionless obelisks propping up the distracted skies, the palaces of the popes opposite the beehives of their servants, the martial towers and peaceful belfries, the remains reduced to cats' cradles and the monuments to birds' nests, the turgescent domes and hidden cloisters, the red tennis courts like chips on the green baize of the meadows on the Via Cassia, the unauthorized swimming pools in the villas on the Via Appia and the luxuriant palms in the gardens of the Quirinale, the abandoned parks and muddy ponds, the gilded bridges over the river that descends to the sea escorted by the traffic, which follows the current or rows against it, swimming as if with flippers towards the mountains that feed the Tiber, the jungles of aerials and satellite dishes on the sun-baked roofs, the pines and lime trees and bitter oleanders along the avenues, the geraniums on the balconies and the brazen jasmine and the discreet lemons on the terraces of apartment buildings. From above, ours is quite another story.

PART TWO

(One month to The Ceremony)

You KNOW THAT EXERCISE they do in theatre workshops and in workplace groups to increase collective harmony and mutual trust among the members? Blindfolded or with our eyes closed, we let ourselves fall backwards, into the arms of the person behind us, who is waiting there ready to catch us.

The only person into whose arms The Writer would have let himself fall backwards, blindfolded or with his eyes closed, was The Publisher.

That was why, when The Publisher had invited him one bright Sunday to lunch in a restaurant not far from the Villa Borghese, even though it was a place they never went, The Writer had been trusting, and had let himself fall backwards into his arms. And when, after octopus in jelly with potatoes and a fillet of monkfish, a bottle of Sauvignon and another of Rhine Riesling, The Publisher had suggested they go for a walk in the zoo to clear their heads of the wine and pointless chatter, The Writer, even though he had found the suggestion unusual, had been as trusting as before. And again he had let himself fall backwards into The Publisher's arms.

"Poor things," The Writer said, stopping in front of the aviary where the birds of prey were kept. "Don't you feel sorry for them?"

The big, dark birds looked like monks sleeping on the roofs of their hermitages.

"Not me," The Publisher said. "They're the stupidest and laziest animals in the entire zoo."

The Writer was surprised by this statement and looked at the aviary with closer attention. A falcon (*Falco peregrinus*) was cleaning its feathers with its beak, hiding its head beneath its wing. A condor (*Vultur gryphus*) with an obscene bare neck was scouring the ground in search of leftover food.

"Everyone feels sorry for them because they think they're intelligent. But what they have in their eyes isn't sadness or resignation. It's emptiness. Absence of thought. People say 'He's as sharp as an eagle' when they ought to say exactly the opposite."

The Writer watched as a majestic eagle (*Aquila chrysaetos*), sitting dark and motionless on a branch, let out a powerful stream of excrement that fell to the ground like huge drops of rain after a tremendous drought.

"Everyone feels sorry for the birds. Nobody feels sorry for the foxes."

"The foxes?"

"Did you know that foxes are tireless walkers? They can cover more than eighty kilometres a day, and they go crazy in that shitty enclosure that's no more than half a hectare."

The Writer didn't know that.

"They grind their teeth, their eyes are bloodshot, they tear out their claws because they're constantly trying to dig their way out under the fence, can you believe that? Come, I'll show you the foxes."

The Publisher took a threatening step towards The Writer, who raised his hand compliantly as if to say, "I believe you."

"How many votes do we have?" he said, in order to change the subject and chase from his mind the image of those mangy crazed foxes, walking round in circles behind the barbed wire.

"A hundred and thirty for sure."

"And how many do we need to win?"

"A hundred and fifty to be home and dry. But a hundred and forty, a hundred and forty-five might be enough."

"Should we beware of The Master?"

"You mean the old man?"

The Writer nodded.

The Publisher shook his head. "The Master's all washed up. He won't even get to The Ceremony."

"But he's a finalist."

"He's sick. He has cancer."

"Are you sure? How do you know?"

"I have my sources. I'm a friend of The Urologist who's treating him."

"Well, that's good, isn't it?"

"No. It's bad. If he gave an interview about his illness, or talked about it on TV, he could gain votes. But he'd never do it, he's too proud."

"I hadn't thought of that."

"I had. Thinking for my authors… of my authors," he corrected himself, "is my job. Anyway his publisher's a small one, he doesn't scare me. They won't be able to raise many votes, just a few old acquaintances who are so desperate they'd sell their souls for a reprint."

The Writer laughed, though he wasn't sure it had been a joke.

"And what about The Beginner?"

"He's the horse to bet on."

"But his book's no great shakes, is it?"

"Have you read it?"

"No, but I've been told that—"

"Read it. Now there's a book."

"…"

"And how many votes do they have?"

"A hundred and twenty, a hundred and thirty. More or less. Like us."

"How come they've got so many?"

"It's his first book. And when it's your first book, they forgive you everything. Don't you remember?"

"No."

"And besides, he's young. Do you remember the 'brand new' sticker we put on the cover of your book? He doesn't need it: his face is the sticker."

"But he's a greenhorn, I read his interview, a naïve mishmash of clichés…"

"Listen, I'm going to be frank. We've known each other for thirty years. You know how much I respect you as a man, and how much I admire you as an artist. You also know that a powerful press office and the biggest publisher on the market aren't enough by themselves. You also need the books, and yours—no offence intended—isn't a good book."

The Writer did not take offence, but those angry foxes grinding their teeth behind the barbed wire had appeared in his mind again.

"In fact, to be quite honest, your last three books were nothing to write home about."

"…"

Rabid foxes were throwing themselves against the electrified fence of The Writer's thoughts. The Publisher took him by the arm and started walking, pulling The Writer's compliant body after him.

"Let's say a trapeze artist in a circus gets one of his moves wrong on the first night of the show. Luckily, his partner has good reflexes and catches him. The number goes down well, the audience don't notice a thing and happily applaud. Then, when the show is over, the two of them clear things up in the caravan, and that's the end of it."

The two men began circumnavigating the aviary.

"Now let's say the trapeze artist makes the same mistake on the second night. This time his partner misses him… The audience hold their breath, then applaud in relief. There was a net underneath. When the show's over the owner of the circus goes to the trapeze artist's caravan. He comes out after a while…"

The Publisher stopped—they had now walked halfway round the aviary—then resumed walking, again slowly dragging The Writer with him.

"Now, let's say the trapeze artist gets the same move wrong for a third night running. There's complete silence under the big top. Everyone's holding their breath, thinking—"

"As long as there's a net," said The Writer, interpreting the audience's thoughts.

"There had been. The circus owner had had it taken away."

" . . ."

"And you know why he had it taken away?"

" . . . ."

"Because he loved the circus more than he loved the trapeze artist."

The two men fell silent. They had done a complete circuit of the aviary and had come back to their starting point. Were there foxes in circuses? Trained foxes? Were there even such people as fox-trainers? The Writer wasn't sure. It might be impossible to train them, but surely they could be tamed. Once, as a child, he had seen a fox come and eat at the back of a restaurant, taking the food from the hands of a kitchen porter who had managed to overcome its mistrust. Word had got around and people talked about the restaurant more because of that tame fox than because of the cooking, and over time the kitchen porter had ended up becoming more famous than the cook. The kitchen porter had continued putting aside leftovers, until one day he had waited a long time but the fox had not appeared, and was never to appear again.

The Publisher resumed his speech, shooing the foxes away from The Writer's thoughts with a stick.

"On the fourth evening, the circus has a new trapeze artist. You have to win. That Prize is a multiplier."

"What do you mean?"

"How many copies do you usually sell?"

The Writer said a number that wasn't too far from the truth.

"Multiply it by ten."

"Tell me what I have to do."

"When the time is right, when the time is right... Look." The Publisher pointed at a sleepy eagle which had broken the enchantment of the aviary by throwing itself on the condor: it was flapping its wings and jabbing with its beak, trying to tear a fragment of rotten flesh from the claws of that lugubrious road-sweeper.

"Don't you feel sorry for them?"

"No."

The Publisher and The Writer headed for the exit.

"And how are you getting on with the next one?" said The Publisher just before stepping into the chauffeur-driven saloon that was waiting for him outside the zoo gate.

"The next what?"

The Writer was distracted: he was thinking again about the birds of prey dozing slothfully on their perches.

"Come on, now, the next book, wake up!" said The Publisher, getting in the car and pulling the heavy door shut before hearing the usual disappointing reply:

"It's coming along."

A writer is strong only when he is writing. He is respected and feared as long as the others don't know what he is writing. When the book comes out, in the light of day, he becomes vulnerable. A writer writing a novel is like a serial killer who's keeping a victim locked in a cellar. Every evening, he slides under the cellar door a tray with a little water and stale bread, just enough to keep his victim alive, anticipating the moment when he descends the cellar stairs to have his fun with her...

But what happens if the victim manages to break free? To escape from her cell, run out in the street and scream HELP at the top of her voice? Then the serial killer is in danger. But not because he's afraid of being caught, that's the least of it. Now that he's lost his toy, the partner in his secret games, whom will he torture when he goes down to the cellar?

Himself, would seem to be the most reliable answer.

So was our Writer strong, sitting there in his study? And how did his victim in the cellar feel? Did she shake with fear every time she heard footsteps in the corridor?

No, sir. The victim in the cellar wasn't trembling or laughing. There wasn't actually anyone in The Writer's cellar. Only dust and odds and ends accumulated during a lifetime.

The Writer wasn't strong for a simple reason: he was not writing. But it wasn't one of those terrible writer's blocks that reduce writers to impotence, like those clients who weep and cry for their mothers in a prostitute's lap—no, it was nothing like that at all. It wasn't that our Writer wasn't writing now, at this precise moment, or even during this period of time, or in the last few years. He really wasn't writing. Or rather, let's be quite open about this: he had never written.

Yes, all right, in his computer there were endless strings of 0s and 1s, which, joined together in bits, and subsequently in bytes, would form words, and these words in their turn, recombined in syntagma and paragraphs and chapters, would go to make up something that by pure convention human beings called "a novel".

What the strings did not say, and would never say, was that The Writer was not the author of his last novel, the one with which he was competing for The Prize, nor of the others that he had published. Or to put it another way: his novels were not his.

Of course, for his readers, his publisher, his fans, and for the aspiring novelists who clogged his letter box with bundles of letters and carcasses of manuscripts, this might be one of those items of news that make your glasses drop to the floor and bookshelves collapse. But it's important to quickly pick up the books and put your glasses back on the tip of your nose before you hear "who wrote The Writer's books". Because if he didn't write them, someone else did. And that's the point we've reached.

But who could it be? Well, in such delicate matters, it's important to put yourself in the hands of someone you trust. Someone you more than trust, someone who's family. MAXIMUM CAPACITY 8 PERSONS. The words were on a metal plate on the wall of the lift in the clinic. So yes, The Writer could read. As for writing...

As soon as he had arrived in the city from the provinces, he really had tried.

Big novels, filled with love affairs, lonely desperate men throwing stones at the stars, missed dates, ashtrays overflowing with cigarette ends and women dragged by their hair, raincoated figures walking the night streets, cars speeding by beneath the streetlamps, the glances of strange women behind the windows of buses: that was how he imagined the stories he would one day write.

Corduroy jackets with patches at the elbows, long walks in autumnal parks, aged rum, cigars in a cork humidor, desks with leather tops and cherrywood bookshelves: that was how he imagined himself at the time when he'd be writing these stories.

Dipping his croissant into his cappuccino at dawn, after a night spent scouring the bars, studying the transsexuals and street-cleaners to gain an insight into the darkest, most brutish of minds. Opening his notebook at the outdoor tables of gilded cafés in the centre, lying on the grass in parks on bright summer afternoons with a cigarette between his lips and the clouds for a hat. Anxiously opening the letter box and taking out the post in the expectation of the Minoan verdicts of publishers, not yet disappointed by meeting the writers he admired, challenging the critics to duels and filling diary after diary. In short, a time when he still desired to write more ardently than to become a writer. But things had worked out differently.

His novels had been born as blind as kittens, his stories had kept slipping away from him, his sentences had jammed like rusty revolvers.

In short, he had tried to write. He had tried with all his might. But it hadn't worked. Such things do happen.

Talent isn't a gift, it's the conviction that you are better than the others. That was what he'd thought, what he'd kept telling himself as he looked at himself in the mirror when he was young, but he'd had to think again. It really was a gift. One that he—who had wanted it so much—hadn't been given.

Even so, he was still convinced that he was better than the others, which was why he had a first great problem: he didn't know what he was better at. He had to discover it. And that was a second, very big problem.

Of course he was good at typing. Nobody could beat him at that. Which was why, if anybody had said that The Writer "wrote very well", in the broadest sense of the phrase they wouldn't have been too far from the truth. The Writer had the dexterity of a professional typist and tapped at his "qwerty" like a consummate lounge bar pianist.

But what was the use of this skill? If he couldn't write, what the hell was he typing all day long on the keyboard of his PC?

It could be said that The Writer was copying out manuscripts onto the computer. He would add a few commas, correct little typos, start a new paragraph, nothing more.

Because, even if he had wanted to, he couldn't—or wouldn't—really add anything to, or subtract anything from, what was already there, which had been given to him in an almost definitive form.

This was more or less the position of The Writer with regard to writing, and life. His, and other people's.

A good day can start with the transfer of an advance from a publisher, news of a reissue, an invitation to an important conference abroad, the reading of an interview with himself in a high-circulation magazine, a telephone number on the back of a photograph of a woman left on his car windscreen. In other words, it can start in many ways.

A bad day, on the other hand, begins like this.

The Writer walked down the long corridors of the clinic, which smelt of mashed potatoes and disinfectant, led by a middle-aged nun who could have turned out to be a man beneath her surplice without anyone being shocked. Passing the single rooms on either side of the corridor, The Writer glimpsed the pyjamas of the sick under the wool-mix blankets that gave off sparks at night.

Through the windows that looked out on the world of the living, the morning light poured cruelly into the rooms of the sick along with the sadistic scent of the flowering wisteria.

In the corridor, hordes of assistants skated on wooden overshoes, trudging after consultants who advanced through the wards driven by their own prestige, white coats unbuttoned and gold chains on their tanned chests, exchanging opinions on boats and publications, diagnoses and restaurants, their breath thick with coffee and cigarettes.

"Please, this way…"

The long corridor had come to an end and the nun gestured to The Writer to go in through the last door on the right. The door opened, and a man appeared in the doorway, an elegantly dressed man in a light-coloured suit and a blue tie, a man The Writer knew well.

The Publisher nodded in greeting, to which The Writer responded without enthusiasm, in fact with a certain displeasure. The nun, reassured by the unmistakable familiarity demonstrated by the two men, persuaded herself to leave them alone.

"What are you doing here?"

"It seemed the least I—"

"Thanks, but you shouldn't have."

"I brought some flowers. Orange carnations. The colour of determination. She'll need it."

The Publisher tilted his head back slightly, indicating the interior of the room.

"And so will we."

"Why?"

"The Prize. It's not going well. Drop by the office tomorrow."

"Leave me alone with her."

"Remember to change the water for the flowers. Carnations need lots of water."

The Publisher gently closed the door behind him and set off along the corridor.

Idiot, thought The Writer. All flowers need water. He walked into the room.

The Writer has done everything to keep bad things out of his life. Suffering is a leper who walks with bells on his feet, and The Writer can recognize that sinister ringing from a distance of kilometres. And when he hears it, he barricades himself in his house, or walks faster.

Now he lives in the city with his beautiful young wife and his daughter, in a residential complex with alarms and private surveillance, and nobody will ever be able to undermine his—sorry, their—happiness.

When The Baby starts to crawl, exploring every corner of the house, sticking her little fingers in every hole she can, The Writer will carpet the house with socket protectors; when she makes her first unsteady steps he will cover the sharp corners of the furniture with foam rubber; and when, at the glorious climax of her oral phase, she puts every object she finds in her mouth, he will get rid of anything that might be indigestible and potentially dangerous, and will lock all the drawers, because that's what you do.

And not so much for The Baby—that's what you tell other people—as for himself, for The Second Wife, for The Filipino, for The Ukrainian Nanny, for The Human Race. Nobody should ever again hurt himself, nobody should ever again suffer, at least in his house. Let them go somewhere else to suffer.

The Writer can't stand suffering. Especially other people's, that's why he insists on eating with the television off. The news must be blacked out, television must regress to being little more than a screen on which to show cartoons for The Baby, pay-TV films for daddy and mummy, or at a pinch that quiz the porter was watching, which wasn't bad, come on.

And even outside the house things aren't much better. When he bought the house he made sure that the neighbourhood attracted the right sort, that only respectable people lived in the area. And that's how it was, until a few days ago—the episode disturbed him so much that he hasn't told anyone about it yet—a few metres from the automatic gate—thinking about it again, it's inconceivable—just in front of the recycling bins, he saw a man, an old man with stooped back, searching angrily in the rubbish. It had never happened since he had come to live in this neighbourhood. If something like that ever happens again, The Writer will sell the house. Forget about compassion.

Life is too short to be devoted to suffering, people who suffer *want to suffer*, suffering is an invention of man: above the clouds the sun is always shining.

That's what The Writer thinks. That's why he has learnt to turn the pillow on the side that's less creased, to winter somewhere warm and spend the summers somewhere cool, to leave for his holidays when everybody is coming back from theirs, to spend the weekends in the city and the weekdays outside—in other words, for him the glass is never half full, but always full, full to the brim.

The day of his divorce? A liberation. His father's death? The deposition of a weary king. The end of a friendship?

Social cleansing. Everything that happens can become an opportunity.

In all these years, The Writer has been the personal gardener of his own success. He has carefully mown, watered and fenced off the evergreen lawn of his well-being. And now? Now he won't allow anyone to get close, and fires off a volley if he so much as sees anyone lurking around the fence of his life. The obvious threat comes from outside, because inside his garden there is nothing and nobody that can harm him, he can run free without fear of tripping up: there are no obstacles or rusty tools in his garden. No offence can come from The Baby or The Second Wife—they are pure, innocent creatures who are unacquainted with evil, and wouldn't even know how to do anything wrong. He does.

That is why now, faced with his intubated Mother, her artificial breathing, the skein of grey hair on her pillow, her nightdress with its faded colours, he can't really forgive the salty tear that streaks his face like sea spray.

And what about this unheard-of second tear following the first? Why? Why? Why? Something has gone wrong, this wasn't the agreement, this wasn't planned.

"Mother..." whispers The Writer in a thin voice. "Don't leave me... What will I do without you?"

He squeezes The Mother's little hand, the hand of an old child, and holds it in his own, strong, masculine hand.

"I know you can hear me..."

The room is silent apart from the regular breathing of the mechanical ventilator, the working machinery, the monitors. The cold eyes of the LED lights watch discreetly over the patient.

"You can hear me, can't you? I know you're there..."

An imperceptible variation in the heartbeat.

"Don't let go, mother, don't let go, not now. There's not long to go, we're almost there, we're going to win this time, it's for sure, The Prize is ours, it's ours and nobody can take it away from us. Hold on mother, hold on. Think of the advance we'll get next time…"

"Life is merely passing time and the desire to be loved. Nothing else."

Life, life, life… How unbearable they were, these writers always talking about life. What do they even know of life? Have they ever lived? Poets, yes, they know about it. Other writers only imagine it. Scoundrels who climb naked onto a ledge and threaten to throw themselves off if nobody will listen to them, that's what writers are. If it wasn't for poets, who question every certainty in order to climb higher, and who extend to them the support of poetry in order to get them down like firemen with a scared cat… Life, yes, but other people's, thought The Master.

If at least they had a bit of modesty, they'd only need a little possessive adjective, a hygienic grammatical precaution: *My* life has been, etc., etc., there's yours, speak for yourselves. What do you know about my life? *The desire to be loved?* I never loved my wife. Nor did I ever want her to love me. At most, I desired her and that was it, but that was a long, long time ago. And she never wanted to be loved by me—by someone else perhaps, certainly not by me. She married me only to be able to despise me, to have someone to insult, to hear how her own voice sounded against a man who had run out of arguments, ultrasonic waves hitting an obstacle and turning back: the same physical principle that is the basis of radar is also the foundation of marriage. But I don't feel sorry for her, let the old girl rest in peace, or rather, let her rest, full stop, clad in the fur coat of hate that she took with her into the grave. She wasn't a wife, she was a factory of negatives. As for *time passing*, that was more nonsense. Time never passes, if it ever did. Time is always in the past, in the present there is only space, looking at the objects that surround us, filling our lungs with air, listening to the sounds of our environment. And the future is anxiety, insomnia and fear of dying. But before I die, I'll have what I'm due.

The Master angrily closed The Writer's book and placed it with a little bang on the counter of the library.

"I'll take this, too," he said to the bespectacled library assistant.

We should know our enemy before the battle.

From an experiment conducted by the Max Planck Institute, it appears that dogs are capable of understanding and recognizing at least 200 words. Some breeds, like border collies, even 1,000.

For now, The Beginner's parrot couldn't understand a single one. All it seemed to be doing was looking across the room with its icy eyes towards the window and the faded blue of the sky. It was as if it were suffused with an impenetrable magnetic field.

A gangster who'd turned State's evidence and was appearing in court behind bullet-proof glass: that was what the parrot looked like.

But with time it would speak, oh, yes, it would speak. The Beginner, who was getting his bag ready for his game of five-a-side and couldn't find his boots, was sure of that at least.

Even though the *Manual on the Raising and Care of Parrots* which he had bought along with the cage suggested, on page 78, "do not leave parrots alone for too long in order to avoid the onset of psychotic behaviour of a self-harming nature (it is typical of parrots to pluck their own feathers)" and, on page 79, urged the reader to "spend more time with the bird, talking to it a lot and letting it explore your home", it was also true that on page 80, almost at the bottom, it said that "if you really have no choice but to leave it alone, it is best to leave a radio or tape recorder on".

That was why The Beginner, who in the meantime had found a single boot and, given how late it was, had contented himself with that, took from the bathroom the portable radio that enlivened his showers, tuned in to a private station where they talked twenty-four hours a day (even when the championship was over) about the most popular football team in the capital: "...*Right now there are people who don't want the best for the team, but are only thinking of their own interests. And I don't only blame the players, because although they're professionals, let's not forget that they're just kids... If a strong hand is missing at management level...*", positioned it close to the cage, put his bag over his shoulder, looked fleetingly at the parrot, which was still as imperturbably silent as ever, pulled the door behind him, and set off for the five-a-side football pitch in the Viale Tor di Quinto. Where, out of the other nine players minus one, someone must surely have an extra boot to lend him.

Today must be the first or third Friday of the month because, as agreed with The First Wife, it is up to The Writer to go and pick up the children. That's why The Writer's SUV is parked just outside the Irish school from which in a few minutes The Boy and The Girl will come out, the miraculous duo resulting from the encounter of his chromosomes with those of The First Wife. Two finely crafted little jewels the court preferred to entrust to their mother, a decision that even The Writer found fair and reasonable. Seeing them less means enjoying them more, it means making do with being a distributor of Gormiti cards and figures and putting on those ridiculous 3D glasses in the promiscuous darkness of a multiplex cinema from time to time. But, above all, it means having peace and quiet and enough time at his disposal to read and write. Or rather, to copy his mother's novels in peace.

Of course, the arrival of The Baby was completely unexpected, and at first seemed a threat to a family order he had rebuilt with no little effort after the turbulent years of the divorce. Because although it may be true that opposites attract, it is no less certain that if they are too opposite they part. Take The Writer and The First Wife. Impossible to imagine any two people more different. And to think that once upon a time they had called each other darling.

Be that as it may, the siblings have emerged from the storms of that marriage without any obvious trauma—although it may be too early to say: in order to proclaim victory it is necessary to wait for the cyclone of adolescence. In their relationship with their father, they limit themselves to a few sudden whims of little importance, nothing that can't be solved with a new accessory for the Nintendo Wii (the canyon wheel, for example) or a Winx colouring book. Speaking of which, it is worth noting that The Boy is more demanding and costs more, whereas The Girl is more affectionate and costs less. In future, The Writer is convinced, the proportions are likely to be reversed.

For the moment they have demonstrated incredible maturity. Both The Boy and The Girl greeted with indifference and fatalism (or maybe they just couldn't care less?) the arrival of that little creature with its vague smell of dairy products and its bald head covered with silky down: The Baby.

In a few moments, they will come out of school in their nice uniforms, cross the garden beneath the attentive gaze of the Irish nuns, and with their colourful school bags, bigger than their backs, run lightly across that no man's land between the exit from school and the return to the family, a no man's land where children enjoy extraterritorial immunity and indulge in little impertinences, fierce discriminatory jokes and aggressive games, before they recognize among the cars parked in the first and second row those of their mummies and daddies, or whoever is driving them, and resign themselves to the authority of adults.

Zzz zzz zzz zzzz... The Writer's mobile was vibrating. The number of an intern from the publishing company appeared on the display.

"Hello, I'll pass you to..."

"Hello," he replied.

"Hello."

Through the invisible Bluetooth connection, a sombre voice echoed in the car's loudspeakers.

"We're in a meeting. We're checking the votes."

"Oh... And how are they going?"

"Badly. You have to come."

"When?"

"Right now."

"But... but... I can't right now."

"Why? Where are you?"

"I'm with the kids."

"Say hello to them for me. And say goodbye to The Prize."

"Why do you say that?"

"Are you coming or not?"

"..."

"..."

"I'll be right there."

The Writer started the car. The engine fired up just as a distant bell announced the end of lessons. The SUV made its way nimbly between the parked cars and turned onto the main road, which was jammed with light and smog.

In a moment, The Writer will look in the rear-view mirror and think that he's a terrible father, in a moment the children will come out and look apprehensively for their daddy's car, and won't find it. And then they will feel the atavistic fear of abandonment, and this fear will mature in their undeveloped minds until it becomes a trauma, and one day, with sweaty hands, they will recall that moment of terror on a psychiatrist's couch. And their account will become disjointed, and their eyes will fill with tears, because that fear controls almost all our actions and thoughts. In the name of that fear, human beings perform senseless acts, rise through the ranks until they reach the top, become rock stars, compete for literary prizes. Fear of being abandoned, that's precisely what it is.

Returning to The Writer's children: after seeing them and realizing, with a lump in the throat, how lost and disappointed they look, the considerate mother or father of a classmate will offer to take them home. And they will accept, with the resignation with which an adopted child enters a new family.

What if that doesn't happen? Unlikely, of course. But if it doesn't happen, didn't The Boy want an iPhone with unlimited voice and data for his tenth birthday? And doesn't his mother always put at least twenty euros in his pocket (you never know...)?

Let's go then, how much will it cost them to call a taxi?

Five-four. To the opposing team, obviously. That was how the five-a-side game had finished.

The two teams had transferred to the bar for their usual after-game aperitif, a ritual which The Beginner could happily have skipped. He could particularly have skipped the dreary conversation, which, as soon as it ventured beyond technical commentary on the game or deviated from the required "update on the championship", demonstrated a crude truth: which was that, once the game was over, those ten people had nothing in common off the field. Maybe on the field, too, judging by how they had played.

The Beginner had eaten hardly anything, half a rice croquette, two bites of an open sandwich. His stomach couldn't face food after the effort of the game and the cold, foamy beer he had knocked back greedily, which was now descending into his innards to appease his mysterious sense of unease.

After the aperitif, with lactic acid in his muscles, he had accepted a lift from one of his team who had a Japanese sports car and who played with the head of a Brazilian and the feet of a Faroe Islander. Now, as he pressed the lift button with his painful finger (his team didn't have a goalie and took turns in goal), it struck him that maybe he ought to stop playing five-a-side. After all, he wasn't a little boy any more, he was a successful writer and successful writers don't play football, the critics would smell a rat immediately. To have a modicum of credibility, writers have to be wimps or misanthropes.

The lift doors opened, and as The Beginner started up the final flight of stairs that separated him from The Girlfriend's loft he felt as though his calves were made of wood and his bones had been reduced to tiny pods, like bags of pellets.

Why did he persist with the five-a-side? Hadn't he had enough of shin pads and stinking feet, sweaty underwear and humiliating genital comparisons in the shower? Yes, he had definitely had enough.

The five-a-side was an unhealthy, typically Roman habit which he could abandon without regret. The next time he was summoned on the noticeboard on Facebook, he wouldn't even reply.

With a final effort, he inserted the keys in the defective lock and entered the apartment. Silence. The Girlfriend was going to dinner with her female colleagues at a Greek restaurant directly after work. So The Beginner was alone. Alone with his parrot. He threw his bags down in the entrance, as The Girlfriend had told him a thousand times not to do, flopped onto the sofa, as The Girlfriend had told him a thousand times not to do, laid his head back, closed his eyes and saw again that moment when, unmarked, he had found himself alone in front of the goalkeeper and had made an unforgivable shot that had ended up beyond the—

"*In the Christian vision, sacrifice does not essentially mean renunciation, so why is obedience a virtue? Because it has the ability to give substance to the ties...*"

Who was speaking? From whose mouth had those words come? Who was in the apartment? The Beginner felt his blood freeze and his muscles stiffen. Slowly he turned. And fear took hold of him. The words were coming from the parrot's cage.

"*Obedience is the only way we can speak to the children of Jesus, for if obedience is a virtue, it is something greater than submission...*"

The Beginner overcame his fear, got up from the sofa and went to the cage. The parrot was frozen, its eyes half closed, its beak clenched, as if reciting a prayer by heart. The Beginner walked round the cage twice. The motionless feathers, the legs hooked over the perch...

"*Obedience to the true, the right, the good, because those who obey and those who demand obedience...*"

The words continued to fill the room.

"*...are both servants... servants in the service of the truth.*"

The radio! The radio was still on, standing on the bookcase. Idiot idiot idiot, stupid bloody idiot. Not even a savage faced with the white man's tricks would have behaved like that. How could he have let himself be scared by a stupid radio? A stupid portable radio broadcasting a religious programme...

A religious programme? But hadn't he tuned the radio to a station that was all about football?

The Beginner picked up the radio, looked at it, then looked at the parrot, which was staring at him with its cold eyes. The Beginner switched off the radio. The parrot hid its head under its wing.

*

The vibrant light reaches the top floors of the buildings, and slices them open.

Spring is here, in the cafés with their tables in the open air, in the women tourists sunbathing on the steps of the monuments, in the reawakening of the parks after their long slumber beneath a covering of leaves. But not everyone is able to enjoy it. There are also those who work and look outside with a sigh.

In the office of the NGO, The Girlfriend is sitting at her desk, too tired to search on the Internet for the best combination of flights for her boss's complicated movements (Copenhagen–Oslo and Oslo–London by plane, London–Paris by train, and Paris–Rome by plane), waiting only to knock off and go to the Greek restaurant with her colleagues.

The spring is of no concern to The Master either: he has other things to think about. He is in a bar, one of those bars where estate agents in pointed boots and office workers with synthetic ties go to eat, where the sandwiches in the windows are covered with paper napkins as if they were corpses wrapped in shrouds, and where there is always a strange stench, as if the barman had left his hand on the hotplate.

The Master is at a table, looking at the entrance, through which, in a moment, a thin, olive-skinned, distinguished-looking man will pass, carrying a showy leather briefcase stuffed as full as a roll: all of which details are necessary but not sufficient to identify the man as The Master's Lawyer.

But what is an artist—and poets and writers are surely entitled so to define themselves—doing with a lawyer? He could be availing himself of his services for matters of contracts and royalties, of course, but such is not the case with The Master. Unfortunately, life has no pity on artists, because the sickness of living which they carry with them does not exempt them from being ordinary citizens. How immeasurably distant, for example, a fine may be from a poem.

"Very nice… Where did you get it?"

The Lawyer had had no difficulty in spotting The Master sitting in a corner of the bar, and had walked up to his table. His curiosity aroused by The Master's sports jacket, The Lawyer, when he was close enough to touch it, took the material of the sleeve between his thumb and index finger.

"It was a gift."

The Master was very proud of that sailcloth jacket, perhaps the only fashionable garment he owned. It was one of the unmissable gifts from Torchio Wines, a company that boasted an enviable catalogue of prizes that could be won by collecting points. The Master was a regular customer, and every month, together with the wine, received sealed envelopes marked PERSONAL and FINAL OPPORTUNITY, which contained exclusive offers. You just had to order the wine by phone—it arrived by courier within three working days—keep aside the stickers over the corks, and return them by post to the offices of Torchio Wines, and that was it.

With the first two cases (only twenty-four stickers) had come a small portable TV set, which couldn't be configured for digital terrestrial but had an attractive design anyway. Then, with thirty-six stickers, it had been the turn of this jacket, made with the same material from which they make the sails for the America's Cup. And much else: a set of ceramic pans, an electric knife, a mountain bike with thirty-two gears, a two-speed hairdryer, a wine-making set complete with professional corkscrew, thermometer, capsule-cutter and wine-pourer, a robot vacuum cleaner and other things too numerous to mention. But for the forbidden prize, the prize of prizes, you needed 360 stickers—in other words, almost a bottle a day for a year, which might seem an unattainable goal, but only if you look at it with the obtuse eyes of a valley-dweller staring at a fearsome mountain peak.

In fact, Torchio Wines are generous to their long-term customers. In spite of the prizes, the points obtained are not gradual, but accumulate. Torchio Wines really have thought of everything. And that is why The Master is now close to his goal. He only needs a handful of stickers to get the object of his desire.

The super prize: a modern laptop with lithium batteries, ultra flat screen, and DVD writer, together with a printer, a scanner and a distance-learning course in IT, all paid for by Torchio Wines, of course.

The Master is convinced that with a machine like that he will finally be able to plug his technology gap and rival other writers in creativity. Because in his opinion (he has no rational explanation for this, it's just a powerful feeling), the fiendish secret of the success of many modern writers is concealed in such machines and their circuits of red-hot silicon, and it is only thanks to the agility of word processing that these writers' torrential prose and labyrinthine plots are able to take shape. Thanks to that marvel, he, too, will be able to erase an entire sentence by simply pressing a button. The Master is excited just thinking about it. He even called Torchio Wines for information: "Can you tell me, signorina, is it just like a typewriter?" "Much more!" was the reply from the operator.

"Here, these are the last ones..."

The Lawyer had placed a ream of papers on the table.

"We've appealed to the justice of the peace, now we just have to wait and see."

"So I don't have to pay them?"

"No, not for the moment. But we'll have to see if the judge accepts the appeal."

"And if he doesn't?"

"If he doesn't... you'll have to pay."

"But I thought we just had to appeal..."

"That does work sometimes—what are you having?" The Lawyer had signalled to the young man behind the counter to come and take their order, and the young man had arrived in no time at all.

"A decaf coffee in a glass… How so?"

"Because… A small glass of prosecco for me, please."

"In the afternoon?"

"Why? Is there an hour for drinking prosecco?"

"Go on with what you were saying."

"No, I was saying that sometimes it's enough to appeal and the justice of the peace—"

"You did say in a glass?"

"Yes, thanks."

The young man had left them alone.

"Why do you take your coffee in a glass?"

"Because that's how I like it. Go on."

"So in theory the justice of the peace would be obliged…" The Lawyer had taken a mobile from his pocket and was looking at it vibrate. "I'm sorry, I have to take this… My dear fellow!"

The Lawyer had got up from the table and moved to an area of the bar where there was a better signal. He gesticulated a great deal as he conferred with his mystery caller, then returned to the table just as the young man was arriving with the coffee and the prosecco.

"I'm sorry, it was an important matter."

"Are you going to get to the end of your sentence?"

"OK, if the justice of the peace doesn't summon you within a certain length of time—"

"How long's a certain length?"

"I don't remember, I have to check in the office… How many?" asked The Lawyer, having already poured two spoonfuls of sugar into The Master's decaffeinated coffee.

"I usually take it without. Usually."

"Quite right, too. Too much sugar is bad for you."

"Anyway, what the hell happens if he doesn't summon you?"

The Lawyer had already drunk the prosecco and was draining the bottom of the glass. The Master watched him irritably.

"We win the appeal and you don't have to pay the fines!"

Fines. Even though he had sold the car years before, The Master was still being pursued over the fines he owed. Old fines, lost fines, fines never withdrawn, never paid, or paid but without keeping the receipts, fines that had slumbered for years in the dusty files of some office, like bacteria surviving under ice, only to then proliferate and spread until they infected him, just when The Master thought he was immune. That was why he had got himself a lawyer, a good one. "He helped me win my appeal against the admissions procedure at Rome University," the intern from The Small Publishing Company had told him.

"Listen, I have to go, I have to be in the office in half an hour…"

The Lawyer had stood up, gathered his leather briefcase and put on his cream-coloured jacket.

"Before I forget, that's thirty-seven euros for expenses."

"What expenses?"

"Administrative costs. Lodging an appeal used to be free. Now you have to pay. They do it to discourage appeals."

The Master had thirty-five euros in his wallet, and knew he had no coins in his pockets, but he had to perform the act of searching for them anyway. The Lawyer was a man of the world, and knew certain things, too.

"Thirty-five will do."

"Come in, come in, sit down…"

It was The Publisher who had spoken. He was sitting at a futuristic glass table in the conference room on the top floor of the publishing company's offices. Also at the table were the press officer, an androgynous woman with angular cheekbones and the husky voice of an inveterate smoker, the designer, a bald man with elusive features and of indeterminate age, and his editor, a small, cultivated man who despised writers almost as much as he despised himself for not having become one. The Writer smiled stiffly, took two steps across the carpet towards the table, but remained standing. The Publisher noticed his hesitation.

"Leave us alone."

"No, why—"

"We've finished anyway," he said, dismissing his colleagues with a glance. They gathered their papers, stood up from the leather and metal chairs, and left the room one after the other, smiling politely as they paraded in front of The Writer.

When they had all gone, The Publisher also stood up.

"Let's go to my office."

The Publisher left the room and The Writer followed him.

"They're a bunch of incompetents," he said out loud as they walked down the corridor. On either side, behind glass doors with small plates on them—VARIOUS, FOREIGN, ITALIAN—employees could be glimpsed bent over voluminous files or half-hidden behind their computers.

"Do you know what one of my recurring dreams is?"

"…"

"I dream that I come in here with a can of petrol and set fire to everything."

"…"

They turned at the end of the corridor.

"A bonfire of all the paper in here. A huge bonfire of proofs, manuscripts, contracts and bills. Seen from a satellite, it would look as if someone had lit a birthday candle over the city."

The Publisher could not suppress his excitement at the thought.

"Come, we'll be quieter in here."

They went through a door with a plate that led to a room decorated with paintings and rugs, at the end of which stood a massive desk cluttered with papers.

"And you know why I don't do it?"

"Do what?"

"Set fire to the place." The Publisher closed the door, walked to the desk and sank into the armchair.

The Writer shook his head.

"Because I don't have the guts. I'd pay someone to do it for me... Would you like to do it? Do you feel up to it?"

Even though the question was obviously a rhetorical one, The Writer wondered for a moment if he was expected to answer it.

"What are you doing standing there? Sit down."

As he said this, he indicated an uncomfortable chair with a steel frame and a leather seat facing the desk. The Writer obeyed. Only then did he become aware of the silence in the room, an artificial silence, as if all the sounds had been sucked out of it for an experiment.

"We're behind."

"It's so quiet."

"What?"

"In here. It's too quiet."

"Acoustic panels."

"What?"

"Do you see that?"

The Publisher pointed to a strange coloured board hanging on the wall, which The Writer had taken for a piece of abstract art.

"It's an acoustic panel. It absorbs all the sounds in the room."

"Get away!"

"If you like it, I can get you one."

"When?"

"Later. Now listen to me. Do you or don't you realize that we're behind?"

"Oh."

"A hundred and thirty-five votes, we can't seem to budge from that."

"Are you sure you've called everyone? Isn't there anyone you've forgotten?"

"The press officer is never off the phone, we've raked through our diaries, done recalls, those are the votes we have. It's because, compared with last year, at least a dozen are gone."

"How do you mean, gone?"

"Dead."

" . . . "

"That's the real problem. Otherwise it'd be perfect. We'd win every year."

"Why do you say perfect? They've been talking about renewal for years, a change among the voters wouldn't be a bad idea."

"What do you mean, a change! You really don't get it, do you? The older they are, the better. What little time they have left isn't enough to read all the books in the competition. So they have to choose: read or live. They can't do both. That's why they have to trust what we tell them."

"And if they don't?"

"They have to. Obviously, they want something in return. But they make do with not very much."

" . . . "

"Every voter who dies is a ballot paper up in flames. One vote less for us. The younger voters aren't so easily persuaded. A change would be a real disaster."

"I'm sorry, we're always complaining that this country is in the hands of the old, and when the young arrive—"

"As if being 'young' was something praiseworthy in itself. What does it take to be young? Who wouldn't like to be young? Wouldn't you like to be young again?"

"Excuse me, I'm not old."

"It takes courage to be old. To climb to the top floor of a building when the lift has broken down just to hand over a ballot paper, queue for ten minutes to grab a sandwich, skip an afternoon nap to sit through some dreary presentation, those people are real heroes."

"Well, if you put it like that…"

"It's not how I put it. It's the way it is. The young, *your* young"—The Publisher paused here, and filled the pause with a mocking smile—"are the people who aren't voting for you. They think your book's an embarrassment. They're voting for The Beginner."

"…"

"There's no use your making that face at me. That's how things are. They've done a good job with The Beginner. They've had him park his arse on the right sofas, on TV and in drawing rooms, they've stuck him on the covers of women's magazines. He isn't very intelligent but it's not vital for him to be intelligent—on the contrary. He's polite, good-looking, blue eyes, women have a soft spot for him."

"I don't think he's that good-looking, he has a stupid face."

"We're not going to beat him."

"Think of something!"

"Maybe I haven't made myself clear. We've done everything we were supposed to. Now it's up to *you* to think of something."

"Me?"

"…"

"What am I supposed to come up with?"

"Well…"

The Publisher stood up and slipped behind the desk. The Writer twisted his neck to keep him within his field of vision. The Publisher walked to a wooden door built into the wall and opened it. Behind one leaf was a battery of bottles, while the other concealed a small modern fridge, like a hotel minibar.

"Nothing for me, thanks."

The Publisher had taken something from the refrigerator, something small which The Writer hadn't been able to see.

"What's that?"

"An egg."

Holding the egg between his thumb and index finger, The Publisher shook his head, went slowly back behind his desk and sat down again. The Writer smiled, like someone who believes he's understood everything.

"What better to get rid of a hangover than an egg... eh?"

But The Publisher ignored The Writer's words, and continued to gaze at his egg as if it were a diamond.

"This isn't an egg. It's a book. And all of you"—there was pride in his voice—"are my hens."

He delicately put down the egg, which oscillated and then righted itself on the shiny surface of the desk. The Publisher picked up a metal paper clip, bent it and twisted it until it was a kind of stiletto.

"Watch very carefully," he said, taking the egg in his hand. "What am I now?"

"A farmer?"

"A reader. I'm holding the book, I'm a reader."

He slowly sank the point of the paper clip into the shell, making a tiny hole. Then he lifted the egg to his lips and sucked greedily. The Writer watched him in disgust. The Publisher moved his lips, shiny and dripping with fresh albumen, away from the egg and smiled at The Writer. Then he flung away the empty shell, which landed in a bin beneath the desk, making the noise of a paper ball.

"What did I do?"

"You had breakfast."

"No. I read a book."

"And what was it like?"

"Good."

"..."

"You know what the eggs you bring me are like?"

"..."

"I'll tell you. Rotten. They're rotten."

"…"

"And I can't take rotten eggs to market."

"But they've sold hundreds of thousands of copies!"

"Precisely. We've poisoned hundreds of thousands of people."

"…"

"And now we have to reassure these people before they bring a class action against us. They can eat rotten food for months, maybe years, because they have very powerful gastric juices, they're like hyenas. But when they realize that you've poisoned them, they may warn the rest of the pack to stop eating. And we don't want that to happen, do we? So we need a certificate of quality, something that guarantees the provenance and origin of the product."

The Writer was nodding mechanically.

"Good. I see we're starting to think properly. That's why, seeing that the last egg you brought me was rotten, we must at least put a sticker on it that says it's fresh. And that sticker is The Prize."

"But how are we going to win? You just told me there's no way we can."

"I didn't say there's no way. I said 'there's only one way'."

"And what's that?"

"It's time we talked man to man," The Publisher said, leaning forward threateningly and putting his elbows on the desk. "What are you willing to do?"

After the five-a-side match, The Beginner ran to the station and was just in time to catch a train for the small provincial town where there was to be an event that night. The umpteenth blind date his publisher had arranged for him.

In the foyer of the hotel, there is a green velvet sofa that looks like a mushroom grown during the night. On that sofa The Beginner, in order to hand over his documents and sign the privacy form, threw his light, functional rucksack, the kind a young explorer would carry. The dusty smell of the curtains, the burnished brass, the wallpaper swollen by damp—everything was sweet and familiar to him in this decadent place.

He was given the keys of his room by the concierge and grasped the cold brass of the heavy keyholder in the palm of his hand.

"Maybe you want to freshen up or rest a bit, you must be tired from the journey…" the organizers said to him as they escorted him down the padded corridors, as if he had just been given a life sentence. Yes, a life sentence, because he's realized that this is how his life will be from now on. He has signed a confession and registered the sentence with a single unconsidered gesture: putting his signature to that wretched novel. From now on, if only he has enough faith and strength, this will be his life. The most difficult part, making a hole in the ice, is over. All he has to do now is start fishing. The fish will come. It all depends on him.

"If you need anything…" No, he doesn't need anything. Thank you. The Beginner smiled politely—he would be capable even of killing politely—and withdrew to his room. Shall we wager that the first thing he will do as soon as the door has closed behind him will be to clean out the minibar and throw himself down on the big bed in the middle of this strange room, open his eyes wide and spin round with the ceiling while the world outside stops and waits for him? There, look. Wager won.

Over the course of the densely packed calendar of events, The Beginner has developed a harmless fetish for hotels. Deep-core sampling in his memory reveals that this weakness lies in one of the oldest layers of his consciousness, where there are fossil memories of distant, legendary journeys with his grandparents to tourist locations with a decadent reputation.

What he loves more than anything are provincial hotels, like the one he is in now, and of these provincial hotels, he prefers the down-at-heel ones, like the one he is in now, which still preserve traces of an old, corrupt luxury, like the one he is in now. It's an old hotel in the main square of the town, just opposite the theatre. Once the haunt of actors, commercial travellers and clandestine lovers, today it is a place for lost tourists who, over breakfast in the morning, take another look at their guidebooks to see if this really is the hotel recommended, or for solitary travellers who exchange glances of mutual suspicion in the lift. In short, the feeling is that the hotel is kept open only out of a stubborn desire not to acknowledge its own downfall.

The Beginner wishes he never again has to get up from the mattress into which he has sunk, wishes he could spend the rest of his days in this room like a convalescent. He has two pillows behind his head. He is tired but not sleepy. With the remote control in his hand, he hops between shopping channels and erotic chatlines, the images and voices follow one another without his brain being able to put them together to make any kind of sense. He thinks again about his day. The whole of his day.

The afternoon arrival by train, the verdant countryside outside the window, then the ring of speculative building that besieges the historic centres of Italian towns. On the platform, the embarrassment of the person sent to pick up a stranger he had only seen in a photograph on the back cover of a novel, the exaggeratedly cordial welcome by the patroness of the local book club, and a certain tangible nervousness over the organization of the event.

A nervousness which in the evening was transformed into embarrassment. And then into melancholy, given that the event turned out so pitiful.

Nobody came, almost nobody. The frescoed hall placed at their disposal by the municipality, freezing cold and barely warmed by two stoves, was deserted.

When the appointed hour had long passed and it was obvious that the plastic chairs would remain empty, the patroness of the book club plucked up courage, abandoned her indefatigable smile for a moment and apologized. "I'm so sorry, there's this flu going round… Half the town have come down with vomiting and diarrhoea…"

What about the other half, why hadn't they come? he would have liked to ask. What he said, though, was: "I understand. I've had it too…"

Those are the words that come out of his mouth. But they aren't true at all, The Beginner hasn't had any kind of gastro-intestinal problem, he's fine, in fact he's in perfect health. At most a burning in his stomach because of those miniature drinks he knocked back in his hotel room. Why did he say it, then? Partly to relieve the patroness of any remorse she might feel at having made the beginner travel so many kilometres for nothing (he had always been more embarrassed for other people than for himself), but because in the end he loves to make allowances for his fellow man. He may not be able to forgive the indifference of these townspeople towards his book, but he can understand it: when you came down to it, thinks The Beginner, he himself would never have gone to the presentation of *their* books.

But he knows perfectly well that basically he did it for himself, because to The Beginner the idea (just the idea) of being ill was not an unpleasant one at that moment, the warm dream of being able to stay in bed, in his pyjamas, with a cup of soup on the bedside table and a good book in his hands instead of persevering with that literary event, treating those two or three yawning customers with the same respect and the same enthusiasm he would show an adoring multitude.

It's one of the riskiest of situations. An author offering himself as a sacrifice to a handful of torturers who have emerged from their houses, defying the tiredness and sadness of the evening with a single intention: to see the writer, to hear the writer, to touch the writer. To have him in front of them, naked, bound to the stake of the event, a Saint Sebastian ready to be transfixed by the arrows of stupid questions and executed by the intelligent ones. Here he is, at last defenceless in front of his executioner, in plain clothes, stripped of his fragile armour of paper, demonstrating his fatal ignorance, his brazen mediocrity. A unique opportunity to give him the admiration, and the contempt, he deserves.

The Beginner had looked at them, inspected them anthro-pologically: a man in a jacket and tie, two ladies in furs, a young girl, a middle-aged man who had left in a great hurry before the end, as if he had suddenly remembered an engagement, or as if that infamous intestinal virus had finally struck him, too. The young girl might have been one of those precocious, sensitive adolescents who devour novels and poetry on the bus taking them to school while their companions share the earphones of their iPods and copy each other's homework. From her, he had nothing to fear. She would ask him for his address and he would give her his publisher's as a precaution, and she would send him a letter, in an envelope sprinkled with beads and scrawled over in coloured inks, in which she confessed she was in love with him. The gentleman in jacket and tie was a trickier proposition, a typical example of a provincial pedant, who would first put forward some criticisms of his book but then become unctuous and servile at the end of the event and present him with a small self-published book signed by himself in fine handwriting (a compendium of local history), begging him to pass it on to his publisher. And that was indeed what had happened.

Luckily, it was then time for dinner, and the patroness of the event and her ladies had transferred The Beginner to a small restaurant chosen by the book club, a place which, if it had not been for the booking, would have already been closed for a while at that hour. During the dinner he had drunk himself silly with carafes of white wine, had ignored the advances of a retired female teacher who proposed grim toasts to nothingness and smiled every time their eyes met. Feeling immune because of his youth and his immature talent, he had pretended to have read a whole lot of books, and lavished scandalous and almost offensive judgements on most current books and authors (all of them very much respected by his dinner companions). Outside the restaurant, with the shutter already lowered, he had lit a cigarette and blandly thanked the patroness, and she had withdrawn together with the other dinner guests, who were by now overcome by sleep and the effort of being sociable. Pleased that he had eaten yet another meal without paying—there had been many of them since his book had been in contention for The Prize—The Beginner breathed in deep mouthfuls of smoke and contemplated the midweek desolation of that decorous little town. Now, between the restaurant and his hotel room, there remained only one final formidable enemy, an enemy he had been trying to avoid all day: the neglected provincial writer chosen to chair the debate.

A debate without disagreements, an argument without arguments, the only sticking point being that a successful young beginner and an unsuccessful and less young writer had been seated side by side at the same table.

As had been predictable from the start, after an initial half-hearted rejection of the patroness's polite proposition, the provincial writer had accepted the invitation to dinner and had tagged along with the others. But The Beginner had managed, by changing places surreptitiously while his failed colleague had gone to wash his hands, to relegate him to the other end of the table, thus attracting hostile looks from him all through dinner—looks to which The Beginner could find nothing better to respond with than vague smiles.

Because he could well imagine ending up there himself, The Beginner had immediately recognized the type, universally known as "provincial writer who hasn't made it". It was a very specific, widespread and in no way innocuous anthropological and literary category. Poisoned by the suspicion, if not the contempt, of their own fellow citizens, hurt by the smugness of literary society towards them, worn down by rejection and their own inadmissible lack of talent, such people spent their wretched days exiled to their desks, writing imaginary reviews, updating their blogs, working away at novels doomed to the eternal darkness of a drawer. With the passing of the years, they ended up suppressing their feelings of failure and converting them into a sense of martyrdom. They constructed vast conspiracy theories in which powerful publishers, ensconced in the centre of things, did all they could to crush anyone outside their own charmed circle—the only proof of this conspiracy, of course, being their own misfortune. They founded small and apparently crusading publishing houses in some cellar, or directly in their own homes, clandestine distilleries where they got drunk on the very spirits they sold under the counter. By so doing, they were finally able to realize their dream and see some of their own manuscripts in printed form, just for the fetishistic orgasm of touching the cover, leafing through the pages, arranging them on display on the mantelpiece in their best room. The more enterprising of them even managed to found schools of creative writing—on the pattern of the more famous ones—in premises placed at their disposal by co-operatives or local authorities, more as an opportunity to exchange a few words with some human beings on autistic winter evenings than as an assertion of their own debatable teaching skills.

This was what had happened to our provincial writer, who had actually had leaflets printed advertising his school of writing, leaflets of which he had given whole bunches to The Beginner, asking him to circulate them once he was back in Rome. "If it's no bother..." "Oh, no bother..." The Beginner had replied, thinking as he said this, not "Would it be right of me to throw them away?"—he was already beyond that—but only "Where can I throw them?"

"Would you like a drink? I have some friends waiting for me in a bar…"

The provincial writer was looking at him with a treacherous smile. But the question had not caught him unawares. Prepared by the psychological analysis he had made, The Beginner had in his pocket the one answer which his colleague the writer could not counter without disavowing his nature and his character.

"Thanks. I'd like to come but… I'm going to take advantage of the time to do a bit of work. I have a piece to hand in tomorrow…"

The provincial writer nodded bitterly. He knew perfectly well what that meant. Mutual solidarity between colleagues.

Now The Beginner is cold, he shrinks inside his jacket, which is too casual for the way the temperature has dropped since the sun went down. If only he had been more sensible, and less trusting in tomorrow, he would have brought with him at least a sweatshirt to offer to the wind which has suddenly risen in the square, stirring the leaves on the branches in the park.

He has preferred to take a detour through side streets which, sooner or later, must any way lead him back to his hotel. And in fact there it is: at the end of the alley, he glimpses the dim sign on the other side of the square. An inevitable doubt accompanies him during the last metres that separate him from the revolving door. Will there be a night porter? If there isn't one, all it takes to get any porter to transform himself into a night porter is to have the courage to ring and put aside every scruple and sense of guilt at dragging a sleeping man from his bed. Here he comes, looking sleepy, his uniform creased. The Beginner just has to pretend that everything is normal, that he feels no embarrassment, no scruples, he just has to dismiss the porter with a hygienic "good night". It's his job anyway, just as it's the job of writers to stay out late. So the night porter who comes and opens the door to a night-loving writer and the writer himself are two professionals of the night, made for each other. There's no lift, but never mind, at The Beginner's age two flights of stairs are nothing. Here is the room. We're almost at the end of this long day.

It's time to sleep. The Beginner undresses, cleans his teeth, turns on the tap and thirstily gulps down two glasses full of water... Oh God, is it drinkable? But why does he always have these doubts after, instead of before, drinking? It's ridiculous anyway, with what he's drunk lately it certainly won't be water that kills him. He slips under the blankets. He hears a noise, a dull thudding. The Beginner gets up and walks barefoot—the carpet filthy beneath his feet—to the window and moves aside the shutter that's banging. There's nobody outside. Who are those streetlamps lit for? The main square of the town looks like a bathtub without water. A cat crosses it quickly and mysteriously, dedicated to God knows what nocturnal mission. The sky above the dark roofs is starless. It will rain tomorrow, there is a smell like damp sand in the air. Back under the blankets.

The Beginner's final—or rather, penultimate—thought before turning out the light is for The Girlfriend: how is she getting on with the parrot?

It wasn't easy to get her to accept the presence—which is a little unsettling, she isn't completely wrong about that—of that black bird in her colourful little loft. To persuade her, The Beginner had to exhume the old, but still valid, argument about moving: they'll look for somewhere new to live, somewhere more spacious, the old promise of a love nest works every time. If only he knew that The Girlfriend is pregnant, he wouldn't be so flippant about it. The Beginner turns out the light and falls asleep thinking—and this really is his last thought—about the hotel room in London. A bright room with lacquered furniture, clean wallpaper with bright colours, soft beds, shiny tiles in the scented bathroom, the capacious bathtub edged in marble and the sanitized toilet sealed with a paper band around it, so similar to the one they put on his book with a quotation from a rave review.

How different the bathroom is in this provincial hotel: the dead hairs tangled in the shower ring, the disposable bars of soap so small they risk ending up in the plughole, the musty odour of stale smoke, the worn appearance of the mattress, the faded wallpaper. But the main difference is that the translator of his book isn't here.

The translator of his book, blonde-haired, big-eyed, firm-breasted, with agile, muscular thighs that encircled him as she moaned above him, blowing her fresh, sweet breath smelling of mojito in his face. And what about that farewell kiss (or was it just au revoir)? That unforgettable kiss in the morning light, with his rucksack on the pavement beside him, the porter looking on indifferently, a kiss both brazen and shy, a kiss which at sunrise had lost its nocturnal boldness and become knowing, intimate, almost dignified. Yes, that's the real difference, the indelible difference, between that never-to-be-repeated hotel room in London and this shabby provincial hotel room.

One moment before closing his eyes and falling asleep, the beginner seems to smell a smell of fresh mint hovering in the room. Where does it come from? Has the young translator been lying in wait in the shadows, jingling the ice in her mojito? Has she taken a flight from London just to give her Italian lover a surprise? Is it an olfactory epiphany? A deception of the senses? Not a bit of it.

A smudge of toothpaste on the collar of his pyjamas. That's where the smell comes from. It doesn't matter, the important thing is to fall asleep caressing the charm of an image. Because the last thing you think before falling asleep must always be the most beautiful.

*

For The Master, the night is the most difficult time. He is assailed by a flock of memories, which he tries to shake off but can't, they're on his back, tearing him to pieces. Among these hungry beasts, there is a bit of everything: the prizes he hasn't won, the recognition he hasn't obtained, the festivals that haven't invited him, and those that have invited him without thinking much of him, the pans from the critics, the books he has finished and those he left half-finished. The Master glimpses an abandoned hut and breaks into a run. He's being pursued. The memories are hot on his heels, sharpening their fangs. Luckily the hut is close. He reaches it, goes in and pulls the ramshackle door shut behind him. He stands there panting, his back to the door. Out there, beyond those planks of wood, the memories are barking furiously, he's the one they want. But inside the hut The Master realizes he is not alone.

There is a figure in the shadows. He can hear its hostile breathing. The figure emerges from the darkness and takes a step towards him. It's a woman, he recognizes her, and that doesn't make him feel any safer: she's his wife.

She's the age she was when she died: it's the only way he remembers her, he never sees her looking young and beautiful, or rather, young, because she was never beautiful. Not even in his dreams. That last version of her—and the last image we have of a human being is usually the worst—has chased from his mind those that came before. The wife gives The Master a nasty look. She starts to speak. She attacks him for all the times he cheated on her, the blonde hairs on the shoulders of his jackets and the smudges of lipstick on the collars of his shirts, all the hours he stole from her, the lies he concocted. The Master says nothing.

After her death, everything changed. His life became easy, light. The world was once again available: he was like someone who has trained for a marathon with weights on his calves and suddenly finds himself without them.

But she isn't the type to be intimidated by any words that old braggart utters, they're only meant for effect anyway. She resumes her statement for the prosecution...

Deep down, she had known it from the start. Why did he get married? The profession he chose—or rather, the vocation, because it chose him and not the other way round—can't be reconciled with a family. Poets can't have wives because they can't be faithful except to beauty, nor can they have children, because nobody is more childlike than they are. To an artist, the family is a calamity to be warded off, a perversion to be cured of. If you give in to it, you either have to change profession or change family.

At last, in order not to hear her any more, The Master flings the door wide open and throws himself to his hungry memories to be devoured. Better to let himself be torn to pieces in the sunlight than suffocate in the dark. They leap on him, sink their teeth into his flesh, pick his bones clean. But the bites of the past are less painful than he expected, they hurt less than the scratches of the present.

Eat me. Chew me to the last mouthful, dine out on my misery. On the edges of pain you can always discover the beginnings of pleasure.

He has woken in a pool of sweat. It isn't the first time his night bed has become a kind of raft, a raft adrift. Sometimes a hand emerges from the mattress, like a shipwrecked sailor might do in the swell of a southern sea. He would like to row with both arms, convey that bed of anguish safely to dry land. He switches on the light, feels the urge. He sits up on the edge of the bed, takes the measuring cup from below and pisses into it. The urine foams in the opaque plastic. He pees and suddenly feels thirsty. A two-stroke engine. He goes into the kitchen. No wine, he's already drunk enough for today. What he wants is a glass of water, a nice glass of water. He doesn't even have the strength to wash the glass, he takes one at random from the sink, pours some warm, gassy water into it, and drinks. An aftertaste of medicine: he must have dissolved some effervescent tablets in that glass. He goes back to bed. But he can't get to sleep again. He's more tired than when he first went to bed.

How well he slept when he was young! Sleep is the one true privilege of youth. After a game of football, a day spent running in the fields, a fuck at the brothel, he would sink into a sleep as thick and dark as sludge, from which he emerged only when his mother pulled him out of bed.

Now he can't sleep any more, the night brings inevitable anguish with it. He goes to bed late and wakes up early. By day he is tired. So tired that for years he hasn't managed to write anything, not even his name on a cheque, not even a telephone number in a diary, a line of poetry on a box of matches.

He can't manage it not because he can't think of anything to write about, but because the very act disgusts him. A disgust superior to any effort, dispiriting, unimaginable, verging on revulsion. Every word that comes out of his head is like molten metal that solidifies in contact with the air, becomes heavy, very heavy, falls and crushes everything beneath it. The problem is with words. Because when wine lubricates thoughts, they still flow as fast and light as they used to.

He would like to be capable of writing as he thinks, quickly, without effort, the words as agile and dynamic as athletes in a race, jumping over hurdles, one after the other, go, go, go, flying towards the finishing post, faster than the disgust limping behind them. Well, maybe writing with a computer can really transform the page into a velodrome where you sprint to the finish, maybe that's what intoxicates young writers, what makes them write so much, what grants them the impudence to talk more about life than they've actually lived, what makes them believe they are so brilliant, so witty, so omnipotent and immortal. Because you can't die while you still have something to say. Witnesses should be spared. Speak now, or for ever hold your peace.

And he, our Master, is about to hold his peace for ever. Because what he had to say he said when he was young, in the season without seasons. When we are old we may say wise things, but when we are young we say true things. Now he is only waiting to leave this world, but he would like to do so in the best way possible, with a plaque on his bedside table. The Prize isn't just the best, it's the only way to take leave of the world with dignity, because there are too many sins and too many sinners, and he would haven't enough time, or enough of a voice, to ask forgiveness of everyone.

Poor Master, he doesn't have much time left. Even though the tests are good, even though his prostate ended up in some plastic bag in the basement of a hospital, even though his daughter doesn't speak to him but sent him her best wishes for Christmas, there isn't long to go now until the final Ceremony of all.

Nor until the other prize, the one from Torchio Wines, the one that means almost as much to The Master as the literary one, there aren't many bottles of wine left—he drank one just this evening—a handful of stickers and he'll finally have his computer. And maybe write a fine novel worthy of the name.

The same cannot be said of the book with which he is competing. A kind of slender literary Frankenstein incapable of speaking (let alone of moving up the best-seller lists), assembled by emptying drawers, turning out pockets, combing through scattered sheets and notes... The Master went through his house with a fine tooth comb in search of unpublished material. Or at least publishable material: once you get to a certain age, the two words become synonymous. Who gives a damn anyway? There is no modesty or shame when you're old.

So many thoughts tonight, too many. Better to sleep, come on. Good night, Master. Not a bit of it. No sleep tonight. All he can do is go to the chessboard and get the king out of an uncomfortable position. Though still not as uncomfortable as his own.

"What's the name of the hotel you stayed in when you were in London?"

The Beginner switched off the electric hair-clipper. In the bathroom, the only sound now was the drip of the water filling the toilet cistern. He put his head round the door.

The Girlfriend was sitting on the bed, putting on her sandals.

"Why do you ask?"

"Because my boss has to go to London and wants a different hotel, he says he's bored with the usual hotels in Covent Garden... I'm sorry, can you do me up?"

The Girlfriend had performed a half pirouette and was now offering her back to The Beginner, who went to her and tied a neat bow at the back of her blouse.

"Thanks... Well?"

"Well what?"

"Do you remember the name of the hotel or not?"

Sometimes, it's when we feel too sure of ourselves that we make the most unforgivable slips, the kind that turn in a moment into the most irremediable of errors.

Like when The Beginner, coming out of the offices of the publishing company, beside himself with joy, with the contract for his novel in his pocket, had bent down to drink from a drinking fountain, forgetting that he had his mobile in his shirt pocket...

"The Old England Hotel."

Or like now, when he has nonchalantly answered The Girlfriend's question, blurting out the name of the hotel with the timidity of an innocent child, or the boldness of a murderer (there's quite a resemblance between the two) before going back

128

to clipping his beard with the electric hair-clipper, completely unaware—but maybe as he's very young it might be better to say "not yet completely conscious"—of what a simple sequence of words can cause. The wrong words.

.

The Writer was sitting on a park bench, blissfully happy in the morning light.

He was thinking again about how he had left The Old Flame on the island. Without regret. Without smugness. He had left her as it was right to leave her, as you should get rid of the past when you realize it is the past. If he thought about The Old Flame he was reminded of the cans tied to the cars of newly-weds going off on their honeymoon, something jolly but vulgar, something from which to free yourself once you've turned the bend of happiness. He'd felt immense joy, and relief at having liberated himself. But he'd still ended that day in the red, because although he'd got rid of one useless person, he'd lost another who was indispensable.

His mother was in a coma, struggling between life and death, in a room in a very expensive clinic. Yes, his "poor" mum. Whom he was starting to conjugate "in the past tense", to get used to the idea of her passing.

From the cradle, and then putting him to bed at night, she had kept him spellbound with her stories and tales. Incredible stories, always the same and always new, which blossomed magically on her lips like buds on a branch. Stories that she invented with naturalness and ease time after time, borrowing people they knew (relatives, friends) and transforming them into fantastic heroes, magical creatures issuing from her heated imagination.

An inborn gift, a natural talent which she had exercised with passion until her child, almost an adolescent, had given her to understand that he had better things to do than listen to her fairy tales.

That was why, years later, when The Mother had handed him a manuscript in her beautiful, neat, joyful handwriting, consisting of big sheets torn from notepads, she had done so with a hesitation that concealed respect for, and reverential fear of, her male child's wide knowledge. "I've been bored since your father left," she said, "and so…"

And so it was only then that The Writer realized that The Mother had never stopped inventing stories since the days of fairy tales, because when passions are suppressed, they don't dry up, but are practised in secret, like heretic cults.

And turning those pages feverishly by the light of his bedside lamp, he had been struck by a mixture of stinging humiliation and boundless admiration. Here it was, at last: the novel he had never managed to write.

Which was why The Writer had gone back to The Mother, tongue-tied, and handed back the folder with his head bowed, as a sign of devout repentance.

"It's yours," The Mother had said. "Do whatever you want with it."

And he had. Publishing it under his own name.

At that moment, sitting on that park bench, The Writer was overcome by an indefinable sadness not completely ascribable to the state in which The Mother was now, nor the desperation of his decades-long creative crisis, a sadness so strong he could have peddled it to all the enthusiasts in the world and turned them into depressives, and would still have had some left over. Because he no longer knew what to do with so much sadness. And sometimes he didn't even know what to do with himself.

When he felt this way, being at home was almost worse. The Second Wife's reassurances, her stubborn optimism (Your mum will get better, you'll see, everything will be fine, you'll see, you'll see...), her unconditional trust in love and its infinite healing capacities (Come here, give me a hug...), instead of comforting him, irritated him. He was even upset by the superficial way The Second Wife had swallowed the excuse he had improvised on his return from his excursion with The Old Flame and the exchange that had followed:

"Am I allowed to ask where you've been?"

"To the sea. Following the line of my thoughts. Even thoughts lead to the sea."

And whenever he gave that awful, enigmatic kind of reply, she, instead of returning to the charge and pulling his answer apart piece by piece, would fall silent, still admiring, as if refuting him were an insult to his intelligence, something her upbringing and her docile nature wouldn't allow her to do.

When he was in a bad mood, The Writer went to the park. The only place he considered friendly. Not the bookshops crammed with titles, with those harsh lights and those piles of books that seemed like barricades, not the street with its narrow, dirty pavements overhanging the traffic, not the noisy restaurants stinking of fried food, not the sweltering buses, not the deserted shops with their assistants waiting for customers like hungry cannibals, not the cinemas with numbered seats in which it only took one transgressor to screw up the whole auditorium, but the park.

The only place where you could still stroll without having a destination, sit down without consuming, drink without paying. A kind of refuge for the incapable and the idle, a fortified citadel in which, especially in the morning, all the most unproductive elements in the city arranged to meet: tramps, pensioners, the unemployed, truants, clandestine lovers, directors in search of a film to make—and writers, obviously. In the park he frequented, fortunately, he had rarely met any.

The Writer would collapse onto a bench, happy to feel the spartan hardness of the iron bars on the small of his back, let his arms droop by his sides and look at the people without thinking of anything.

Legions of old people in wheelchairs, pushed by hard-faced foreign women chattering into their mobiles in unknown languages, advanced beneath the sun. Pale expectant mothers pushing their prams along the paths of the park, looking with disapproval at children sleeping in the pushchairs of young foreign nannies who swayed their hips provocatively in front of tramps with cigarettes in their mouths and bottles of beer in their hands. Squadrons of crows (*Corvus corone cornix*) overturning baskets and spreading rubbish all over the lawns, owners at the mercy of dogs driven mad by living in apartments, fountains gushing murky water, light filtering through the web of branches: this was the park.

But more than anything else, The Writer liked to watch the little children playing football on a small, scrubby patch of grass. Overflowing with indulgence, he envied them, he felt an incurable discontent at not being their contemporary, not being able to join in the game. What he would have given to run down the middle, feint away from a marker and shout at the top of his voice "Paaaasss!"

"May I?"

While The Writer was immersed in his thoughts, a thin, olive-skinned, distinguished-looking man had taken up position in front of him, face stretched in a broad smile.

The Writer shrugged.

The man sat down with the air of a person waiting for someone.

The Writer stood up and walked towards the gate of the park. He hated sharing benches. And not only benches.

A pity. If he had remained just a few minutes longer, he would have discovered who the man sitting next to him was waiting for, and what had become of The Filipino.

Nobody, only the owner of the bar who no longer gave him credit, could know with certainty that this apparently elegant man was not a law professor or an eminent barrister, that he did not have files, law books or doctoral theses in his swollen briefcase, but creased shirts and dirty laundry, that he had neither an office nor a fixed abode, and that he was only a poor alcoholic lawyer who had been struck off but continued to exercise his profession illicitly and when he was broke suggested claims and lawsuits to immigrants or people who were worse off than him. The problem was that there were always fewer people worse off than him.

Right now, The Lawyer had two clients. One was The Master, on whose behalf he was dealing with the matter of the fines, and the other was about to arrive. This other was The Writer's Filipino, who was in the country illegally. And Filipinos should always be helped to be legal.

Sooner or later, all writers come to Rome. Even those who do not want to come there, who say, "I'm not going to Rome even when I'm dead…" Because writers don't come to Rome to write, to work in films, contribute to newspapers, appear as guests on television or present their books.

They come to live there, or to say that they have lived there. But above all, they come to Rome to die. And when they die, a church is built around them. In every church in Rome, if you look carefully in the crypts, in the shrines, in the sarcophagi, beneath those of popes and cardinals, painters and captains are wedged the bones of dead writers.

Some died in restaurants as they were waiting for the bill, or in drawing rooms because they couldn't think of a word (a pity, they had it on the tip of their tongues), some were found stone-dead in the armchairs of their apartments with a better book than theirs on their lap, some died of exertion in bookshops because they couldn't find their books, or collapsed at the tables of bars because their pen had run out before they could finish a beautiful sentence, some died of hunger in parks while they were in search of an idea, or were run over while crossing the street because the idea had come to them at that moment, or dived into the Tiber to make an impression on a girl and didn't come up again, some died because no reviews had come out in the newspapers, or because nobody was publishing them, and those who were published because nobody was reading them, and those who were read because nobody understood them.

All very sad and painful, of course, but most died—let's be honest about it—without ever having written a decent line. With the belief, though, that they had inside them that damned book that would shake the walls of the bookshops and make other writers' books fall from the shelves. Except that if they had it inside them, they couldn't find it. Maybe because they had hidden it too well. Which is what happens with things we really care about.

As for ours (our Writer that is), he was on top, very much on top. On the terrace of the five-star hotel to which The Publisher had invited him for a drink.

"If you're not capable of creating a work of art, you have to become a work of art."

From the terrace you could see the whole of Rome. The golden light of sunset fell like honey on the roofs and the hanging gardens. From that height the Spanish Steps were like the ribs of a strange fossil that had remained imprisoned in stone, the people became the tiny tips of coloured pencils and the chaotic, untidy streets converged towards the Piazza di Spagna, acquiring a glorious, unquestionable order and perspective which they never had in the cramped vision from below. In the distance, the profiles of the churches, the pinnacles of the monuments, the jagged foliage of the pines embraced the limits of the city.

"You're not listening to me."

"Sorry, what did you say?"

"That if you're not capable of creating a work of art, you have to become a work of art."

"Who said that?"

The Writer tilted his glass because the straw could no longer extract any of the cocktail from the fruit in which it was drowned. He sucked hard, emitting a vulgar sound.

"Never mind. It's the substance that counts. Don't you think?"

"Oh, yes."

The Writer was watching a pair of seagulls who were hovering in the sky, enjoying the heat that rose from the cobbles and the asphalt made red-hot by the first warm day of the year. The birds were sailing with their wings motionless and arched, like handlebars taut in the evening sky.

"Listen, did you call the person I told you to call?"

"Who?"

"Are you listening to me?"

"Why?"

"Sometimes I don't think you realize you're a finalist for The Prize."

The fact was, lately The Writer hadn't been feeling much of anything. If he had looked for metaphors to describe the state of his brain, he would have come up with things like a disused warehouse, a closed airport, a terrain to be cleared of landmines.

"We're doing so much for you, but you're doing little or nothing for us."

"Can't *you* call?"

"Me?"

"What about the press officer? I'm sorry, it's your job."

"Some people don't like being called by the press officer, they want the writer in person to call them."

"Or the publisher."

"No, the writer. It makes them feel important. They expect a gesture of humility, a testimonial of affection…"

"Sycophancy, not affection."

"The fact remains, you didn't call."

"No. But the man's always reviewed my books sympathetically, he's hardly likely not to vote for me."

"No, not that. If you're going to be smug like that, we're not getting anywhere."

"Oh, come on. I'm sorry, I was just talking."

The Writer attracted the barman's attention and quickly rotated his index finger in a horizontal direction, as if rewinding a roll of film. The barman understood the sign, filled a glass with ice and immediately started cutting fresh fruit for another Pimm's.

"In my opinion, you're tired. You need rest."

"Yes, you're right. I really do. When we're at the end of this thing, I'm taking a holiday. There's a cruise that leaves from Hamburg on board an ice-breaker and sails to Greenland by way of the Svalbard Islands, where they organize a photographic safari to look for polar bears, and they also stop in a bay where, according to the brochure, if you're lucky you can watch the humpback whales reproducing and—"

"If I fell off this terrace accidentally," said The Publisher, getting to his feet and solemnly approaching the parapet, "what would the newspapers write tomorrow?"

"Why on earth should you fall from the terrace?"

"Come here."

The Publisher leant forward, pushing his chest beyond the parapet.

"Get away from there, you're scaring me!"

"Come."

The Writer got up from his chair and joined The Publisher.

"If I fell off this terrace accidentally, what would the newspapers write?"

"…"

"Look down."

"Come on, stop it. Let's go back to the table. I suffer from vertigo."

"Wait. They wouldn't write anything. Because nobody remembers publishers. They only remember writers. Which is only fair. You get the glory, we get the dividends."

"Well…"

"But what if *you* fell? What would the papers write then?"

"I don't know, and I don't want to know."

"I can tell you what they'd write. Nothing. If you fell accidentally they wouldn't write anything. But let's say you wrote a letter, and then fell off this terrace."

"What letter?"

"A beautiful letter, full of anger and poetry, a letter condemning prizes and their corrupt workings, the intrigues, the slander, the backstabbing…"

"…"

"They'd say the only true winner of The Prize had died."

"…"

"…"

"You think so?"

"I do."

"…"

"…And you know why?"

"No."

"Because if a writer kills himself, he's only doing his duty."

Between an action and a reaction, between a gesture and its consequences, everybody agrees that there is an exact relationship, but not necessarily a proportionate one. As an example of a gesture, let's take the simple light pressure of a right index finger (with the nail painted scarlet red) on a plastic surface, and indicate that gesture with the onomatopoeia "click" or "double click". As an example of a consequence, on the other hand, let's take the page of the website maps.google.it that appeared to The Beginner's Girlfriend as she tried to visualize the façade of the Old England Hotel, the hotel which the young secretary had booked for her boss on The Beginner's recommendation. Or rather, what appeared on the screen when, because of her harmless but unfortunate desire to check everything down to the smallest detail—which we should never be do: let what follows serve as a warning—The Girlfriend clicked on the *street view* option offered by Google Maps; and she did so, not because she didn't trust her boyfriend but, on the contrary, precisely because she trusted him, in order to go down those streets, with the charitable illusion of being there, of escaping her desk and the air-conditioning for a few moments; she did so in order to see the hotel and its aristocratic façade, without any ulterior motive, without any second thoughts; she did so to give her pride a polish, her pride at having sent her boss to an important hotel, that *contemporary luxury hotel where the City meets the West End*, as its website said, a really elegant place in which her boyfriend had been put up when he had gone to London to present his book. That was why she did so.

And precisely because she was not prepared, because she did not deserve it, because certain things are best not known about, and if you really have to know about them there are many ways of finding out about them, there are no cures for her disappointment or alibis for her anger.

When, off-centre in relation to the limp flags outside the hotel, to the left of the glittering entrance, next to a stone planter, almost at the edge of the image, she saw a rucksack placed on the pavement, a rucksack she thought she knew, and next to the rucksack the entire figure of a man, or rather, a boy she thought she knew but for reasons other than the rucksack, a boy who was holding between his hands the head of a blonde woman, a woman who on the other hand she was certain she did not know, a tall, slim woman with prominent breasts beneath her dark dress, her face up against his face, as if they were looking each other in the eyes before—or as if they had just moved apart after—a languid kiss (this was impossible to establish), and his head appeared—though it might only have been a suggestion—to have been caught in a slight, lazy rotation towards the lens of the camera, as if someone had called him from the other side of the street before photographing him. Extracting more details would have been impossible because of the not very high definition of the image, the angle of the light, the excessive distance from the lens. But, above all, it would have been pointless. Because a woman can recognize her man kissing another woman even if she's blindfolded.

What followed the conversation that had taken place on the terrace of the five-star hotel is difficult to reconstruct. The words fired from The Publisher's mouth like darts from a blowpipe could have been listened to by the lizards crouching in the cracks in the warm walls, could have been crushed in their hard beaks by the crows, like seagulls' eggs, or pecked at like seeds by the pigeons with coral-coloured feet, or maybe they could have been seized in flight by the falcon, and would have emitted the soft noise of a swallowed mouse or the electric quiver of a lizard's thrashing tail. But the only one who could not have reported them was The Writer.

On that terrace, with those sentences vibrating in the sunset, with the ice melting in his third (or fourth? or fifth?) drink left half drunk, with the wind drying his sweat-streaked forehead and sliding beneath his linen shirt, making him feel itchy, with The Publisher silent at last, staring at the motionless horizon—it was there, on that terrace, for the first time since he had started to write, or rather, for the first time since he had come into the world, with the city of Rome as the one unreliable witness, that The Writer saw, with superhuman clarity, the pallor of his existence compared with the blinding glitter of legend.

And for a brief moment he saw them flying together, and then separate. Like that pair of seagulls in the sunset.

Kissing a woman who isn't your wife or girlfriend while the curious white Google Maps car complete with cameras and periscopes is passing cannot be dismissed as mere misfortune. Let alone as fate. It is a privilege. A privilege granted only to a chosen few, a stern divine warning that serves to remind you of your own finiteness, your own smallness, your pathetic attempt to elevate yourself above your own irredeemably mediocre nature. That was why destiny, or whatever, had chosen The Beginner's book from a pile of manuscripts that had arrived by post, that was why it had had it published, that was why it had entered it for an important prize, that was why against every expectation it had made sure it became a finalist, that was why it had given it wide coverage in the press (much more than it deserved), that was why it had made sure a small publishing company on the other side of the English Channel had noticed it, acquired it, translated it, that was why it had invited The Beginner to London to present it, that was why it had put him up in an exclusive hotel, that was why it had equipped his translator with a C-cup bra size and a weakness for Italy and Italian wines, that was why it had made sure that, after a night of sex, the two of them had said goodbye and kissed with their feet on that stone pavement, at the very moment the stereoscopic Google Maps camera was capturing, with a wealth of details, one of the many insignificant frames to be sewn into its stunning urban patchwork. That was why destiny, which is the hitman of chance, had conceived all this. To remind him that such things are not done.

"Which language?"

"Italian."

The Writer mumbled the words and absorbed the cautious scepticism of the guide who was barring his way on the running board of the bus. She must have assumed he was an American, or at least a German. And with his baseball cap and his shirt unbuttoned over his chest and his aviator sunglasses he could easily have been either. But no, he was only an Italian.

The guide held out her hand and gave The Writer a pair of headphones in a cellophane packet.

The Writer instinctively put his hand on his wallet, as he did every time he was in difficulty, every time he wasn't sure what he was supposed to do, to check that that reassuring swelling was still there with him, that it hadn't abandoned him, because in his life money had got him out of trouble every time he had got into it. He took out the shiny wallet, stuffed with large, colourful banknotes, and offered one at random to the young woman.

The guide gave an embarrassed smile and with her hand invited him to put his weapon back in its holster: he'd already bought a ticket, and the headphones were included in the price of the tour.

"Channel 1 for Italian."

The Writer nodded, without really understanding. He could not even have said what route he had taken to get here from the hotel terrace, let alone what he would do afterwards. He was so drunk that he would have stubbornly denied that he was.

But his stomach was a cloudy fish tank, and the drinks he had had a school of tropical fish eating each other. He got on, his heart swelling with every step, and with difficulty climbed to the light-drenched upper deck. He had been preceded only by a couple of tourists, who, as they took their seats in the front, passed each other a camera with a telephoto lens.

The colours of the world seemed brighter, the tones more vivid, the light clearer, more transparent. And that must be an effect of the gin, the clear alcohol that leads to levity and clear-headedness. But the noises—of the bus with its big engines, the pneumatic drills on the building sites, the cars rolling over the cobbles—were becoming dark and menacing, and this was because of the rum, the dark alcohol that weighs down the senses and discourages all initiative. And his cheeks were red, which must be due to the Aperols and Camparis, which excite and exaggerate; his forehead sweaty because of the wine, which congeals thoughts and makes them jingle like coins; his lips salty and his tongue parched because of the tequila and the salt in the margarita, which leave you feeling as tired and thirsty as a shipwrecked sailor.

And his mind... Well, his mind was a prodigy of sensations, imbued with a reckless beatitude that would soon abandon him, but for the moment was keeping him going. Indeed, encouraging him. Even though his anxiety was merely suspended, taking the form of a premonition that would soon come crashing down on him, along with a hangover. Right now, though, on the upper deck of that double-decker bus, as the last light of day gave way to a grey dusk, between heaven and hell it was—for a while yet—heaven that was closer.

He staggered down the aisle to the front, and sat down. Once seated, he put on the headphones and after a couple of attempts managed to insert the jack in the socket on the armrest. He heard a crackling. He took off the headphones. But the world outside sounded the same.

In the meantime the bus was filling up, but he didn't see anyone, didn't hear anyone, didn't think about anyone. His only desire was to get moving, to break this stasis he couldn't bear much longer. Fortunately, the bus now set off, shaking like the deck of a ferry when they switch on the turbines in the engine room.

Slowly, the bus moved out of the noisy dock of the station. The Writer took off his sunglasses and tipped his cap back. He looked at the sky, vast and impregnable above the heads of the tourists. He reached out a hand to touch it. And this time the sky did not retreat, but let itself be caressed.

The imposing brick structure of the baths of Diocletian
   If a writer kills himself he's only doing his duty
   Built in only eight years at the end of the second century AD
   You'd get all the critics on your side
   They could accommodate up to 8,000 people
   Nobody would ever again be able to pan a book of yours
   Both sexes were admitted to the baths but at different times
   Home and dry at last
   The Aqua Marcia aqueduct that supplied
   The Olympus of writers
   From which the name "Termini" derives
   Top of the best-seller lists
   Via Nazionale, decreed by the government of the newly unified country
   Never mind fiction, top of the general list
   Quirinale, the highest of the seven hills
   You'll never again be able to ruin your reputation with a minor novel
   The great basin of the Dioscuri, which the poet Shelley
   There'll be tons of reviews

The fountains are enough to justify a trip to Rome
Reassessing is their job
Torre delle Milizie, from the top of which, according to legend, Nero
Nobody will be able to deny your stature
Thirteenth-century fortress built on the remains of the Servian Wall
We'll reissue the complete works
The transept windows lighten the volumes
Of course we'll choose the paper together
Which later became the Embassy of the Republic of Venice
A lovely Morocco leather cover
Famous balcony from which Benito Mussolini
Red with gold lettering
Vamos a tomar la via de los foros imperiales
With his elbow, The Writer had inadvertently pressed the button on the audio guide and was now on channel 2.
Back to 1
Known as the Coliseum. It could accommodate up to 300,000 people
On 2
Gladiatores destinados a ser devorados por las fieras
1
The classis pretoria, the famous military fleet
Channel 3
Trois niveaux d'escaliers ici se chevauchent
1
In the first sat the emperor, in the second the senators
Your opportunity
Used as a quarry for material
Revenge on other writers
After the sack of Rome by the Goths
Front pages of the newspapers
Now running alongside the cavea of the Circus Maximus
A street or a university course
Velabrum or river port

Piles of books

Boarian Forum

The windows of the bookshops

Here the Sibyl predicted for the emperor the coming of Christ

Maybe a gift edition or a boxed set

Sacred area of greatest architectural importance from the fourth century

Boxed set

Palace of the Chancellery

Boxed set

Marbles plundered from the Theatre of Pompey

Boxed set

Clement VI

If it's gratuitous it's a cowardly act

Alexander II

But if it's a protest

The magnificence of the Castel Sant'Angelo

Think about it

Formerly Hadrian's Mausoleum

An act of humility

The Vatican. The oldest absolute monarchy in the world

We're sure to win

Transformed into a fortress and finally a prison

To leave a mark on history

Tosca, the lover of Cavaradossi

The road to immortality

Typical colours of Rome are pink, orange and peach-yellow

Take all the time you need

Piazza del Popolo

Remember it's a week to The Ceremony

The work of Valadier, who was also responsible for the slopes of the Pincio

A week

Along the kilometre and a quarter that goes from the Piazza del Popolo to

You have a young wife

A race between Berber horses

Your children have their whole lives in front of them

The weakest set off from what is now the Via del Vantaggio

Time heals everything

Belonging to the Barberini family

Life isn't a solution

Taxes and tallage, which earned him the famous comment Quod non fecerunt barbari

It can be done

Which the Romans call Esedra

Think it over

Palazzo Massimo, now the Museum of Civilization

Give me an answer

In 1964 the mummified corpse of a little girl was found during excavations

It depends on how you see it

A discovery that moved the entire city

It isn't the end

Next to the little girl's body

It may be only the beginning

A small treasure

If you want to win The Prize

A splendid ivory doll

If

That is the end of our tour

You want

The commentary was written by Professor

To win

Thank you for choosing

The

Rome Open Bus

Prize

Wishes you

(If you want to win)

Goodbye
It
All
Depends
On
You

When an attack is made on our lives, we are usually the last to know. The attack is prepared in distant places, far from us and our insignificant little daily gestures. The fuse is lit, sometimes it burns for a very long time, it crackles, almost risks going out, has a little strangled sob, then starts burning again, inexorably.

At other times, though, the explosion is sudden, and takes even the attacker by surprise. But that's of little importance, because in both cases the fuse burns. We bustle about, minding our own business, and the fuse burns, we follow our dreams, and the fuse burns, we sin, and the fuse burns, we are absolved of our sins, and the fuse burns, in parallel, behind the scenes, the fuse burns. And we can't snuff it out or cut it. Because we are the ones who thought up the attack, made the home-made device by assembling mistakes, triggering lies and mixing the weaknesses according to an infallible recipe, and then planted the bomb in the unlikeliest corner of our lives, in the knowledge that one day, when the fuse has burnt all the way down, then we will indeed hear a great bang.

A boom that will make us as free, fast and light as a blast, an explosion that will break everything that enchains us, so that everything is recomposed in a new, different order of rank and meaning. And the firework display is so spectacular, it's worth an entire life.

The Beginner had been prostituting himself at a book-signing in a bookshop in the city centre. He hadn't called The Girlfriend to tell her he'd be late. If he had, she wouldn't have answered the phone. But he couldn't have known that.

He had stayed longer than he should have in the bookshop. Answering people's questions (questions from which it was obvious that almost nobody had read his book) without losing your mind was a task that required commitment and thought.

His unsteady, irregular handwriting, the pen wandering desperately over the page in search of support, the constant anxious request for the date—What day is it today? What day is it today? What day is it today?—as if with each inscription his brain wiped out the chronology, and his constantly changing signature, as if there wasn't just one person signing but many, like a primary school pupil doing his first spelling exercises, or a schizophrenic with multiple personalities: all these details revealed with incontrovertible clarity that he was merely a beginner, because professionals adopt an initial, a cryptogram like a national health doctor's, or a kind of monogram like the one you find on shirts, and, if they are actually forced to write a whole sentence, always write the same one, all their lives.

It wasn't just a question of signing, there were also the confessions, the outpouring of feelings, because that was another reason—the main one, in fact—why the people waiting their turn had come. A middle-aged woman had declared that she was in love with him, a pensioner had handed him a typed manuscript, a housewife even confessed to him that she never read books because she was too tired in the evening after she had finished her work.

However, there had been a shock during the procession of signatures. Emerging from signing one particular book and handing it back to its owner, he had raised his head and found himself looking at an unmistakable face. A sagging face, furrowed with deep lines, framing a sardonic smile ruined by yellow teeth: The Master.

The Beginner smiled nervously, completely unprepared for this encounter. During this whole process, with all the public events the three finalists were obliged to attend, The Beginner had become familiar with the figure of The Master. He would have recognized him even in the midst of other people, from a distance, from the back, half-length, in hotel foyers, in terraces laid for receptions, and so on. The same thing, obviously, was true when it came to The Writer. *Never let your enemies out of your sight* is one of the basic rules for achieving victory. Keeping up a conversation at a reception after an event and pretending to listen, while actually following your enemies out of the corner of your eye, observing their movements through the golden lens of your glass, recognizing the people they are talking to (pests, journalists, agents, editors) and—if possible—moving closer while pretending to be searching for something or somebody, maybe saying hello to a stranger or a distant acquaintance within range with the sole purpose of overhearing fragments of conversation…

All skills which are not inborn, but are acquired with the experience of literature and already figured in The Beginner's armoury. In spite of what The Master and The Writer thought, he wasn't as innocent as all that.

So from what dark abyss of the bookshop had that stooped figure emerged? In which lair of books had that denizen of the deep been lurking? How had he managed to materialize out of nowhere, with such a sulphurous, unpredictable appearance? But above all—and this question surpassed all the others—what the hell was he doing at The Beginner's book-signing?

All these doubts crossed, and filled, the distance separating The Beginner from The Master, the former sitting, the latter standing, the older man bold in handing over the book, the young man embarrassed in signing it. And they rumbled, in all their inappropriate obtrusiveness, in the head of The Beginner with the slowness with which an idiot grasps a concept. Late, too late, when The Master had already disappeared into the crowd and the anti-shoplifting alarm had started ringing…

On the way home, in a half-empty bus driving through the sunset to take him back to The Girlfriend, The Beginner tried to shake off that unpleasant contact, and to think of something else. He thought of the dinner awaiting him, a dinner on the terrace—the first of the season—which The Girlfriend had announced, he thought about his parrot, silent, off its food, and vowed to devote more time to its upbringing (as suggested by the *Manual on the Raising and Care of Parrots*) and thought about various other pointless things, whose only purpose was to keep at bay the unpleasant impression left on him by that close encounter with The Master. Hoping to throw it into some well of his consciousness, he decided he would not tell anyone about the regrettable episode. But the apparition presented itself again at every street corner with shameless tenacity: the anti-cholesterol testimonial of a bold advertising poster assumed the semblance of The Master, the siren of an ambulance speeding past on the Via Nomentana modulated into the bookshop's insistent alarm… every involuntary distortion his nervous system imposed on reality helped to evoke the unpleasantness of the incident. Fortunately, his was the next stop.

The Master was sitting on the toilet, his trousers down around his hairless legs (after a certain age, hair deserts the body like rats leaving a sinking ship), his feet wide apart and facing in different directions like the needles of a broken compass, his clogs on the faded tiles. He had The Beginner's book in his hand, and was looking through it in search of—let's say inspiration.

He leafed through it without interest, as if it were the phone book of a foreign city in which he did not know anybody. He looked at the pages and they seemed to him like hieroglyphics, Sumerian tablets, Sanskrit inscriptions. However hard he tried, he really couldn't grasp the meaning of those typographical characters lined up in neat rows. Not that this was particularly surprising, given that The Master did not have the slightest intention of actually reading the book. Heaven forbid! The only thing that intrigued him was the dedication: "with affection", "with irritation", "wrong direction"—he couldn't even read what the hell was written in that dedication... With a modicum of imagination you could even read "big erection" in that rickety handwriting. Could that be the outrageous tribute The Beginner had dared pay The Master?

This thought horrified him. To someone like him, the thought of being mocked by such a novice was truly inconceivable. The suspicion was enough, and the book fell from The Master's hands to the floor. The Master grabbed the book from where it lay open and face down on the tiles, pulled it up by the spine and turned it over slowly. The book had opened at random at the acknowledgements page.

A long, a very long list of acknowledgements, which overflowed from one page, occupied the following one, moved on treacherously as far as the one after that. It was like the end credits of a Hollywood film. The Master started going through these acknowledgements, shaking his head, but persevering, if only to measure the full extent of his distaste.

Beginners. Yuk. Disgusting.

Naïve, amorous idealists, they write acknowledgements longer than their novels and think they are in debt to the whole human race. To the writers who helped them find a publisher, to the publisher who took them on, to the friend who consoled them when they broke up with their girlfriend... They all feel it's their duty to thank everybody, a kind of pointless family tree of gratitude, from the mother who brought them into the world to the lowliest doorman in their publisher's offices.

At least—and this thought moved what had to be moved in the delicate position he was in—in *his* book and in The Writer's (which, now that he thought about it, was almost due back at the library…) there weren't any acknowledgements. Keep it clean, keep it simple.

The Master turned to get the toilet paper but found only the grey cardboard tube. There was no more toilet paper.

He tore a page out of The Beginner's book and wiped himself with the acknowledgements. As they get older, writers get better, or maybe more ungrateful.

The Girlfriend was in evening dress, as if instead of having dinner at home she was about to go out, as if that long black gown with the slit and those high-heeled shoes were for a date with a man she had only just met instead of with The Beginner, whom she had been with for three and a half years (according to him) or almost four (according to her). Before she had started cooking, she had taken down the parrot's cage and put it on the terrace, and now in the reconquered space of her little loft she was nervously pacing back and forth between the oven and the table, which was laid with wine glasses and her best cutlery. She kept raising and lowering the lid of the wok and the non-stick white ceramic saucepan to check if the basmati rice and the chicken curry were where she had left them a moment earlier, and opening and closing the fridge door and pouring herself small quantities of white wine which she then drank apprehensively before putting the bottle straight back in the fridge. With her heavily made-up, swollen eyes (and the onion she had fried tonight had little to do with the swelling) she looked like a woman who had things to say.

Because women wait to say certain things. They keep them aside to use at the appropriate moment, like an anti-rape spray at the bottom of a handbag. This time, what awaited The Beginner, whose keys were turning at that very moment in the defective lock of The Girlfriend's apartment, were unconventional weapons.

One was hidden in her belly, the other beneath the lid of the plate on the perfectly laid table.

"Here I am!"

"…"

"I'm late, aren't I? Sorry, darling, but they just wouldn't let me go at the bookshop!"

"…"

"What's for dinner? I'm so hungry, I…"

"…"

"How smart you look! Are you expecting anyone? Only joking!"

"…"

"I'll just go and wash my hands and…"

"…"

"But…"

"…"

"Where's the cage?"

"…"

"What happened to the parrot?"

"Sit down."

The Beginner at last realized that things were serious. Slowly and pensively, he sat down at the table, throwing an alarmed sidelong glance at the terrace barely illuminated by the moonlight: the dark shape of the cage was in a corner, but in that blackness it was hard to say whether or not its mystery tenant was at home.

"I don't understand."

"Eat."

"But…"

The flickering candle flame was between them. The Girlfriend moved the tip of her nose imperceptibly, indicated The Beginner's covered plate, and with a nod invited him, or rather, challenged him to lift the lid.

"Eat, before it gets cold."

The Beginner summoned up courage and lifted the lid. At the bottom of the empty plate lay a strange object. A kind of plastic thermometer with one vertical line and one horizontal.

"What's this?"

"A pregnancy test."

"What… what…"

"I'm pregnant."

"…"

"Wait there, let me get the second course."

"But—"

"Here you are, help yourself."

The Girlfriend was on her feet in front of The Beginner, holding with one hand—holding it nice and high, level with her prominent cheekbones—a glittering silver tray with a domed lid that looked like a Trojan shield.

She moved the tray closer to The Beginner's face, put it right under his nose, then grabbed the lid by the knob, and removed it with a theatrical gesture.

The Beginner just had time to see a sheet of paper imbued with the dull colours of an ink jet printer before the colours came together to form an image that struck him at the same time as strange and yet familiar: a photograph of the main entrance of a hotel in London, of a stretch of pavement in London, of a rucksack placed on that stretch of pavement in London, and a young man and a young woman who had just kissed each other in the open air of London.

Then the tray came down on his head with a furious clang. This was followed by screams and tears.

"Now get out," she said when she had calmed down. "You and that damned parrot."

When he was small, in the endless prairies of time of his childhood, before the world of adults snatched him from freedom with the sadistic institution of school, he would spend whole days playing alone on a sun-drenched veranda, silently concentrating on deploying toy soldiers in imaginary battles. Even though he could not see his mother, and for long periods was so absorbed in his games that he forgot all about her, and even about himself, deep down he knew that her love was watching over him.

He could feel the warmth of her affectionate presence, the invisible gusts of wind stirred by her movements, hear her walking down the corridors, crossing the rooms. Now she was in the kitchen, now in the bedroom, now she had gone down into the cellar to get firewood for the stove. He never wondered about her whereabouts, but at every moment he'd have been able to say where she was and what she was doing.

Every now and again she would pass to check up on him, she would look through the doorway, lean in slightly and watch him from the back as he sat on the rug, bent over his battling armies. He would immediately be aware of that gentle intrusion (it was his loyal soldiers who warned him that there was an enemy behind him), but he would pretend he hadn't noticed and actually increase his concentration on his games, striving to find a difficult balance for the one-legged soldier or for the sniper lying in wait on the roof, pretending to be even more engrossed in the game, thinking she would never want to break the fragile spell of his games.

Sometimes, when his deception didn't work and their eyes and smiles met, she would pass her hand through his hair and she would ask him what he wanted for a snack. It was always bread and jam in winter, and bread rubbed with tomato in summer.

Now, in the air-conditioned room in the intensive care unit of the luxurious clinic in which The Mother was a patient, The Writer contemplated the carnations wilting in the vase (even though he'd watered them), and looked at his mother lying in the bed, somehow shrunken, enveloped in a spider's web of sleep. He found it hard to recognize in her that attentive young woman who had passed her hand through his hair and made him so many snacks.

And was that greying man at the foot of the bed really the natural development of the child who had played with his toy soldiers? Was that creature the result of the growth—and deterioration—of the organs and cellular structures generated by the woman now lying on the sheets?

What malign kinship was there between these people? Through what perverse line had evolution passed?

"What should I do, mother? Tell me! What should I do?"

The Writer started crying.

And now it wasn't just a single tear, or watery eyes. No, The Writer was weeping shamelessly, the way we weep only when we think we are alone.

His tears and sobs drew one of the nuns into the room. The Writer turned towards the door, mortified. Thanks to her boundless familiarity with suffering it only took the nun a moment to understand that there are moments when we do not need to offer comfort or consolation, but only to stand aside and let the spasm subside, the tears cease, in the expectation that life will regain the upper hand over death. She left the room.

"I know you're there. I know you know. I can feel it. So help me, mother. Help me. What should I do? Because I... I really don't know any more... I... I'm so confused."

The Writer passed his hands through his hair and squeezed the bridge of his nose with his index finger and thumb.

"I want to win, I want it more than anything, is that wrong of me? Is it wrong of me if that's the only thing I really want? If I had something else, I'd care about that, but I don't have anything, I mean I have a lot of things, but it's as if I didn't have them, as if they weren't mine, do you understand? They're things I don't need, things that if I didn't have them, I wouldn't even notice I didn't have them. It's like when a friend, someone you're really familiar with, asks you what you want for Christmas or your birthday, and you start to think about what you'd like, and you can't think of anything, then you think about what you need and you can't think of anything, then you think about what might suit you and you can't think of anything, and that means either that you have everything or that your mind has turned to mush, and you say, I can't think of anything right now, I'll think it over and tell you tomorrow, but then you think it over and you still can't think of anything so you say just anything, something you already have, or at best something you can't find, maybe you don't know where it is but you don't feel like looking for it, and I've thought this over, I've thought it over a lot, and I don't know why, but this Prize really is the only thing I want, it's my one wish, am I asking too much? I don't think so. I don't care about the next novel, I don't want to write any more, or rather, I promise that if I win, I won't write another line, yes, I know, mother, I didn't write anything before either... but try to understand, it'll be different, I swear that... we won't write any more, you and I, I promise I'll get you published under your name, from now on I'll let you sign everything you write..."

The Writer took a bottle of water from the bedside table and drank. Then, feeling really hot, he undid one button of his shirt and sat down again next to the bed.

"I've been told that… that there's only one way to win, and you can't even imagine which way, mother, or rather, maybe yes, maybe where you are now there's no need to imagine, from there you just have to… to see. But… but it's a very cruel way, a way that… that… You can't ask a man to do something like that, because I really want to win The Prize, I told them, and they said, what are you willing to do? And I said, anything, I'm willing to do anything, and they said, if you're willing to do anything, what's the problem? Just do it. They're persuasive, but it isn't as simple as that, because this thing they're asking for is… how can I explain, it's all or nothing, it's not just one thing and that's it, it's everything, it includes everything, it contains everything, do you understand what I'm trying to say?… I mean, how can I give up everything? I have kids, a beautiful wife, a dog, a house, a publisher, and that's a lot, but it's not everything… I don't know if I'm making myself clear, I mean how can anyone ask you for everything? They can ask you for a lot, but not everything, that isn't the same thing, don't you see? I'm sorry, mother, I'm sorry if I'm boring you with all this… But I don't know who to ask these questions, I don't have anyone who'll listen to me, I don't even have anyone to speak to, I mean speak to openly, as we always did, you and I, I don't have a dog to… or rather, yes, I do have a dog, but it's not even mine, it's my wife's… and it doesn't understand anything… but anyway I don't have anyone, do you understand? Anyone of my… of our level, I mean… So where should I go? How's this story going to end? Not the novel that's in the running for The Prize, and not even the next one, I don't care about that any more, partly because if you're like this… and you don't recover, then the novel stays as it is, the way you left it, half-finished… even though, if you made a little effort to recover, maybe in a couple of months we could finish it… but let's forget about that, it doesn't matter right now, what matters is that I want to know how *this* story is going to end. *My* story! I don't know anything any more, mother, help me, I beg you, I feel so alone. Wake up, mother, wake up. And give me a sign, mother. What should I do, mother? Should I accept the proposition they made me?"

Now you can choose to believe what happened in that room or not, because some people believe in souls, some in angels and some in devils, some believe they have been abducted by aliens, some believe in ghosts and some in voices, some believe they have come back from the afterlife just as there are some who believe in novels, and luckily every now and again there are also some who do not believe—and we are among them. The fact is that even the most sceptical will agree that if it hadn't really happened it would be difficult, if not impossible, to believe that at the very moment The Writer calmed down and the room fell silent again like the burial chamber at the heart of a pyramid, the line of the EEG and that of the ECG underwent a sudden variation at the same time, the former registering the exceptional presence of beta waves among the predominant delta and theta waves, typical of the EEG of a patient in a coma following a stroke, and the latter the sudden rise of the heart rate from 90 bpm to 104, then an abrupt fall to 24 bpm.

He looked at The Mother lying in the bed: she seemed like the princess in a fairy tale grown old inside her glass case because of a thin crack that had let in the mortal breath of time.

He felt his strength fail him, his knees gave way faced with the gravity of the task, and he could not stop himself from kneeling at the foot of the bed. But it was not a nervous kneeling, a kneeling of surrender, rather a gentle bending, the inflection of a young tree to the imperium of the wind. The Writer laid his head on the sheet and closed his eyes. He again smelt The Mother's smell, a mixture of roses, beeswax and corn, the smell his mother had had when she was young. Then he took off his moccasins, easing them off with the tips of the toe against the heel, and let them drop noiselessly to the floor. He got up on the bed, edging his mum across to find a place for himself, made himself as small as possible, his legs gathered under him, his back curved, his head tilted back, and lay down next to her.

"So is that what you want, mummy?"

Immature, false, cowardly, opportunistic, and then obviously arsehole, bastard, son of a bitch and more of the most common insults that go through the head of a betrayed woman and which it is unseemly to list to excess. Many of these words yelled by The Girlfriend echoed in The Beginner's head like the gong ending a contest that hasn't gone well: with such wake-up calls, it wasn't easy to recover even a shred of concentration, not so much to confront fatherhood (but was that even true?) as to fill his rucksack with a few things and go and spend the night on a friend's sofa, in obedience to The Girlfriend's stern ultimatum.

But the operation was more complicated than he had anticipated, and the rucksack had filled up with terry-cloth ankle socks, shin pads, knee-length socks, spare pants and shorts, but without a shirt, a pair of trousers or a jacket... as if The Beginner were not totally conscious of the gravity of the moment and was getting ready for his usual weekly game of five-a-side football.

The Beginner emptied the rucksack and, for the third time, arranged—completely illogically but in perfect order—its contents on the bed, stubbornly determined to start again from scratch, because packing and unpacking that rucksack granted him the momentary illusion that it was possible to do the same with his life.

A father. He was going to be a father. Was it possible? Ever since he was born he had always been a son, and in the eternal struggle between parents and children he had always been on the side of the children, serving the cause with loyalty and self-denial.

Now he was being called on to betray that cause, to cross over and join the enemy...

With these thoughts hanging over him, The Beginner lost himself in what he was doing, lifted his head from his rucksack and looked at the loft in which he had spent the last year of his life, and for the first time it seemed to him less ugly than he had always found it. Did he really have to leave this apartment? Was The Girlfriend quite serious? The modular bookcase with the hanging lamps, the kitchenette with the sink in which he had strained pasta al dente, the little fridge that had housed his cold beers, the tottering plastic tower of obsolete CDs, the little corner into which his computer had been squeezed, even the cage seemed to him...

The cage.

After the quarrel, in the indefinite interval that had gone by since The Girlfriend had gone out through the door and he had started fiddling with rucksack, wardrobe and drawers, The Beginner had forgotten all about the cage and his parrot. He had performed every action as if he were alone. And in a way he was, given that the bird's state was just as inanimate as that of a mineral. Now that he thought about it, all his problems had begun with the arrival of that plumed guest. The Beginner went out on the terrace and looked at the cage where it stood shrouded in darkness.

The parrot was motionless and black inside his cage, as if carved out of peat, with its head under its wing, almost as if ashamed for him, and for his wretched fate.

"If it's all your fault, I, I..."

He approached threateningly, but was overcome with a sense of unease. Once the adrenaline of the quarrel had worn off, a blanket of despair had fallen over him: without The Girlfriend, without the security and strength she instilled in him, he felt lost. Finished.

161

To face the last part of the competition tormented by the sorrows of love, to reply to the questions of the public in mono-syllables, to sign every copy as if it were a notice of dismissal, to wander without appetite through the final—but crucial—cocktail parties, to appear tired and rumpled in interviews: no, now was not the moment to let go. He who needed peace and quiet to calm his basest instincts... What unforgivable carelessness!

The Beginner leant on the window sill. An impertinent breeze was blowing over Rome, whispering to the flowers and trees wait-ing in the darkness to keep themselves ready for the arrival of the summer—and The Ceremony, of course. When The Beginner would raise The Prize in victory and dedicate it to...

That was it. Now he no longer had anybody to dedicate it to. This sentimental accident was the last thing he needed. If he couldn't somehow heal the split, he would have to find himself temporary accommodation, move his things, find a new girl-friend... all things that sucked energy, time and concentration away from writing, but above all away from the competition. Because only someone who has never taken part is unaware how stressful and demanding it is to win, or even to just try and win (nobody in his right mind tries to lose).

Had the lucky star that had guided him so far abandoned him for good? The Beginner looked up in search of stars. But no star was shining for him. The sky, grey and orange with the reflection of the city's lights, was like the unsafe ceiling of a tunnel full of seepage.

He had to find some way to repair the damage. The Beginner still loved The Girlfriend. He loved her, and that meant a lot. Her gentle tolerance, her radiant good humour, her soft skin, her full lips like the beautiful, fatal fruit of a carnivorous plant, her ripe breasts, her long raven-black hair. Finding another woman, or women, wouldn't of course be difficult. But one like her, so good-natured and easy-going, so patient and courageous, a woman who didn't make waves, who wasn't demanding but let him write in relative peace—well, a woman like that deserved to be reconquered. But how? Not with scenes, not with bouquets of flowers, not with grand gestures. A letter. Yes, that was it, The Beginner would write her a letter. An old-fashioned, irresistible, desperate—or rather, heart-rending—love letter, handwritten. Was he or wasn't he a good writer? No woman, let alone someone like her, would be able to resist a letter like that. Anxiously, The Girlfriend would gently peel the flap of the envelope and be infected with love, as if the missive contained anthrax.

Pen and paper, then. The Beginner went back inside, carrying the cage with the parrot, thinking that it might inspire him at such a delicate moment.

Then he took a sheet of paper from the ream in the printer and a pen from a glass at the entrance. He sat down, shifted about in the chair until he felt comfortable, spread the sheet of paper on the table, tried out the pen on a shop receipt, neatly wrote the date in the top right hand corner and… stopped. How did you write a letter to make a woman fall in love with you? How did you talk about love? The only things he knew about love at his age he had put in his novel, all of them, and now it was as if the cupboard were bare, and all that remained in him was an unquenchable languor.

Maybe it was all down to the fact that, being accustomed to typing on a computer, the pen made him uncomfortable. How long was it since he had last written a letter by hand? In fact, apart from signing cheques, writing Christmas cards, dedicating books, making shopping lists, how long was it since he had last written *anything* by hand? But he didn't have time to go that far back in thought, because there was suddenly a voice in the room.

"Come on now, write a nice letter…"

The Beginner wheeled round in fright and looked at the room. The objects lay motionless, the half-light making their outlines vague and unreliable. But there was nobody else here. That was a pleonastic observation, of course: after all, who could there have been?

"…if you can," the voice continued from its hidden pulpit.

The Beginner got to his feet and ran to the light switch.

Defiled by the artificial light, the furniture and objects had lost the threatening appearance they had harboured in the darkness and appeared now in all their disconcerting banality. Not that this was much comfort to The Beginner. On the contrary, to observe that everything was stupidly in its place merely increased his anxiety.

"You know why you can't write?" said the voice.

All right, it had been a difficult day, a colleague had got him to autograph one of his books then stolen it, The Girlfriend had found out by surfing on the Internet that he had cheated on her, then he had discovered that she was pregnant, and finally she had thrown him out of the apartment. More than a difficult day it might be more correct to call it an unrepeatable day (let's hope so for his sake). His nervous system had been put to the test, what's more it was late, and he was tired and confused, but he hadn't drunk anything, or taken drugs… he hadn't eaten anything either, but could not eating cause such powerful hallucinations in a young male in otherwise perfect health?

"I'll tell you why you can't write," said the voice. "Because you don't know how to write."

And this time The Beginner realized whose voice it was and where it came from, but the mere fact of having realized it did not make it any easier to accept.

The cage was empty and the door open. The perch was swaying.

The parrot was perched now on the back of a chair, staring at him with a defiant air.

The Beginner retreated in terror. The bird, on the other hand, fluttered through the room and landed on the tap of the sink. It raised its head and swelled its breast. Then it spoke.

"You think you're a writer?"

"You... you're talking!"

"There are those who talk and those who write," the bird said, sharpening its beak.

The Beginner pressed himself against the wall, aghast. It isn't possible. I'm going mad. Or else I'm dreaming, yes, that must be it, I'm dreaming, he thought. A waking dream. I'll go to the tap, pour a glass of water over my T-shirt and if this is a dream, when I wake up the T-shirt won't be wet, right?

The Beginner went to the sink, opened the tap and let the water run a little. He filled a glass which was drying on the sink. He emptied it over himself and felt the T-shirt stick to his skin and the cold water spread over his belly. He wasn't dreaming. Unfortunately.

"You wrote a book. It came out well. But that was a lucky chance."

"What the hell are you talking about?"

And here The Beginner made a fatal mistake: he replied.

Because if there's one sure way to make a hallucination real, it's to give it a consideration it doesn't deserve.

"Anybody can write a book."

"That's not true."

From the living area, The Beginner crossed the loft to the bedroom. The parrot flew past him and glided onto the head of the bed.

"You don't even know how you managed to write the first book."

"Of course I do!"

"Oh, come on! The first book is like a foundling wheel in the Middle Ages. Someone arrives, leaves a baby wrapped in a bundle outside a monastery, rings the bell and runs away."

"It wasn't like that at all! It was three years of hard work!"

"You just happen to be the monk who picked up the bundle."

"That book is my child. I'm the father. And I'm proud of it."

"I bet there are times you can't even remember when and how you wrote it."

The Beginner turned his back on the parrot and went to the other side of the room. Beating its wings sharply, the bird joined him and perched on the curtain rail.

"I also bet you sometimes wonder if you really wrote it yourself. Am I right or am I wrong?"

"…"

"I knew I was right. Let me give you some advice—"

"I don't want your advice!"

The Beginner drew back the curtain and opened the window.

"Quit writing, you're only wasting your time."

"…"

"Do you ever ask yourself if you have talent?"

"Get out!" screamed The Beginner, showing the bird the darkness awaiting him outside the room.

"You're right to ask yourself that. It means you don't have any."

"Who the hell are you?"

"Oh, please. I'm a parrot."

"Leave me alone!" screamed The Beginner, abandoning the consideration he had so far shown that hallucination. "What have you got against me? What have I ever done to you?"

"I'm here to save you."

"I can save myself."

"By yourself you're not going anywhere."

"Well, I know where you're going."

"Do you want success? Do you want fame? Do you want The Prize? If you do as I say, if you follow my advice, there may be some hope…"

For a moment, The Beginner left the parrot in the living room and in a convulsive frenzy rushed to the bathroom and pulled the door shut behind him, while the parrot continued speaking.

"For a start, you have to change publisher, because small publishers don't have distribution. Tell me the truth: how often have you heard people say, 'I looked for your book, but I couldn't find it anywhere'?"

The Beginner emptied the canvas bag for dirty washing onto the floor. Pants, socks, vests and nightdresses spilt over the floor.

"Because if you want to compete for prizes (and maybe have a chance of winning) you need a big publisher, one with lots of votes in his pocket and a good press officer, and one who pays handsome advances, not that pittance they gave you. And sooner or later, we'll also have to tackle the matter of your agent, because you really need to change, you know? We'll go with the best, the one who managed to—"

But the parrot was unable to finish the sentence because just then The Beginner came out of the bathroom carrying the canvas bag, and in a fury threw himself on it and literally bagged it.

Shutting the top of the bag tightly, with the parrot writhing inside and screaming furiously, he dragged it to the bookcase. He took a heavy dictionary of synonyms and antonyms from one of the shelves and slipped it into the bag, then, still holding the bag shut with one hand, with the other he pulled down other books from the shelves. Books that had been given to him as presents but which he already had, masterpieces he had pretended for years that he had read, books that already struck him as too long by page 10, books he'd been ashamed not to have at home, books not to be missed and books that you "couldn't not have read" all slipped one by one into the bag. The bird had stopped moving: even if it hadn't been knocked unconscious by the hail of volumes and crushed by the weight of culture, it couldn't have been feeling very well. The Beginner took a roll of packing tape, put it round the top of the bag countless times until the bag looked like one gigantic candy. He dragged the bag onto the landing, pulled the door shut behind him and called the lift.

A faint gleam announced that dawn was on the way. The traffic was still human, but within an hour all hell would break loose. The Beginner parked the car at the side of the road, switched on all four indicator lights, opened the boot and filled his lungs with the unhealthy early morning air. With the bag on his back, and taking care not to fall, he descended the embankment amid reeds and ferns and nettles and brushwood, following a path marked by dirty handkerchiefs, beer bottles and condoms, and reached the banks of the Aniene. A sickening smell of stagnant water and sewage caught him by the throat. The water, of an indefinable dark colour, was moving so slowly that it seemed to be refusing to follow the current. On the opposite bank, metal sheets covered with a plastic tarpaulin revealed the squalor of a desperate human settlement. As the pale sun rose behind the concrete roofs of the apartment buildings, The Beginner contemplated the bleakness of this place with a fatal resignation.

Then, with both hands, he lifted the bag, whirled it round in the air and flung it a long way, as far as he could, into the middle of the river. And the Aniene, with a splash and a gush of bubbles, indifferently swallowed the umpteenth rotten morsel offered it as a gift by men.

Explanations are even worse than goodbyes. In the following few days, The Beginner didn't write a letter, but there were difficult phone calls and delicate exchanges of e-mails. In the end he was granted an opportunity to explain. They arranged to meet in a well-known café in the centre. The Beginner had arrived early, nervous but guardedly optimistic, a newspaper under his arm. Amid the precise trajectories of the industrious pedestrians, aimed at their targets like missiles, and the lazy, nonchalant trajectories of the tourists, he set an unhappy pace, without rhythm and without destination. To interrupt his anguished wandering, he had gone into a café just round the corner from the one where they had agreed to meet and ordered a coffee. With the next one, that would be three, not bad for someone already feeling palpitations. In the end, thinking that in order to kill time it might be less ridiculous to sit and wait than wander about pretending to have something to do, he had decided to take his place beneath the white umbrella of the café where The Girlfriend should be arriving at any moment. Half hidden by the planters, a newspaper of property ads unfolded on the table, he looked at the comings and goings in the light-drenched street. The disc of the sun rotating high in the sky made the shop windows gleam, and cast veils of shadow that slowly devoured the pink façades of the buildings. From a distance every girl—at least for a fraction of a second—looked to him like The Girlfriend (or should he call her The Ex-Girlfriend? Come on, cheer up: all was not lost yet) until a detail or an obvious incongruity—a showy hat she would never have worn, thick calves, a blonde streak, exaggeratedly high heels—told him that his senses were deceiving him.

The Beginner had already repulsed two assaults by the waiter, the first politely ("What can I get you?" "Thanks, I'm waiting for someone..."), the second with a touch of annoyance ("Can I get you anything?" "I told you I'm waiting for someone!"), and by the time the third came around he would certainly have capitulated had he not at last spotted a woman at the end of the street whose features were compatible with the one he was waiting for. As she approached, every detail stood up to examination, indeed grew stronger, forming a female figure which at that distance seemed as familiar to him as it was strange.

She was advancing with a martial stride, dressed in blue linen. The light make-up, the metaphysical pallor and hardened features suggested that whatever his arguments, The Beginner would have to work hard not so much to impose them as to expose them. She flung her handbag on the table and sat down.

"You're looking beautiful," The Beginner said with a gentle smile, clinging to the comfort of habit. But The Girlfriend's look was eloquent, like an air-conditioner pointed at a naked, sweaty man.

"Look, I haven't forgiven you. I came to talk about the baby."

"Hold on, wait a minute. Isn't it possible the test—"

"False alarms are very rare."

"Oh. So what do I do now? I mean, what do *we* do?"

The Beginner anxiously noted an imperceptible swelling beneath The Girlfriend's dress. But it was only a fold.

"What I'm asking of you is a gesture."

"Right, that's what I wanted to talk to you about. I gave the parrot away."

"Who cares about the parrot?"

"I've arranged to see an apartment. Aren't you pleased? It's quite close to here, we can go together if you like."

The Beginner underlined his words by showing The Girlfriend a page full of ads, some of them circled with a marker. The Girlfriend ignored them.

"I want you to give up The Prize."

"What?"

"You heard me."

"You can't ask me to do that, I'm already a finalist."

"Either the baby or The Prize."

"…"

"…"

"What do you mean?"

"What I said."

"Blackmail?"

"An abortion."

"You… you can't do that."

170

"Oh, yes, I can."

"Try to be reasonable."

"No, you try. You haven't been reasonable since you published that fucking book."

"That's not true!"

"You've become cynical, selfish, vain."

"Me?"

"You'd never have been capable of doing something like that before."

Here, The Beginner was wise enough to keep silent, stifling his wounded pride, which would have liked to counter these insinuations.

"Fortunately you're still nobody."

"In what sense?"

"In the sense that you haven't yet won anything, you haven't been successful, you're not famous. Even though you already behave as if you were."

"You're paranoid."

"No, you're the one who needs to regain a little humility. I don't want to bring a child into this world with a father like the one I saw on Street View."

"You should be put away. In a clinic."

"That's where I'm going. To get an abortion."

"Are you joking?"

To make sure she wasn't joking, he should have looked that proud, wounded girl straight in the eye. But that was something The Beginner hadn't been able to do for some time now.

Let's face it, having your books brought out by small publishers can have its advantages: it's a bit like eating in a family restaurant. That was what The Master often said, more to convince himself than to answer the doubts of those who asked him how come he had never changed publishers in his long career, and why he had entrusted his books to a publishing company so small it was little more than a print shop.

Let's be clear about this. The Small Publishing Company that issued The Master's books was a fully fledged publisher with a back catalogue that brought out at least ten to fifteen new titles a year, a director who dictated the editorial line with the same love and the same care with which a grandmother knitted bonnets for her grandchildren, a press officer who worked hard (The Director's daughter), a meticulous proofreader (The Director's wife), a dynamic, fully computerized copy-editor who laid out the texts and took care of the various series (The Director's daughter again), a sensitive and perceptive editor (The Director again) and an innovative young graphic artist (an unpaid intern).

And its office was The Director's apartment. A small apartment in a somewhat dilapidated but lively multi-ethnic building in the Esquilino, populated by Sinhalese and Africans who had never complained about the presence of that unobtrusive publishing company on the first floor, so unobtrusive that it held down its expenses by "borrowing" the wi-fi from a Chinese hairdresser on the ground floor.

In other words, a small, family-run publishing company (hence The Master's comparison with a restaurant), a closely knit team that would sooner or later take him to the top, to the victorious heights of literature, validating the nimble revenge of the glider over the mammoth power of the fighter-bomber.

But who are you trying to kid, Master? You're perfectly well aware of the real truth. Come on, be brave, tell us how you felt every time you looked with indignant embarrassment for one of your books in a bookshop and they didn't have it, how your hands sweated as you went through the newspaper from first page to last looking for the review you had been promised and which wasn't there, make an effort to remember the taste of the canned meat you were eating as you watched your young colleagues smiling at the flirtatious questions of female TV presenters.

A prisoner: that was how he had really felt all these years. But in that case, why hadn't he dumped The Director of The Small Publishing Company? Why hadn't he abandoned him like a dog on a motorway, as everyone does as soon as they realize how things work here? Hard to say.

Maybe because being faithful to his own publisher was the only vice an unfaithful man could allow himself. In his long, foolish life, The Master had betrayed everything and everyone, his friends, his wife... oh yes, even poetry—let's drop this farce about loyalty to ideals—but the only person he hadn't betrayed was The Director of The Small Publishing Company. A simple, energetic man who wore sleeveless synthetic shirts and had a thick, grizzled beard which had once been dark—rather like his past, as it happens. He had long been active on the extra-parliamentary Left, until one day he had set up as a semi-clandestine publisher, starting by printing political texts of a Marxist-Leninist orientation, and emerging little by little from the shadows, only to plunge straight back into them by specializing in the publication of poetry.

Sometimes accompanied by his wife, but usually alone, The Director of The Small Publishing Company drove around in his noisy diesel van, with a mattress and the entire stock of titles in the back (this was his solution to the problem of distribution). He was like a carnival barker or street vendor, criss-crossing the country and clocking up thousands of kilometres every year to attend every Party festival, fair, exhibition and book-related event, finding any mangy patch of grass he could as long as it gave him a few square metres free to pitch his rickety stand. He would spend summer evenings drinking warm beer and eating salty rolls with roast pork and chips in plastic bowls without moving away from the stand, then sit down on a folding stool like a Sunday angler and read books that confirmed what he had always known about men and their destiny.

The Director and The Master, two foreign bodies that society had never been able to assimilate—or even to expel—the former as sturdy and well-built as the latter was thin and unsteady, a couple about whom, if you saw them a hundred metres away, you would wonder, Where are those two going? And at fifty metres, Where do they think they're going? And yet they keep going, The Master and The Director keep going. But to do what? To capture The Prize? Do they really have any hope of winning? One thing at a time. In the meantime they're going.

They've just left the van in the semi-deserted car park of the Parco della Musica auditorium, which from a distance appears to The Master like a huge mussel with valves made of silicon.

Unobserved by the world, sharing the weight of a large box filled with books, they cross the sun-drenched square, and their linked shadows are forced to follow them.

It was two in the afternoon, and there was almost nobody about. Which was understandable, given that the auditorium only comes to life in the evening.

Despite the modicum of visibility that The Prize had conferred on the book, it was no easy matter for The Master and The Director to get hold of this space for the presentation. The only time the owners said they were available was early afternoon on a weekday. An unusual time, nothing to boast about, agreed, but what can you do?

Nothing. You can't do anything. You can only enter the book-shop and hope there'll be someone there.

And that was what The Master had done. He had gone in through the automatic door, nervously, afraid it might close on him at any moment. This was a recent fear of his: that of being invisible, bodiless.

He had felt it for the first time one winter's evening, when the automatic door of a supermarket on the outskirts of the city had refused to open. The Master had been overwhelmed by an unknown sensation. He had stood there as if paralysed outside the clamped jaws of the door. The little red light of the sensor stared at him with scorn. The Master had started shaking and through the big windows had looked imploringly into the supermarket. Beneath the fluorescent lights, the colourful merchandise glittered on the shelves, weary women bent down to grab products and impatient men trudged along pushing trolleys. Immersed as he was in the semi-darkness of the pavement, although lit by the reflected light from inside, nobody had noticed him. And yet, as never before in his life, The Master had felt an all-consuming desire to belong to something, to be part of something, to be there, in the midst of those commonplace people performing the even more commonplace act of doing the shopping. He had inflicted a secluded life on himself, had always derived pride from being an exile and comfort from his isolation, had found strength in solitude, had disdained drawing rooms, steered clear of cliques, mocked high society—and now all at once he wanted more than anything to belong to the most anonymous of societies, to join the most resigned of armies. Entering that supermarket and queuing at the checkout with other strangers was more than a desire at that moment, as he stood outside that blocked door: it was an urge to live.

For the first time in his life, The Master had felt as though he were a ghost knocking at the doors of the living.

He had started shaking, screaming, beating his fists violently on the glass. A cashier had come running and activated the door from the inside. Other people had arrived. They had tried to calm him down. They had brought him a glass of water. The Master had been unable to give any explanation, he had simply kept silent, trapped in his own shame.

He had returned home without doing his shopping, drunk a cup of milk with honey and gone to bed. The same night that horrible sensation had assailed him again, reaching the centre of his consciousness, and The Master had wept, making the pillow wet. Then he had got up and started emptying the drawers in search of old photographs and yellowed newspaper cuttings, scouring his bookshelves, throwing out other people's books to find his own. Reading his own name in black-and-white capitals on a poetry collection had brought him a modicum of relief, a photograph showing him looking tanned and stern beneath a palm tree had alleviated his anguish for a moment, and a favourable review had eased his torment.

He had rushed to the bathroom in search of a mirror in which to see himself, but all he had seen was a scared old man. What had become of the young poet in the photograph? Somebody must have killed him and buried him in the garden. The thought had made him shudder, and he had felt dizzy. He had run into the bathroom and thrown up the wretched cup of milk he had been unable to digest. Then he had wiped his mouth with the back of his hand, gone to the telephone and, before the fear could completely overwhelm him, had phoned The Director of The Small Publishing Company, who was, if not the only friend he had, certainly the only one whose number he knew by heart. "I have a new book," he had said to the irritable voice at the other end of the line. "It's very good. You have to enter me for The Prize." It was a lie to say the book was new, nothing that came from The Master could be new. Whether or not it was good was not for him to judge.

The fact was that The Director, being a man of powerful intelligence and strong temperament, had taken advantage of the situation, riding the regular controversy that flared up every year the day after The Prize had been awarded, a controversy in which (some) newspapers, (some) writers and (some) readers waxed indignant over the excessive power concentrated in the big publishing groups, as well as the lack of turnover in the ranks of those allocated votes. With perfect timing, The Director had managed to obtain an interview with a little-read but crusading newspaper, in which he demanded more space for small independent publishers and—why not?—for books of quality.

The controversy had been taken up by other organs of the press and had made a dent in the impenetrable armour of The Academy. The Director had taken advantage of it to get The Master's book, printed in haste for the occasion, considered for The Prize.

In truth, the campaign had only succeeded because it enjoyed the consent of the big publishers, who were happy to have a third competitor in the race as an unquestionable demonstration of their openness and of the equal opportunities represented by The Prize.

That was how The Master and The Director of The Small Publishing Company had ended up, miraculously, as finalists.

And that was also how, miraculously, they had ended up in this bookshop.

As soon as they entered, The Director noticed that there was almost nobody there, and The Master noticed that there was not even a poster advertising the event.

The female cashier looked at this pair less with curiosity than with anxiety. The Director and The Master came straight to the cash desk, and with a joint effort placed the big box noisily on the counter.

"Shall we leave it here and you'll see to it?"

"Sorry, I don't understand, see to what?"

"In case you don't have enough copies of the books, we've brought these."

"What books?"

"For the event (clever this one, eh?)," said The Director with a nudge in the elbow to The Master, who was looking around uneasily.

"But... I don't know anything about it..."

"Listen, signorina, don't make us waste time," The Master intervened, The Director stepping aside for him. "Call your manager."

"The manager's on his break."

"Call him anyway."

"I told you he's—"

"Call the assistant manager, and if he's on his break too, call whatever damned person is responsible, and if you can't find that person either, call the delivery man—I just want to speak to someone."

"Maybe I can be of help."

"Anyone but you, damn it!"

The girl lost her veneer of false confidence, pressed a button and put her pale lips to a microphone.

"Someone in charge to the cash desk, someone in charge to the cash desk, please."

The announcement echoed around the shop, like a voice in an empty stadium.

Time passed, during which the three of them avoided one another's eyes.

As they waited, The Director guarded the cash desk and The Master moved away and, with his hands behind his back, started strolling between the shelves. In the whole shop there were a handful of potential readers, who were wandering listlessly around the various sections. Without too much conviction, they extracted books from the shelves, picked up the suggestions of the month, read the blurbs, turned them back and forth like fans, opened them halfway through and pushed their noses into the hollow between the pages, then put them back again, disappointed.

Beneath the artificial light, piles of thrillers blew ice or dripped blood from their glossy covers, blocks of best-sellers marked an obligatory route, a gallery of faces of well-known TV comedians stared out from other covers. In the Italian Fiction section, The Master looked for his book: it wasn't there. He checked to see if the titles were in alphabetical order: it wasn't there. He felt a lump in this throat. With long strides he reached the Poetry section and, by now in a state of some confusion, started running through the names on the spines of the books: at last, at the end of a row, right in the corner, jammed against the wall of the shelf, he found an old book of his. His anguish eased, and he felt a deep love suffuse him. As if it were a sparrow caught in a trap, he freed his book and took it in his hand. He blew away the dust, stroked the book, leafed through it as gently as if it were a living creature: if it had been possible he would have liked to throw it in the air and let it take flight. A heavily made-up middle-aged woman, hair dyed a Titian red, looked at him curiously. The Master held out the book, inviting her to take it. The woman took it reluctantly and examined it.

"Do you know his work?"

The woman shook her head.

"He's a great poet."

"…"

"The greatest poet alive today."

"Thank you, but I was looking for a cookery book," said the woman, handing him back the book. "Can you tell where I could find one?"

The Director called The Master, who joined him.

"We can't find the person in charge."

"Go and find him!"

"But I can't leave the—"

"Go!" The Master roared, and banged his fist on the counter, making the coins in the till jingle.

His temples throbbing, his hair unkempt over his thin skull, his face no longer just pale but ashen, The Master was beginning to look like a demonic mask.

Afraid of him now, the girl came out from behind the till, slamming the flap. The Master remained motionless, stunned by his own outburst.

The Director of The Small Publishing Company passed his thick fingers through his beard as if they were the widely spaced teeth of a comb. "I just thought of something," he said.

"…"

"What day is today?"

"How should I know?"

"I can't remember if it was the 15th at 16:00…"

"What are you talking about?"

"No, the event, I mean…"

"…"

"I hope it wasn't the 16th at 15:00…"

In an instant, the error pierced The Master's weary heart like a stiletto.

"I mean, my daughter left me a note and I couldn't find it… But I could have sworn…"

The Director wiped the sweat from his forehead with the back of his hand. The Master bowed his head, defeated. Then he looked up again, grabbed the microphone stem, bent it towards him and pressed the button.

"Summer is coming. If you're looking for a book to read on the beach, you've found it. It's waiting for you at the cash desk, in a limited edition at a discount price, copies signed by the author…"

The starlings at the Termini Station don't read books and don't compete for prizes.

They don't care about the traffic, or about the people getting off the trains, eyes swollen with tiredness, and waiting for buses to take them back and forth from home to work and from work to home.

Once seasonal, they would come down from the vastness of the North at the beginning of autumn, meet up in the skies of Rome and then fly together towards the mild African winters. Now they winter in the city and never leave. And that's understandable. The life of a commuter is no great shakes.

There are thousands of them. As they rise into the blue sky, they look like a blossoming rose made up of tiny lead pellets. They throw themselves on the fruit trees and plunder the vineyards. Then, having eaten their fill, they go back to sleep among the oaks and the palms, scattering tons of acrid guano on the benches at bus stops. The Piazza dei Cinquecento smells like one huge henhouse.

The lights from the streetlamps have altered the birds' cycle of sleep and waking, and they chirrup all night long. They sound like babies crying, but what is it they want?

Ornithologists say they are stressed.

They are not the only ones.

PART THREE

(One week to The Ceremony)

T HE WRITER had been unable to sleep a wink. Taking advantage of the short summer night, he had left the house as soon as a diffuse light had brightened the curtains at the window.

He had dressed in the first clothes he could find, then taken the lead and waved it in front of The Dog, which had looked at it without interest, still lazing in its basket. Sometimes he had the feeling the animal would have preferred to give up all bodily functions, to hold everything in until it burst, rather than go out for a short walk with him. With this thought in mind, The Writer had hung the lead back up on the coat stand and gone out alone to face the dawn.

The air was crisp, the city asleep. He had walked for a long time past the old Vatican walls that had led him finally to the Tiber.

Now, leaning with his elbows on the parapet, The Writer was watching the water of the river open upstream of the massive piles and close downstream, forming channels, like enormous wounds that healed instantaneously. Summer was just starting and the level of the river was beginning to fall, but the water was still heavy with the residue of the spring rains. The Tiber flowed placidly, drawing broken branches, plastic bags and scum along with it. And together with the bags it also drew The Writer's thoughts. From the height of the bridge, in sight of the river's eternal flow, his life seemed to him not so much finished as concluded, or rather, accomplished. Accomplished, not like something that has completed its task, but rather like something to which there is nothing to add.

The Writer was looking back at himself, searching for reasons for satisfaction, flashes of joy, detours along the relentless downhill route of his life.

He thought of all the things he had had, the things he had lost, the things he had been given, the things he had been denied—not that there were many of those—and the few he had denied to himself just for the hell of leaving aside something he could still wish for.

He had driven sports cars, he had lain on snow-white beaches and swum among swarms of tropical fish, he had skied on amazing slopes, he had mounted horses glossy with sweat and galloped away into the wind, he had surrounded himself with influential friends and sexy lovers, he had dined in the most exclusive restaurants and slept in the most luxurious hotels. And now, it was as if all that remained of the life he had lived were vague impressions, shadows behind a screen.

Everything seemed to have been carried away by the current of time. How did the champagne he had ordered by the case all the way from Rheims taste? Did the truffle he'd bought for an arm and a leg at the market in Alba really smell great? How many minutes of happiness had the architect given him, showing him the plans for the new house? Had he felt any emotion when he had taken his daughter in his arms for the first time?

The Writer felt a sudden warmth on his back. He turned and saw the sun high in the sky and people coming and going on the bridge. A pair of young foreign priests, with short hair and exposed necks, crossed the bridge with rapid strides, mixing with the tourists. How long had he been here, watching the water flow by?

"Excuse me, could you tell me what time it is?"

The passer-by replied without stopping. It was after midday. The Writer looked around him with the air of someone who has just woken from a dream.

A few paces from him, on the pavement, a Pakistani street vendor was selling his useless merchandise. At his feet, he had stick figures that danced when he clapped his hands and little electric cars that went round in a circle and got in between his legs like scared little mice.

In his hand he had a coloured pistol blowing soap bubbles that the wind immediately dispersed. Driven by a childish curiosity, The Writer approached.

"How much for that?" he asked, pointing at the plastic pistol.

"Ten euros."

"Five. I'll give you five."

The Pakistani nodded, in no way troubled by that abrupt decrease. The Writer extracted a crumpled banknote from his pocket, took the pistol and gazed at it in his hands. He started walking across the bridge in the direction of home. But halfway across, he stopped and sat down on the ledge. With a solemn gesture, he aimed the pistol at his temple and put his finger on the trigger. Then he burst out laughing. Next he aimed his gun at the river and fired.

A swarm of iridescent bubbles flew up into the sky.

Never before had he felt so light and transparent.

The Writer had made his decision.

The Beginner had spent the night on the sofa of an old friend from his university days, but hadn't been able to sleep a wink.

The squeaking of the springs, the heavy material of the smoke-steeped sofa, the damp that hung in the basement apartment his friend shared with a work colleague, the proximity of that apartment to some paleo-Christian catacombs, had given him a grim, restless night, one of those nights when all you can do is keep looking at the luminous hands of your watch and hope it will soon be day. It was only when the longed-for dawn arrived that his eyelids had at last started to close, but he had made an effort and got up. Soon the two clerks would wake up to go and work in an office on the other side of the city: at the thought of having to fight for the little bathroom at the end of the corridor, and of seeing his friend sleepily spreading Nutella on bread beneath the green fluorescent light in the kitchen, with his bum crack visible under the Juventus T-shirt he had been sleeping in, The Beginner felt a kind of disdain. He wasn't a university student any more, he'd had enough of shared bathrooms, hairs stuck on the soap bars, bills divided by calculator and stickers on the juices in the fridge according to whose mother had sent them.

He had already lived that life: but now... now he was a writer, damn it, one of the most promising around (there were even those who maintained he was potentially the greatest). All he had to do was demonstrate it. For a start, he stretched and got to his feet, splashed some water on his face from the kitchen sink, then looked around for a pen and paper, intending to leave a note for his friend. But just as he was thinking about what to write, he was struck by an awful sense of dejection. What was he doing in this place? Who was this friend of his? Why hadn't they seen each other in all these years? The Beginner flopped back on the couch. He felt more alone than he had ever felt, like a writer without a single reader.

To hell with the note, to hell with his friend, and, yes, to hell with The Prize too. Without The Girlfriend The Beginner was lost. He too had made his decision.

> Subject: Your last chance
> Congratulations, you have won our prize!

The Master carefully reread the first line, mentally articulating every syllable. Then he continued.

Dear customer,

To get it all you have to do is hurry up and subscribe to our latest offer.

The offer consists of eight fine red wines, and four crisp whites, and also includes four small bowls ideal for sauces, condiments or appetizers.

Included with the package you will receive a jar of truffle sauce, a jar of stuffed peppers, wild boar sausages cooked in Barolo and some tempting cucumbers in oil.

As soon as your order is received, the package will be conveniently delivered to your home via a reliable courier.

The products will travel at our risk, and in case of damage we will replace the goods at no extra cost.

In the next few days you will be contacted by one of our agents to agree on the details and time of the delivery.

Very best wishes

Torchio Wines

The Master folded the sheet of paper carefully, slipped it in the envelope, and put it back in the inside pocket of his jacket. Then he closed the letter box, leaving two reminders from a debt collection company to germinate in the dark.

Feeling pleased, with the intention of subscribing to the latest offer in his head and the weight of his years on his back, he waved to the Nigerian prostitute who had taken up her usual position outside the gate and walked down the tree-lined drive that led to his house.

In The Writer's house, everyone was asleep: The Second Wife, The Ukrainian Nanny, The Baby, The Filipino (yes, he was asleep, too)—everyone except The Writer.

Locked in his study, his features tense, his face illuminated by the bluish light from the computer screen, he was looking at the website of the biggest online bookseller and reading the comments on The Beginner's novel. There were five in all.

Win4life: A book as irritating as it is ugly. There's no plot, no logical development and, as if that's not enough, there isn't even a main character! The aspiring writer who wrote this rubbish isn't content to tell a simple linear story but, in his conceit, has tried to play around with chronology and interior narration. The result is quite frankly unreadable. I got to page 200, I defy anyone to do any better!!!

Rating: 1/5

Mundialito: The story seems interesting and well written at first, then as it goes on it becomes boring and falls off badly… overall, nothing to write home about…

Rating: 3/5

Tigersden: Likeable, a good read, not bad for a first novel. We'll hear more about this author.

Rating: 4/5

Supersimo@tascaliwebnet.it: I bought this book because I had heard good things about it, because the author is the same age as me and because they said he is a powerful new voice of his generation. Well, I really had trouble finishing the book, which was a great disappointment! A pity, because you feel that basically he can write and the idea is so up-to-date and important that it's really a missed opportunity.

Rating: 2/5

> Arturo: It's a moving novel, I read it in a few hours because the main character is so engaging. Long live the young men with beards!
>
> Rating: 5/5

Confidently excluding "Win4life" (he had written that one himself), and "Arturo", which in all probability had been written by a friend of The Beginner's or maybe his press officer, The Writer could consider himself well pleased with the public's reception of The Beginner's work. So they weren't as naïve as publishers assumed!

The Writer passed on to the older of his two rivals. He typed the title of The Master's book in the database. The result of the search brought a broad smile to The Writer's face. *No matches found*, said the screen.

Which was no great surprise, with the kind of distribution they had. Another point in his favour: if the book couldn't be found, that meant it couldn't be read either. And the jury would take that into account. The Writer yawned complacently.

Gratified by that double victory, The Writer could have calmly switched off the computer and gone to bed undefeated. Instead of which, he was summoned back by an obscure, morbid desire: to look up his own book.

The Writer typed his own name into the database, as if every letter were an organ of an imaginary double that was coming together, piece by piece, on that screen. When he had finished assembling the golem, he pressed *send* to give it the spark of life.

It emerged that the golem had written seven books, some of which sounded so strange and remote they might have been written by someone else (which of course they had been). The Writer clicked on the latest one.

There were ninety-two comments, two more than there had been the day before. The Writer chose the *newest first* option.

<u>Magiccat</u>: This novel isn't bad, though limited by a certain adolescent quality in the writing. On the other hand, it's a quick easy read, which also means it doesn't go very deep.
Rating: 3/5

<u>bertafilava</u>: slow, boring, far-fetched and absurd. Absolutely the worst book I have ever read. A waste of time and money.
Rating: 1/5

He took his eyes off the screen, hurriedly closed the browser window and from the scroll-down menu chose the *Shut down system* option.

With excessive caution, the system asked him if he was really sure he wanted to shut it down. The Writer had never been so sure in his life. This world didn't deserve him.

In the days that followed his decision, The Writer felt a noticeable change. And one of the first visible signs of this change was an erection in the shower. As unexpected as it was surprising, the erection manifested itself in a prodigious manner, like a quack doctor's caravan arriving in a border town. So prodigious was it that The Writer immediately wanted to run and find someone with whom to share this little miracle, but in the end he decided it was best to keep it to himself, and he masturbated in the shower.

Apart from the intense—though very brief—orgasm, the erection had helped above all to reveal a hidden problem: the lack of any desire in his life recently.

Yes, there had been a time when sex had been for him, like art, a noble and important branch of human knowledge. A way to achieve wisdom, a long, effortful road to awareness along which he had stopped only to catch his breath between one fuck and the next, exploiting every opportunity to penetrate different women in different ways.

Every time he set his sights on a woman, he had seen in her the repository of a body of knowledge unknown to him, a priestess guarding an inviolable temple that he had to take by storm at any cost. The ravines and dark caverns of women's bodies, it had seemed to him, concealed initiatory secrets and supreme truths that would finally fling wide open the gates of knowledge. That was why he had tried to penetrate as deep into them as he could, to forage in those viscera in search of priceless treasures. In his impossible journey towards that unreachable goal, he had hoped that every fuck would be the ultimate one, the supreme revelatory one, the magic formula that would put an end to his painful apprenticeship and make him a real wizard.

He had searched everywhere, foraged in every hole, explored every lair, but to no avail. Like a disappointed alchemist, he had finally closed the magic book, drawing a bitter lesson from the experience.

The object that The Writer had been looking for in women, either did not exist, or was so inaccessible it could not be reached with the rudimentary means at his disposal.

The same thing had happened with The Second Wife, his relationship with whom, initially based on sex, had turned into an exchange of devotion and tenderness—her devotion to him, his tenderness towards her, of course.

The erection had been the most visible of the changes, but not the only one. After communicating his decision to The Publisher with a laconic message in the dead of night, other things, too, had changed.

Just for a start, the morning toast: the very next morning it had struck him as fragrant and flavoursome (had The Filipino fallen into line?).

And even in his dealings with people he had regained a sense of involvement and a willingness to help which were surprising, at least to him.

Walking along a street in the centre, he had noticed water gushing from a crack in the pavement and flowing into the gutter. How many litres of water were being wasted like that every hour? Disturbed by the thought, once he reached home he had called the number used to report breakdowns to the municipal water company. But there was no reply, so he had called the fire brigade, who had passed him from one office to another and then kept him on hold for about ten minutes. The strange thing was that as he had sat there listening to the music they played, a nocturne by Mozart on a loop, he hadn't been at all irritable, but had actually hummed along to the pleasant melody with his eyes half closed. When the loud voice of a woman firefighter had interrupted the nocturne, he had almost been upset. The Writer had reported the leak and the woman had thanked him.

There is no way to demonstrate it, but The Writer who had hung up was a better citizen—and man—compared with The Writer who had called. And even if it wasn't true, that was how he had felt.

That night, he had fallen asleep thinking about the municipal workers who would fill in the crack, and had even dreamt of swimming naked in an irrigation ditch of icy transparent water, between the stones and the trout, and immersing himself in the municipal springs that quenched the city's thirst. The benefits of this invisible transformation continued to manifest themselves in the days that followed, making him increasingly open and accessible to the world.

On Sunday, instead of sitting in his study reading the newspapers, he had offered to take The Second Wife and The Baby for a walk.

It was early, and the park was quiet and shady. He could even

hear the murmur of the fountain, which for once was not drowned
by the exhausts of the cars or the ambulances speeding past
with their sirens blaring. The swallows (*Hirundo rustica*) fluttered
through the air like commas and brackets that had escaped from
a giant typewriter. The Writer had offered to push the pram,
and had done so with ease and naturalness, as if this—and not
writing—had always been his profession.

The Second Wife, her heels sinking into the gravel, soon got
tired of walking. The Writer, on the other hand, would have liked
to stay a while longer in the park, because with every circuit it
seemed to him that he was capturing unusual details, details of
the world that only revealed themselves to those who were willing
to capture them: a heart carved into the bark of a tree trunk, a
squirrel clambering up an oak, a porn magazine sticking out of
a rubbish bin.

"Do you want to stop? This isn't some kind of riding school."

The Second Wife collapsed on a bench and lit a cigarette.

"It's really nice here…"

The sun tickled the baby's face, and she laughed without reason,
intoxicated by sensations that were new to her. And not only to her.

"You've always got a cigarette in your mouth…"

The Writer tore the cigarette from The Second Wife's lips and
threw it under the bench. The Second Wife did not know whether
to be surprised or annoyed.

The Writer smiled at her. Then he leant over the pram. The
Baby had just fallen asleep.

"Don't wake her!"

Gently, The Writer picked up The Baby and held her in his
arms. On his shoulder, he could feel the warmth emanating from
that tiny head. The Baby had almond-shaped eyes, a squashed
little nose and a round face. The Writer took one of her little
hands and looked at it: the pink nails, the folds in the soft, thin
skin. More than a hand, it seemed to him the prototype of an

195

organ that would soon be going into production. The Writer put a finger in the palm of her hand, and with an unconditioned reflex The Baby squeezed it hard.

The Writer's mobile vibrated.

"Can you answer that?"

"Where is it?"

"Right-hand pocket of my jacket."

"…"

"I said right."

"…"

"Hello? Hi. Yes, he's with me."

"Who is it?"

"Your publisher."

"What does he want?"

"How should I know?"

"Can't you see I don't want to answer? You talk to him."

"He can't come to the phone right now, can I give him a message?"

"…"

"Hold on. He says can you drop by the office to talk about the cover?"

"Tell him it's Sunday."

"He says it's Sunday."

"…"

"He says it's urgent."

"Then tell him to come to our house."

"He says can you come to our house?"

"…"

"He says all right."

"Tell him we'll expect him for dinner."

"We'll expect you for—hold on a minute." The Second Wife covered the phone with her hand. "The nanny has the day off and you start inviting people to dinner!"

"What's the problem? I'll cook."

The Second Wife was stunned. Since they had known each other she had never seen her husband go in the kitchen, except to look for a corkscrew.

"Are you there? He says… can you come… to… to dinner, he's cooking."

"…"

"Yes that's what he said."

"…"

"Hold on: what time?"

"Half past eight."

"Half past eight."

"…"

"He says bye."

"Tell him goodbye from me."

"He says goodbye."

The Second Wife moved the phone away from her ear and looked at The Writer. The Baby had woken up. The Writer was sitting on the bench and was now jogging her up and down on his lap and singing her a nursery rhyme.

"Careful!" cried The Second Wife.

The Baby was bouncing on her daddy's thighs and laughing like a drunk. A silvery, gurgling laugh, with her mouth and eyes wide open.

"Stop it! She only just pooed and you're going to make her—"

The Baby threw up on The Writer's beige trousers. The Second Wife glared at him.

"They needed washing anyway," he said, with a mischievous gleam in his eye. Even The Baby seemed amused.

*

When you're young it's much easier to be sincere than to be convincing.

It is not at all easy for The Beginner to explain to The Girlfriend that pulling out of The Prize is much more complicated than it seems. No, not easy at all. Especially on the telephone.

"Believe me."

"I don't believe you."

"I tell you that's how it is."

"It can't be."

"If I pull out it'll be a real mess, it'll screw everything up."

"Who gives a damn?"

"Come on, I can't involve other people when it's my fault."

"Then lose."

"How do you mean lose?"

"Lose."

"…"

"Compete and lose."

"And how do I do that?"

"That's up to you."

"Don't you think that's enough? I slept on a sofa bed, my back's broken… If I lose, will you forgive me?"

"Maybe."

"Come on!"

"We'll see."

"…"

"…"

"Why don't we meet?"

"It's too soon."

"Please. I need to see you."

"After The Prize."

"…"

"…"

"Darling?"

"What is it?"

"Tell me the truth. You'd never have done it."

"What?"

"The baby."

"..."

"You'd never have had an abortion."

"..."

"Would you?"

"I don't know."

"I knew it!"

"I really have to go now."

"Do you love me?"

"Hang up."

"Do you love me?"

"..."

"Come back to me."

"Do what you have to do first."

"..."

"Lose. Or at least, try not to win."

The vegetable carbonara was a success. Free-range hen's eggs instead of bacon, courgettes lightly fried in oil, and onions—actually leeks or shallots would have been better, but it was Sunday and everything was closed.

Maybe a little too delicate, according to The Publisher (at any other time he would have openly called it "bland"), maybe "a little undercooked" for The Second Wife—the fact was there wasn't anything left on the plates. Then with what there was in the fridge (veal cutlets and some leftover ham) The Writer had improvised a delicious Roman saltimbocca, picking fresh sage from among the herbs in the garden, herbs The Second Wife was not even capable of recognizing, except on the spice shelf of the supermarket.

It was a small trauma for her to see The Writer standing by the oven in a black apron with the word *Bistrot* on it, nimbly chopping the onion, tossing the pasta with a sharp blow on the handle of the non-stick pan. She had never before seen him cook, and had never suspected that he had a passion for it, let alone the ability.

If the father of her daughter could cook without her being aware of it, what else was the man capable of? The thought made her shudder.

"Where did you learn to cook?" she asked him, her eyes open wide in amazement, as soon as The Publisher had got up from the table and gone to the toilet.

"I learnt when I was young."

"…"

"When I was a student."

"And why have you never cooked before?"

"I didn't feel like it."

Then The Publisher returned, and the conversation turned to other matters. Sitting at that round table in a circle of light, his elbows planted solidly on the peach-coloured tablecloth on either side of the art-nouveau china dinner service and behind the thick palisade of crystal glasses, The Writer struck The Second Wife as more affable and relaxed than she had ever seen him before. There was a light in his eyes, a light that made them gleam more than the silverware. And watching him serve the steaming pasta with a waiter-like allure, uncork the bottle of Bonarda dell'Oltrepò with a mere flick of the wrist, fill the glasses without spilling a drop, eat with a napkin tucked into the neck of his shirt, break the bread with his hands and clean his plate with it, she felt a kind of quiver of excitement: he was so manly and reassuring… For the first time since the birth of The Baby, she wanted to make love to him.

After dinner, while waiting for The Nanny to come home, The

Second Wife lay down in The Baby's room, and the two men withdrew to the study.

The Publisher took with him the crocodile-skin briefcase and the bottle of Japanese whisky with which he had arrived.

They lit two Havana cigars, and beneath a mushroom cloud of smoke, by the light of the desk lamp, like an undertaker dealing with the widow of the dear departed, The Publisher opened the briefcase and showed The Writer every article in his sample selection, one after the other. First they saw the proofs, then the various cover designs, for the soon-to-appear *opera omnia*.

The two men talked for a long time and agreed about many things. For example, about the photograph to appear on the boxed set, the choice of which, after a long and judicious scrutiny, boiled down to a dead heat between a black-and-white portrait of The Writer—a few years younger, with a boastful little smile, his head propped on his fist—and a more recent shot, also in black and white, of The Writer sniffing a small white flower, pushing his nose deep into the corolla. After weighing up the pros and cons, the choice of both of them fell on the photograph with the flower.

It would be a unique edition, a collector's edition, on high-quality paper, binding made by hand according to an old process, Morocco leather cover, tanned using only natural products, with gilded head and tail bands. On this point there arose a brief but lively discussion. For the colour of the cover, The Publisher leant towards an austere Prussian blue but The Writer did not agree. He found that solution, that blue coupled with gold, too aristocratic, a kind of blazer with showy buttons that would make him feel alone and melancholy, like an admiral at rest: to him, it was out of the question. Basically he had always been a popular writer, close to the masses, accommodating to his readers, and that was the image he wanted to leave behind him.

So why not red, stronger but still elegant, maybe in a dark shade?

A wine red, Bordeaux or better still Burgundy—yes that was it, a Burgundy red with gold lettering would be perfect.

The Publisher paused. Gravely, he extinguished his cigar and poured a finger of whisky into his tulip-shaped glass.

"But the collections of complete works have always been blue, we'd have to do it outside the usual collections…"

The Writer relit his cigar, which had gone out, solemnly took the bottle and poured two fingers of whisky into his tulip-shaped glass.

"Then do that."

"Do you know how much this whim of yours over the cover is going to cost me?"

"Would you believe me if I told you that I don't know and don't want to know?"

"I wouldn't do it for anybody else."

"Liar."

"You know how many copies we're going to print?"

"How many?"

"To start, two hundred thousand. That's just to start."

"In such a short time? How will you manage?"

"I've bought an old printing works in Serbia. They used to print phone books under Tito. They're just waiting for a phone call from me."

"I really like you, you son of a bitch."

"I like you too, you bastard."

Quite tipsy by now, the two men embraced with masculine vigour.

"Then we're almost there," said The Publisher when The Writer had let go of him.

"Yes."

The Writer's face clouded over. He stood up abruptly from the desk, went over to his collection of LPs and became absorbed in combing through them.

"I hope you don't mind me asking…"

The Writer still had his back to The Publisher. He chose a record with a colourful sleeve.

"Have you already thought about..."

"About...?"

The Writer turned abruptly and looked The Publisher right in the eyes.

"About 'how'?"

"That's none of your business."

"All right. Besides, in art, we judge by the results, not the process."

The Writer wiped the record with a cloth until it gleamed like petrol and looked at himself in the shiny surface: he saw a handsome man, with an arrogant little smile and a slightly wild look in his eyes.

"It's getting late. I'd better go."

The Writer carefully placed the record on the turntable.

"I'd like to hear a bit of music."

"You can do whatever you want this week. In fact, you should take advantage."

"You can bet on it."

The Publisher left the room.

The needle crackled and the record started turning slowly like an eddy in the middle of a pond. The Writer turned up the volume up to maximum. Heather Parisi's 1980s hit *Cicale* boomed out. The whole house started shaking. He took off his shoes and started dancing barefoot, with his eyes closed, on the cold floor.

"Darling, is everything all right?"

The agreement was clear. He was the one who was confused. If they wanted to get back together, he mustn't win The Prize. "How" didn't matter—what mattered was the result. He had to lose, as The Girlfriend had asked. Or do everything he could not to win, as he preferred to put it in order to beautify the concept.

But was there a way he could make sure of not winning? And above all, was it worth it? Maybe the decision had been a hasty one. Men do unthinkable things for women, that's true, but the proof of his love which The Girlfriend was asking of him was more than unthinkable—it was inconceivable.

How many writers would do it in his place? How many of his colleagues would give up the recognition that would for ever rescue them from the obscurity in which they were vegetating? Very few. Maybe nobody.

Moreover, although it was true that The Beginner was young, and had plenty of time, all the time in the world, to write other books and win other prizes, it was equally true that he also had all the time in the world to make other children, with other women.

Emboldened by these thoughts, and playing on her compassion, he had managed to obtain a late-night confrontation that had begun on the landing and had ended up in the bedroom, demonstrating how even the most implacable logic melts in the heat of bodies.

In again making love with The Girlfriend, instead of smelling the stale odour of burnt soup he had savoured the pulp of a fruit, a semi-adulterous sensation which had reminded him of his adventure in London.

But all these sensations, savoured in the night, had faded by morning, when we repent not only the things we have done but also those we are about to do. As The Girlfriend finished dressing, resentful at having sold her pride so cheaply, The Beginner remained in bed, wrapped in the warmth of his sense of guilt, buried in the certainty that he had once again made a promise he was in no position to keep.

"It was a mistake. It's best if you don't stay here."

"I'm going to take a shower."

"OK, but then go. What happened last night doesn't wipe out our agreement."

"But darling, I—"

"We'll talk about it after The Prize."

"Whatever you like."

"I'm going. Make sure you shut the door when you leave."

The Girlfriend grabbed her handbag, took a light coat from the wardrobe and left.

The Beginner looked at the sliding door that led onto the terrace. The new pane of glass gleamed in the morning light, like a widescreen TV tuned to Rome.

As naked and hairy as a hominid, The Beginner got up and pattered over to the coat stand. He searched in the pocket of his jacket. In his notebook he had numbers his press officer had strongly advised him to call. Numbers of people whose votes counted and could alter the outcome of The Prize.

Uncertain votes, votes offered and suffered, bought and sold, promised and denied, votes that at the uttering of a single word could sway from one side to the other.

"Hello? Good morning! Sorry to disturb you, I'm calling about The Prize... We met at the presentation in the theatre... Do you remember? What? No, the other one, the young one, that's right, that's right... Well, I was calling to... I don't know how to put this, it's about your vote... What? Oh, I'm very pleased you liked it, thank you, thank you, no, as I was saying, about your vote... Of course... I understand... Oh, you've already voted for me... No, no, of course I believe you, I wouldn't dream of... It's just that, actually, I wanted to ask you NOT to vote for me... What?... Am I joking?... Well... Yes, of course I am."

"We're not moving!"

The Director of The Small Publishing Company beat on the steering wheel with his fist.

"What's happening now?"

"How should I know? There's always something in this fucking city!"

"Excuse me, why aren't we moving? Has there been an accident?"

The Master had lowered the grimy window of the van and tackled a traffic policeman who was talking into his walkie-talkie.

"No, there's a transport strike."

The policeman went back to his radio.

"There's a strike."

"I heard."

"What time is it?"

"Six o'clock."

"Shit, we should have been there by now."

"Take the Aurelia Antica, we can cut across."

"If only that guy would move..." The Director of The Small Publishing Company hooted his horn. "That's it, get out of our way!"

The van, once white, now blackened by diesel fumes, managed to free itself from the steel vice of the other cars and turned onto the old Roman road.

"Tell me the street again."

"Lungotevere something... I can't remember the exact address. But I know where it is... Anyway, if it's 'Lungotevere', that means it's by the Tiber. We can't go wrong."

"Yes, just like the event at the Parco della Musica!"

"That again? That was an oversight."

"Let's not get into that. But are you sure there's any point to these things?"

"Of course there is."

"So tell me, what's the point of presenting a poetry book to a rowing club?"

"Don't worry. That's my job."

The Director of The Small Publishing Company accelerated, and a light came on on the dashboard.

"No!"

"What is it?"

"The radiator. The water's overheating."

"Now what do we do?"

"It's the washer on the cylinder head. I was supposed to change it but they were asking eight hundred euros."

"Like my advance! So what do we do now?"

"Let's look for a drinking fountain. The first drinking fountain you see, I'll stop."

"There!"

"Where? That's a rubbish bin!"

"Oh, sorry, I can't see from a distance... There!"

The Director braked suddenly and turned right. A big scooter passed him with a roar.

"You go and get the water, I'll look for a rag to open the valve."

"How do I get the water? I need something, a bottle."

The Director searched in the van. Under the seat he found a bottle of citron juice that had gone flat. "Here."

The Master took it and walked to the drinking fountain. It was a quiet street. Beyond the automatic gates, the perimeter walls and the hedges, there were glimpses of well-tended drives, guard dogs and big, powerful cars.

The Master leant over the drinking fountain. He unscrewed the top of the plastic bottle, which slipped from his hand and fell into the drain below the fountain. Before throwing away the little bit of citron juice that was left, he suddenly felt like tasting it. It was a disgusting, sugary swill.

The Director of The Small Publishing Company was standing by the steaming bonnet with a rag in his hand, trying to unscrew the top of the radiator. The Master started back towards the van, with the water overflowing from the bottle, so icy that it steamed up the plastic. On the way, he slipped on something sticky, lost his balance for a moment, swayed, then straightened, thinking he had been betrayed by his wet shoes.

"Here!"

The Master held out the bottle to The Director, who did not turn, his head still stuck under the bonnet. A cloud of white smoke, like a lighting effect in a disco, billowed from the engine. The two men avoided it with a timely leap backwards. They waited for the water in the radiator to stop boiling. Then The Director topped up the water, slammed the bonnet shut, and the two of them got back in the van, hot and weary.

"Bloody hell, what's that stench?"

"What stench? I can't smell…"

A foul smell of shit seemed to be trapped in the passenger compartment, as if a demon had suddenly appeared from the sulphurous pit of hell. The two men looked at each other in embarrassment, each secretly hoping he was not the source of that stink. Unfortunately one of them had to be. And it wasn't The Director.

The Master hadn't slipped because of the wet ground, but because he had stepped in a huge pile of dogshit, the kind with which the pavements of Rome are covered, yellow and as mould-able as clay, a substance that was no longer shit but was not yet something else different from shit, a product the chemical industry would call "semi-processed".

"It can happen. They say it brings good luck."

"What do you mean, good luck? These things always happen to you."

"That's not true."

"Maybe you have the evil eye."

"What are you talking about?"

"Have you ever checked?"

"I don't believe in such things."

"If I were you—"

"I never thought you could stoop so low."

"I want you to get out now. Go on, move. Get that muck out of here, I can't breathe!"

The Master got out of the van to get a better view of the situation, which was becoming increasingly compromised. Because if there's anything worse than stepping in one of those turds, it's stepping in them with uppers like a tank. And this was the case with The Master: an old pair of worn but magnificent Timberlands, the only decent shoes he had left, which he wore on special occasions.

The Master looked first for a patch of soft grass and started scraping away like a rooster.

"Let's go, get a move on!" The Director roared from the van. "We're an hour late!"

The Master examined the results but was not satisfied. So he started to scratch around, stooping over, with his eyes on the ground. At last he found a piece of wire next to a rubbish bin, took off his shoes, placed them on a low wall, and patiently began the hard work of chiselling away at the cracks in the soles.

"I'm going to leave you here!"

The Director started the engine and set off again.

"No! Wait!"

The Master ran after him barefoot. The Director slammed on the brakes and let him catch up. The Master, hair dishevelled, fringe sticking to his forehead, hoisted himself on board, panting.

"What about my shoes?"

"Leave them here."

"Am I supposed to come barefoot?"

"How do you think Jesus Christ preached?"

"He was a prophet."

"And what are you?"

"A poet."

"Better still. They forgive poets everything."

"…"

"Is there anything else, or can we go?"

"Just one thing."

"Let's hear it."

"Do you really think I have the evil eye?"

"Yes."

From the edge of the little wall, The Master's shoes watched the white van disappear in a cloud of black smoke like a squid in its own ink.

If only The Writer and The Beginner could have exchanged lives! If only they could have swapped their respective miseries and converted them into something very close to happiness! Without realizing it, they were both basically trying to be what they were not. Like everyone else, in fact.

Didn't one of them miss the carefree lightness of his beginnings? What he wouldn't have given to feel again the emotion he had once felt!

And didn't the other perhaps envy the solidity of the veteran? God, what he wouldn't have done to gain a modicum of gravitas!

Unfortunately it couldn't be done. And that was a real problem. Yes, a big problem.

Even more so for The Master, who didn't even have anybody he could have swapped his life with, because, apart from The Prize, behind his wrinkled brow, beneath the stubble of his silvery hair, between the calcareous synapses of his brain, he did not even know what he wanted. Except everyone's harm.

*

Death has an enviable wardrobe. He never wears the same thing twice. On one occasion he knocks at the door modestly dressed, another time he arrives at the appointment in monochrome grey, or we may see him working in blue overalls or moving around the lanes in a green smock. If he presents himself naked, it is only because he has not had time to get dressed.

The Writer, who had time—although not so much now—was hesitating in front of his open wardrobe. He wasn't choosing the clothes in which he would take The Dog for a walk, or even the suit in which to go to that evening's private view. He was choosing something important, the garments he would wear for The Great Moment—that was what he had decided to call it, because it sounded more solemn and reassuring.

The Writer took out the hanger and placed it on the bed as if it were a soldier fallen in war. He removed the cellophane wrapping and gazed at the magnificent morning suit in which he had remarried. Jacket, trousers, shirt, waistcoat... Only socks, tie and braces were missing. The Writer took some underwear from a drawer and put it on. Then he patiently recomposed every piece of that beautifully tailored jigsaw puzzle. As he did up the trousers, he had his first surprise: he had put on weight. In the last few days he had rediscovered many appetites. Apart from making love with The Second Wife almost every day (a fact by which she herself had been surprised, but not annoyed), he had eaten and drunk a lot. He would wander around the house feeling hungry, always returning Oedipally to the fridge. Especially in the dead of night, when everybody was asleep and he was alert, his head burning with thoughts, he liked to violate the territory of the kitchen. To break into that Swiss bank vault and finish whatever leftovers there were, soft cheese in little foil wrappers, slices of cooked ham, cold mashed potatoes and dried-up omelettes, even the leftovers of The Baby's pap had been finished off with cynical, voracious satisfaction.

By holding his breath, The Writer had finally managed to do up his trousers. He buttoned the shirt, which smelt of lavender, and put on the jacket. That was when the second nasty surprise arrived, because it was not only the bottom part of the suit that was narrow, but also the top. The jacket was tight across the back and the sleeves were short. The Writer looked at himself disconsolately in the mirror behind the wardrobe door: he looked like a mafioso at a funeral.

He quickly undressed and, remaining in his pants, recomposed the totem of the morning suit. Then, with an excitement that soon became frenzy, he emptied the wardrobes and drawers. Shirts, sports jackets, polo shirts, jeans, trousers, socks and ties flew around the room, his inexhaustible wardrobe piling up on the bed like a little mound of rags. After a hard struggle with that heap of clothes, The Writer emerged with some clearer ideas: a white shirt with a mandarin collar (a tie would have added a somewhat lugubrious touch), cream-coloured trousers and a blue jacket. Plus a pair of blue socks. He looked at himself in the mirror again.

He was the very image of an immortal writer, with an elegance that was considered but not premeditated, a marriage of tradition and creativity, and that touch of the dishevelled possessed by men who are too intelligent to submit to the dictatorship of fashion. Perfect. This was how he would go to his appointment. All he needed now were the shoes.

"All" was putting it lightly. Because when The Great Moment came, he would be on foot, and that was not an insignificant detail. He would need shoes that were appropriate to the situation, elegant but comfortable. Because you can't die in uncomfortable shoes. So The Writer opened his shoe cupboard and tried on all the footwear he had. French moccasins, decorated Church's, Australian half-boots, sailing shoes, tennis shoes, suede ankle boots, hiking boots, German sandals, espadrilles, even some flip-flops, but couldn't find a single pair that suited him. If they were comfortable they weren't elegant, if they were elegant they weren't comfortable, if they were sporty they weren't in keeping with the situation, if they were in keeping with the situation…

In the end, The Writer chose the least bad pair, a kind of closed sandal (although he already knew they weren't right), practical but inappropriate to The Great Moment. Then he went into the living room, where The Dog was lounging in his basket. He waved the lead and this time, unlike most other times, The Dog overcame the atavistic laziness imprinted in the genes of its vagabond race and came trotting towards him. The animal lifted its eyes to its master, then bent its muzzle to let him attach the lead, submitting to The Writer's authority. This had never happened before. The Dog had always hated the lead. Putting it on was always an exhausting ballet of moves and counter-moves, feints and counter-feints. Only The Filipino had a special technique to keep The Dog still, a skill The Writer assumed was derived from ancient martial arts.

What did the animal feel? Why had it surrendered without resistance this time? Had what was happening inside The Writer created a magnetic field? Something invisible to the naked eye, but perceptible to creatures with senses more developed than ours, like earthquakes sensed by animals before they arrived?

Questions that could not be answered, either by The Writer— looking very elegant apart from his shoes—or by The Dog, calm and compliant, as they went out to have a dress rehearsal for The Great Moment.

Have you thought about how? The Publisher had asked.

Had he thought about it? Since the possibility had been presented to him—officially, so to speak—he hadn't thought about anything else. It wasn't actually the first time the thought had crossed his mind. Even when he was young, very young, the idea had captivated him, almost seduced him, but in a heroic and completely infantile way. Every child is a hero ready for martyrdom purely out of loyalty to his imagination, a valiant warrior ready to fight to the death with his classmate to possess a football card. But now there was nothing heroic in him, or in what he had to do.

It was an ordinary task, a job to be carried out with almost clerical zeal. Once, in a poem, he had come across a great idea: that in performing that extreme gesture there was the possibility of finding oneself in another dimension, not the afterlife, but rather the before-life. Through the looking glass, into a world that existed prior to one's own arrival. The prior-ness of suicide.

Suicide. Yes, for the first time that word had lit up in his mind like the sign over a casino, and seeing it flashing in the darkness scared him.

The Writer, impeccable in his light trousers and blue jacket, and The Dog, its tail erect and its muzzle well forward, were crossing the park. The Dog was aiming its nose right and left like the self-propelled turret of a machine gun and barking at the other dogs, without breaking step. The Writer was looking up, but was not distracted. He was looking at the trees, but not the tops of them, not even the trunks. He was looking at the branches.

Over the past week, knotting his tie, tightening the belt of his dressing gown or looking at the handle of the lead dangling from the coat stand, he had thought a lot about how he would do it. A hunting rifle? No, too noisy and romantic, and above all, too literary. The thought of his body blown to pieces and his clothes ripped open and the smell of burnt flesh made him heave. If he really didn't want a complete break with tradition, why not go for the classic method: barbiturates. But what was the lethal dose? And what if somebody arrived in time and pumped out his stomach? Also to be dismissed was the idea of flinging himself off a flyover, because it was too ostentatious and would inevitably snarl up the traffic, while jumping out of his own window was impracticable because he lived on the ground floor, and gas was out of the question because he had a state-of-the-art halogen oven... How, then?

Maybe there was only the rope. The good old rough, thick rope. Feeling the knot tighten around his neck, his throat close, the air burst in his lungs. How long would it last? Would he lose consciousness? Would his soul abandon his body, or would it remain trapped in the limbs and hang there kicking the air until the last spasm? The thought gave him the shivers. How long would he be suspended there, like game left hanging until it becomes high? He had read that if the collarbone wasn't broken—and his would never break—you could last another ten minutes. No, he had to die more quickly.

As The Writer advanced, pursued by a swarm of dark thoughts, The Dog was marking their route with steaming spurts of urine. They walked for a long time, past the windows of closed shops, office supply showrooms holding closing-down sales, luxury car showrooms and finance companies ready to finance that same luxury, estate agencies and little shops with the sign "WE BUY GOLD", one after the other, scenes from a blockbuster about the kind of life the country could no longer afford (the country couldn't: he could). They walked down the traffic-clogged street as far as the underground stop. Young men in wide trousers and hoodies and tennis shoes were launching their skateboards against the incomprehensible architecture of the station, only to be pushed back by the hardness of the material. The wooden boards scraped on the stone and slipped on the metal with a crash that seemed exaggeratedly loud, given the clumsiness of the moves. In order not to see or hear, The Writer went down into the station, bought two tickets, one for himself and one for The Dog, and plunged into the warm intestines of the underground.

On the platform, as they waited for the arrival announced on the indicator board with the words NEXT TRAIN 1 MINUTE,

The Writer approached the end of the platform and looked into the dark mouth of the tunnel. From that tube came a distant clanking sound, like the shuffling of a chain gang. The Dog, a humble four-legged auxiliary device connected to its master's server through the lead, sensed that something wasn't right. It had lost its self-assurance and was nudging its muzzle in between its master's legs. The noise grew until it became a roar, like a distant roll of drums before a battle. A breath emerged from the tunnel, ruffling The Writer's hair. It was a tickle from the column of air rushing in ahead of the train. The Writer looked at The Dog, and The Dog looked at The Writer, who placed a hand on its head and stroked it.

How long can a minute last? Why wait? What if instead of a dress rehearsal for The Great Moment, The Great Moment had arrived? The Writer thought about The Second Wife (but not The First), thought about The Baby (but not The Boy and The Girl), and about The Publisher, and about The Prize, yes, quite intensely about The Prize. As the brakes of the train bit into the rails, The Writer had a vision: the big posters in the station no longer showed a bottle of perfume and a model with a knowing smile, but the cover of his book, with a band around it mentioning The Prize, the number of reprints and of copies sold...

The Writer took a step towards the yellow line, and The Dog followed him.

The train came down the tunnel, making the arched roof shake.

The Writer took another step, and The Dog dug in its heels.

The leather lead became as taut as a rope.

The Writer pulled and moved one of his feet to the edge of the platform.

The train emerged from the tunnel like an arrow of steel and light.

And The Writer fell.

There are dogs that would die for their masters. There really are.

Not this one. Even if it had never seen an underground train before, it knew at what point to start pulling. To pull with all the strength pumped into its body by the high-energy dog food (*for a glossy coat and perfect health*) The Filipino filled its bowl with every day. To pull with all its pectorals bulging, swollen, its back arched, its tail pointed downwards and its claws scraping on the platform, to pull with its nose wet and its tongue out. To pull so hard that The Writer's shoes skidded on the floor of the platform. To pull so hard...

...that The Writer fell.

But not forwards.

Backwards.

Hitting his coccyx painfully on the platform at the train stopped and the doors were thrown wide open, revealing this ridiculous man to the passengers.

No, those shoes really weren't right.

As he returned home, with his lower back aching from the fall and The Dog more depressed than tired, The Writer, drawn there by some invisible magnetic force, stopped again halfway along the bridge. He placed his hands on the parapet and looked down.

There was the solution, simple and economical. Within everyone's reach. No branches, no tunnels. Water.

Like the legendary Alaric, King of the Visigoths, for whose funeral hundreds of slaves diverted the course of the River Busento so that he could be laid to rest in the river bed, together with his glory, and his legendary treasures.

Well, now the Tiber would welcome *him* to its bed and cover him for ever with its age-old waters.

Pleased to have found such a simple but spectacular solution, The Writer could already imagine the item on the One O'clock News, with the reporter on the bridge, hair ruffled by the breeze, the Castel Sant'Angelo in the background, and the camera

217

panning over the barges and the firemen's dinghies as they dragged the river in search of his body... Talking of which, who would find him? Maybe a fisherman from Fiumicino, or a lifeguard from Ostia. Oh God, let's hope not. Because in such things every detail counts: you can't just be found by the first person who happens to pass by, but nor can you be found by someone who's too important and might overshadow the discovery itself. Perhaps the best thing would be not to be found at all. Immersed in the waters. Then nothing more. And the mystery would become a legend. Brilliant.

It had been a long walk. His back hurt because of the fall, and he needed to be content with doing one thing at a time: that was the way great enterprises were built up.

In the meantime, he had almost reached home. The Dog stopped to drink from the drinking fountain and greedily swallowed big gulps of water, then, at the view of the gate, pricked up its ears and curled its tail: exhausted by the overwork to which its master had forced it, it was already dreaming of its basket and its rubber toys.

The Writer was about to go through the gate into the drive when he noticed something: a pair of shoes on the edge of the low wall on which the perimeter fence stood. He went closer: they were beautiful Timberlands, broken down by time and shaped by thousands of steps, but still in good, in fact excellent, condition.

Was it a joke? Or the missing accessory to complete the outfit for The Great Moment? Who had left them here, and why?

When he picked them up, he at least discovered why. A lethal whiff of shit caught him by the throat. The Writer instinctively moved the shoes away from him and put them back on the low wall. The Dog went closer and started sniffing them and wagging its tail. Then it stuck out the pink spatula of its tongue and tried to lick them, but The Writer tugged at the lead with all the strength he could muster, pulling the animal away from the shoes.

"Don't even think about it!"

And he whipped it on the backside with the handle of the lead. The Dog still didn't understand. After all, it was his thing.

When fate crosses your path, if there's one thing to avoid it isn't turning your back on it. It's turning your head away and pretending not to know it. To recognize the few significant signs amid millions of insignificant signs, to try and bring order to disorder (or vice versa): wasn't that the work of a writer? To ignore that pair of shoes sitting on the low wall around the neighbourhood where you lived would have been more than obtuse, it would have been wicked. When fate shows its hand so clearly, all you can do is submit to its omnipotent will.

That was why The Writer had taken those shit-smeared shoes home. When you come down to it, even shit has its place in the universe, and has as much right to be in this world as we do. There was nothing here that could not be solved with a pair of rubber gloves and an iron brush. The Filipino was an expert at things like that.

To avoid The Second Wife making a scene, The Writer had taken care to leave the shoes outside the door, next to the doormat with the words In&Out.

Once inside the house, he had started looking for The Filipino, an activity that had lately become the domestic sport par excellence.

The Second Wife came out of the bedroom with The Baby in her arms and barred his way threateningly.

"Are you looking for someone?"

"Yes, have you seen…"

The Second Wife said nothing. The Writer waited. The Second Wife walked to the little cabinet by the entrance. Supporting The Baby with just one hand, she picked up an envelope, clearly already opened, and handed it to him. It had been sent by recorded delivery. The Writer took out the contents and read it. It was a letter from a lawyer. The Filipino's lawyer. It mentioned irregular conditions of work. Payment in cash. The threat of action. An employment tribunal.

The Writer looked up.

"And you were always defending him! That skunk!"

"…"

"I should have expected it, he'd been very strange lately…"

"…"

"To think that wretch gave The Baby a little gun to make soap bubbles! I found her playing with it. Can you imagine? She could have swallowed the soap! Or the cap! She could have died! I'm going to report him. Are you even listening to me?"

"…"

"And now what do we do? Can you tell me that? What are we going to do?"

"…"

"Oh, not speaking now, eh?"

"…"

"But you still want your trousers ironed with a crease, your shirts starched, your chicken nicely seasoned, your records dusted…"

"…"

"And still he doesn't speak. Don't you realize we're in trouble?"

"…"

The Writer let the letter fall to the floor.

"That's it, go on! Throw papers on the ground. As long as there's someone to clean up after you, right?"

The Second Wife had raised her voice. The Baby was crying.

"That's it, congratulations, now you've made the little one cry. No, darling, don't cry, yes, I know, daddy's bad…"

The Writer left the room. It wasn't that he couldn't speak. He had other things on his mind. Just imagine. Right now, dealing with the case of The Filipino would have been like stopping to answer a market research questionnaire while the bombs were falling.

He picked up the shoes and went to the garage. There, he put on a pair of rubber gloves and found a brush with steel bristles. He switched on the hose and started cleaning the shoes in the garden. He always had to do everything himself. He couldn't even get a dog to help him die. On the contrary.

"They say it's good luck, signore!"

The porter had stuck his head outside his lodge and had been watching him for a while, but The Writer hadn't noticed. He looked up from the shoes, looked at the porter, shrugged and went back to brushing his good luck.

The Beginner didn't think he could pull it off. That was what always happened. He didn't think he could pull it off, and then he pulled it off. In every single case. This time, though, it was different, this time pulling it off meant not pulling it off. He had started to feel scared. It was the kind of fear that comes over a tennis player when he has three match points in hand and then chalks up three consecutive double faults, a surgeon's assistant before an operation, or a man who at last finds the woman he's been dreaming about naked in his bed. In other words, the fear of winning.

But the fear of winning is only the most presentable aspect of the desire to lose. Difficult? Twisted? Maybe, but that's how it is. Man is an enigma that has swallowed its own solution.

So, faced with the terrifying possibility of being left by The Girlfriend—because even the most misanthropic of writers are terrified at the thought of being left alone with only themselves for company—The Beginner started to feel that he had a good chance of winning. A growing, definite, confident chance of winning. It was something he hadn't thought before. Or rather, he'd thought it but hadn't believed it. What he needed now was reassurance, reassurance that he wouldn't win. To get it, all he really had to do, instead of writing his book, would be to read it. Naïve, openly derivative, imbued with a certain idea of literature (rather than with literature itself). But that was something for the critics to discuss. Now all he needed was someone who could get him out of trouble.

As he drove his moped in and out of the cars and buses walled up in the mortar of the streets of Rome, The Beginner became firmly convinced that the only person who could understand his situation was The Patroness of The Prize.

Of course. The distinguished lady who pulled the strings, hatched all kinds of literary plots and conspiracies, administered a huge cultural inheritance and maintained relations with the sponsor.

He would talk to her openly. The way you do with a mother. No, with an aunt. No, with a grandmother. He would tell her everything. The betrayal. The (incredible) way in which it had been discovered. The baby they were expecting. The dilemma. Or better still. The blackmail. Imposed on him by The Girlfriend. Everything. From first to last. And she would listen. She would understand. She would help him. He felt sure of that. Confident. Because nothing bad can happen. To someone who tells the truth.

The evil eye? The Master didn't believe in such things. He was a man of letters, a man of culture. And yet he couldn't completely leave the irrational out of his cosmogony. If you looked at it the right way, he worked with the irrational. What was poetry if not a spark of irrationality, a match struck on the bare walls of logic? Besides, things had been going so badly for him lately, it was better not to take any risks.

He had been given the name of a witch by the woman who came to clean a couple of times a month. The Witch wasn't a real witch. Assuming there were such things as "real witches". She was a woman from the South who practised her profession from home—her kitchen, to be precise.

The Master had walked for a long time because he couldn't find the address. Then he had asked some immigrants waiting for buses that would never arrive. One of them, who didn't speak Italian well, made some vague gestures with his hands, which at least indicated the direction.

In the end he had found it. The Witch lived in a bleak apartment building on the edge of the city. She spoke with a strong Apulian accent and kept her heavy breasts propped up on the kitchen table. On the table were a plate, a cruet of oil and a pot of salt. You could have used these things for a salad, or to take away the evil eye, depending on what you were hungry for.

The Witch had first wanted to see his money—The Master would have liked to see it, too—then, uttering the name of the Father, had marked the plate with an upside-down cross. Then she had poured three drops of oil into the plate, one at a time. In contact with the water, the oil, instead of floating, had somehow vanished, an unmistakable sign of the evil eye. The Witch had observed an ancient ritual which she had learnt in her native region when she was a child: she had uttered an arcane formula, full of incomprehensible words, and with the salt had drawn an imaginary cross on the four sides of the plate. Then she had poured oil into another plate of water, and this time the drops had stayed on the surface, like floating coins.

"Do you want to know who did it?" she had asked.

The Master was surprised. He didn't know you could actually trace the evil eye back to the person who had given it to you. The Witch had told him it was only possible to find out the initials of the person. But that had been enough to remove any lingering doubt from The Master's mind.

"Do you wish him harm?"

"Yes."

"Do you want to do him harm?"

"Can you turn the evil eye against him?"

"No. A more powerful magic."

"What magic?"

"A spell."

"…"

"I need his shoes. And a nail from a coffin."

"A nail from a coffin? And where would I find that?"

The Witch opened a drawer and took out a handful of nails. From them she chose one that was bent and rusty and put it on the table.

"The nail is a hundred euros."

"Really?"

"And the spell is a thousand."

"And without the spell?"

"What?"

"Nothing, I was joking."

"I wasn't. You don't joke with the evil one. A thousand."

"A thousand, eh?"

"With what we'll do to him he'll never again be able to hurt you."

"…"

"…"

"Are you sure?"

"Do you have a thousand euros?"

"I have them."

No more than that, but he did have a thousand.

"Bring me the shoes."

The evil eye, if it existed, had been defeated. But there was more. Something that The Master, coming out of a small local cinema where he went every now and again with The Lawyer to see second-run films, would soon find out.

"The scene where the husband comes home unexpectedly and the wife hides her lover in the sofa bed and the husband sits on it, takes off his shoes and his feet stink and the other man practically has them in his mouth, that scene really killed me."

"I thought it was disgusting."

"Why? Come on, it was good."

They had been to see a comedy that had cleaned up at the box office, and The Master was lost in thought. But not because of the film.

"Listen, do you believe in the evil eye?"

"Of course I do."

"So everybody believes in it!"

"Why do you ask?"

"I went to see a witch."

"A witch?"

"I had the evil eye."

"Oh!"

The Lawyer's instinctive reaction was to move half a step away from The Master.

"I *had* it. She took it away."

"It's a good thing she did."

"She also told me who gave it to me. Do you want to know?"

"Who could it be?"

The Master looked around as if afraid someone was spying on him. Then he whispered a few words in The Lawyer's ear.

"I can't believe it! Isn't he one of the finalists for The Prize?"

"That's right."

"What a bastard, he wanted to screw you."

"Precisely."

"He must have been scared of you. And in a while he'll be scared of me too."

"Why should he be scared of you?"

"Because his Filipino is bringing an action against him."

"How do you know that?"

"I'm dealing with the case."

"..."

"..."

"Let me talk to this Filipino."

"Why?"

"Let me talk to him."

Who does the darkness belong to? The nocturnal animals? The screech owls (*Tyto alba*) that fly up from the roofs of abandoned apartment buildings? The mice that come out of the manholes to search among the remains in local markets? Or the human beings? The children sleeping in their colourful pyjamas, the wives unable to sleep beside their snoring husbands, the whores walking up and down the Via Salaria, the Sinhalese in the self-service shops? The cooks grilling hamburgers on greasy hotplates, the young men with bottomless appetites waiting for them to get hot? The cleaners sweeping the streets, the car thieves, the police patrols driving around the city? Or the inanimate things? The motionless statues, the cold steps, the deserted benches, the damp parks, the sleeping squares?

Who does the darkness belong to?

An evanescent, intoxicating darkness was sniffing at him with its wet nose like a weasel, and he opened his mouth wide and swallowed it in spoonfuls. It swelled his lungs heavy with the steamroller of night, a cloud of black silk within which to move with legs and hands, to jump from one shadow to the next, gripping them like a lemur. This darkness belonged to The Master. But it wasn't his: he had taken it.

The gate had opened with a click, like the trigger in a game of Russian roulette that he had won. Beyond the gate, silence. And beyond the silence, the little lights at the sides of the drive, tracing the route. The Master had passed the porter's lodge and had introduced himself into the nocturnal calm of the neighbourhood. The swimming pool slept beneath tall palms. The cars were asleep, their powerful engines still warm beneath the bonnets. The inhabitants were sleeping behind their closed shutters. To The Master, this place had seemed almost familiar, as if he had already been here in another life, a life in which he wrote and the world read him. He had looked more closely at the buildings that comprised the area, semi-detached houses, elegant and discreet, with adjoining garages and well-tended lawns to define their borders. Then he had stopped next to a garden spotlight and taken a dirty sheet of paper from his pocket, an arabesque of confused lines traced in pen: the map made for him by The Filipino. Couldn't that madman have drawn it more clearly? The Master had put on his glasses. Left right right left. Had he turned right at the first fork in the road? He had gone round in a circle like the needle of a crazed compass until he managed to realign himself. Yes, it was right. At that exact moment he had heard a noise. A noise of shifting gravel and trampled pine cones. He had flattened himself against a hedge. Nothing. Just a cat on the prowl. He had continued scrupulously following the map, and was now facing a door. Behind it, tucked up in the warm blankets of his certainties, slept his enemy, the man who wanted to win at all costs, the man who was about to get a taste of a mad poet's revenge.

The key turned in the lock of the reinforced door: a soft click, the sound of lubricated gears. The door opened with a bow, as if after years spent protecting a usurper it had finally recognized its true master.

Now he was in the dark. In the dark from which he came, the dark to which he would return. He who had lived in the shadow of others had finally cracked the darkness that imprisoned him. And he felt free and happy. He closed his eyes to fraternize with the darkness. A darkness scented with lavender and lemon, with wax and resin, rubber and freshly mown grass. A darkness so different from his own, which smelt of burnt egg and dirty sheets, cork and expired medicines, dusty books and full ashtrays.

The house was all on one floor, and that was an extra risk. The Master did not have a black uniform like those in the films, but he had dressed himself in dark clothes. Blue velvet trousers in which he was so hot he thought he would burst, a black shirt, a stained waistcoat, a pair of slippers lined with lambswool, an electric torch (the one he used to fix the fuse box whenever the lights went off) and a canvas bag: this was his gear.

Large rooms, windows that by day must let in a good deal of light, clear, scented wooden floors, leather sofas with an all-pervasive smell, like living creatures, designer lamps that looked like sleeping flamingoes in the shadows.

It was easy to move in this darkness, easier than expected. The furniture had rounded edges, and the carpets absorbed his steps. Not a sound, not a moan, not a sigh: everything was silent in the temple of Calliope.

The Master was in control. He knew that, whatever time he had left to live, he would never again get so close, so close to something of which he knew the existence but not the essence.

That was why he was in no hurry. He was savouring this fleeting mastery over people and objects, because being invisible is the privilege of thieves and hunters. It is for that intoxication, rather than for the booty, that they set off every night.

The Master went into one of the rooms. Steel dressers gleamed in the light of his torch, a rectangular table in the middle, a lamp hanging over it. The kitchen. A sickly-sweet smell, most likely apple pie, tickled his nose. The Master spotted a dark sarcophagus, approached it, opened it, and in a shower of light saw a smoked salmon as plump as a ham, truffles in a glass jar, French cheeses in a drawer and rows of wine bottles stored horizontally like mortar shells. This was the diet of a best-selling writer. The Master closed the fridge door.

He wouldn't find what he was looking for in the kitchen. To get his lock of hair, he had to enter the wolf's lair.

He crossed the living room, marching past an eye-catching dark rectangle that he took for a piece of conceptual art (it was a wall-mounted plasma TV screen). He came to the beginning of a long corridor. On the right, a door was ajar. He pushed it slowly and shone his torch inside. A solid wooden desk. Shelves crammed with books. *His* books. The Writer's books. Translated into a dozen languages (there were ideograms and runic characters on the spines and covers). A Persian rug. A hi-fi unit. An LP collection. A drinks trolley. The Master went up to the trolley and flashed his torch at it: bottles of fine whisky and cognac, spirits and liqueurs from the best brand names on the market. He took a bottle at random, pulled the top off with his teeth, and had a swig: gin. It burnt like fire in his dry throat. He wiped his lips with his shirtsleeve. It was what he needed to find the courage to bring his mission to its conclusion. He left the room and ventured along the corridor. From a closed door came laboured breathing. He checked the map: it was The Ukrainian Nanny's room. Again according to the map, he should have the small toilet ahead of him, The Filipino's bedroom to his left—he aimed the torch: empty—and The Baby's bedroom to the right—he aimed the torch: empty. Towards the end of the corridor was the bathroom, and at the end to the right the master bedroom. The secret chamber at the heart of the pyramid. That was where he would carry out his desecration, like an unscrupulous tomb robber. The Master took a deep breath, switched off the torch and pulled the door handle down.

Husband and wife were in the nuptial bed. Abandoned and dreaming like Etruscan sculptures. Here was The Writer with hundreds of thousands of copies read and translated throughout the world, lying on his back, his arms crossed over his chest, as motionless as a corpse. Here was The Second Wife of The Writer with hundreds of thousands of copies read and translated throughout the world, lying face down, the back of her neck bare, given up to her dreams. Between them, a miniature that looked human: The Baby.

The Master looked at the royal dynasty immersed in slumber. They were sleeping a remote, aristocratic sleep, chrysalids waiting to become butterflies. He could kill all three of them, poison them, smother them as they slept, cut their throats, it would be like a palace revolution. But he didn't. He could. But he didn't. He would. But no. He needed only one thing. Just one thing and he would go. The spell would deal with the rest. The Master shielded the mouth of the torch with his hand and aimed it at the back of the room. The light gave form to the solid surface of a modern wardrobe and an armchair on which lay a woman's clothes flung down haphazardly. Next to the armchair, a valet stand, with a jacket and a shirt hanging all neat and tidy, and trousers with a fine, straight crease held in the press. And finally, at the foot of that pagan fetish, the reason why The Master had come so far, both in this story and in this house. The Writer's shoes. They were one metre from him. The Master advanced, bent down and took them.

Son of a bitch, you did it. Now put them in your bag and leave the room immediately. Be brave. Take your stiff legs and get them out of here. Get out while there's still time. Don't stand there gawking. Move. One small effort and in a minute you'll be outside. Get out of here and take those dammed shoes to you know who.

Well? What's come over you? Why aren't you moving? Have you fallen asleep, too? What are you doing standing there? Hey, I'm talking to you! Make a move! Do you want to be discovered? Do you want them to wake up and find you in their room like a mouse? Think of the newspapers! Think of the scandal! Think of The Prize! Think of The Prize, Master. Think of The Prize.

Hold on a minute. The Master was old, and perhaps mad, but he wasn't stupid. If he didn't move, he had his reasons. Trust him.

Someone was licking him. And now sniffing at his crotch.

That there was a dog in the house was something that stupid Filipino hadn't even mentioned.

Incredible as it may seem, there are apparently dogs that can sniff out tumours, sense organic material present in cancer cells, recognize a chemical compound even when it has been diluted down to one part in a trillion.

Was The Writer's Dog sniffing The Master's prostate tumour? Or was it only the pants he'd been wearing for three days? Who can say?

Only The Dog. And, while it was about it, it could also tell its owner who had paid him a visit tonight. But, just like its owner right now, it was speechless.

When The Master at last left that trap of a house, he found the night waiting for him. And in its black depths, a white van was also waiting for him. With its lights off. And its engine off, too—because it had been making too much noise. A grimy van hidden behind the recycling bins. And when The Master climbed in with his ill-gotten gains and his thumb up as a sign of victory, the van's lights went on, its engine started up, and it moved slowly towards even darker territories of the night.

A few hours before The Writer was robbed of his shoes, we find The Beginner in the toilet of a bar. The icy water flows from the tap and collects in the hollow of his hands. He rinses his mouth and spits into the sink. He looks at himself in the mirror.

But what's happened? Just a moment, his mobile is ringing. He looks at the display. It's The Girlfriend. He looks at himself in the mirror again. Interminable seconds pass. Then he takes a deep breath and answers.

"I only just left."

"How did it go?"

To get the answer to that, let's step back in time and imagine we are a robin (*Erithacus rubecula*) that has just come to rest on a window sill in the apartment of The Patroness of The Prize. And let us attribute to the little songbird pronounced audiovisual as well as vocal gifts.

Look, The Beginner is just about to be received. The apartment is crowded, it's teatime. The butler greets him and asks for his jacket, and The Beginner reluctantly hands it over. He waits in a large room. He looks around, threatened by imposing works of art. In the sumptuous drawing rooms, the ladies exchange reviews as if they were recipes while their husbands doze in armchairs. The frescoed ceiling is animated by the warm light of evening. The French windows that lead out onto the balcony are open, the smokers stroll lazily between the thick plants. The butler goes into the main room and whispers something in The Patroness's ear. The lines on her face crease a moment like a ruff, then relax. The Patroness is wearing a cream-coloured tailored suit and white shoes with gold buckles, and she keeps her legs parallel and twisted to one side. She is holding a glass, it isn't tea, it's a flute of champagne. Reluctantly, she stands up, shaking her head at the lady who is in front of her as if to say that they can never get any peace in this place. As she follows the butler, she smiles to a group of guests standing arguing beside a tray of canapés.

Now here she is, receiving the young candidate for The Prize of which she is the undisputed heart and soul. The Beginner gives an embarrassed smile, he has never before kissed a lady's hand in greeting (it even disgusts him slightly), but he does so. The

Patroness smiles to take away his embarrassment, then motions him to follow her: there is a small drawing room where they will be able to talk undisturbed.

They walk towards it, skating on the shiny decorated floors.

They sit down on an uncomfortable little sofa. The Patroness calls the waiter and asks for something to drink. Tea for the young man, a spritzer for her. The Beginner tells his story, in an ardent if confused manner. He tells her The Girlfriend is pregnant, then takes a step back, confesses his betrayal—omitting to mention the absurd way it was discovered because he knows that talking about Google Maps to this lady would be like talking about condoms at the Vatican—then takes a step forward and refers to the blackmail, then steps aside and informs her of his fear of winning, but above all of losing what is dearest to him right now: that germ of life in The Girlfriend's belly. He is speaking like a father, or even like a mother. He gets emotional, lets himself be carried away by his own passion, and for a moment feels so persuasive that he suspects he must be feigning, rather than actually feeling, those emotions.

The Patroness listens to him in silence, while the ice melts in her first spritzer. And in her second. And in her third.

"Poor thing," she says from time to time, as if adding a cross stitch to the weave of his story. And her heavy rings tinkle on the glass as she puts it down and picks it up. The Beginner summons up all his energy, an extreme, painful act of humility in which he declares he doesn't want it, he doesn't deserve it, he wouldn't pull it off anyway (there, once again that damned inadequacy).

"Can you help me not to win?" he asks at the end of his long speech.

The Patroness looks at him, full of understanding. Her eyes are shining, her hair motionless, trapped in a nest of lacquer. She moves closer. The Beginner thinks she wants to tell him something in confidence. She moves even closer. The Beginner smells her breath, it's reminiscent of faded flowers. She passes

a hand through his hair. He sees her powdered face a few centimetres from his. The Beginner barely has time to turn his face
away before a kiss sticky with lipstick is imprinted on his cheek.

He runs away, leaving his jacket in the cloakroom. The Patroness
regains her composure and returns to her guests, whom she has
neglected for far too long.

The robin has seen too much. It flies away, without even a
left-over canapé.

Now that we have an idea of what happened, we can return to
the toilet of the bar in which we left our young writer.

"Well? How did it go?"

"O… K. It went OK."

"Will they vote for you?"

"I don't think so."

*The first specimen arrived from the coast, coming up the mouth of the river while the herons watched anxiously. Urged on by the beautiful sunny day and its own pioneering sense of enterprise, it flew curiously over the great sedimentary terrain, the Pleistocene and continental marine deposits, took advantage of the sweet thermal fumes that rose from the alluvial plain of the Tiber, looked with respect at the enigmatic summit of Mount Soratte to the north, and with scepticism at the spurs of the Sabine and Prenestine Hills to the east. It hovered over the volcanic plateaux carved and dislocated into seven hills by the sinuous course of the river, until at last it hovered over the city and its swarming humanity, eventually landing on the top of the Vittorio Emmanuele Monument, resting its tired wings, right at the tip of the wing of the winged quadriga. Hard to believe, isn't it? And yet that is what happened. From there it had the privilege of enjoying a view of Rome denied to the Romans themselves. And this happened on 7th May 1912, the day on which a Caspian gull (*Larus cachinnans*) was spotted in flight over the city for the first time. Since then, many things have changed.*

PART FOUR

(One day to The Ceremony)

I F WE TOOK THE LIVES of human beings in the hours preceding terrorist attacks, heroic enterprises, brilliant discoveries,
it would be discovered that men are not doing anything exceptional at such times. That is why we say nothing about it, why
we observe a vow of silence over what happens on the eve of
things. Knowing that a general before a crucial battle had been
struggling with his haemorrhoids, or that a scientist before making
a momentous discovery ate a roll with mortadella, would make
heroes too similar to us mortals.

Now that we are on the eve of The Prize, aren't you curious to
know how our friends the writers are spending it?

It may perhaps be worth dropping in on The Master, but
the image of a man sprawled on the sofa with a bottle on the
floor beside him and the TV on is something we can frankly do
without. And what if we sneak into The Beginner's loft, where
he is cleaning his teeth and The Girlfriend is looking through a
dictionary of names in search of inspiration for her as yet unborn
child? Not too captivating, is it?

Better to hover over the usual high-class neighbourhood where
you-know-who lives.

If an alien had landed in The Writer's garden and asked for
information about planet Earth, he would have said to him, "I'm
sorry, I'm not from round here." That gives some idea of his state
of mind with just twenty-four hours to go until The Ceremony.
And even less time until The Great Moment.

The unease began last night, when he had two terrible dreams, the most terrible thing about them being that he remembered them perfectly. In the first, more distressing of the two, he was being spied on by the secret service, who had sneaked into his house and planted bugs and miniature TV cameras all over it. In a small van parked somewhere, a bored but zealous security operative was following, on a screen similar to the baby monitor, his life and that of his family, from the toilet to the bedroom, as if it were a reality show about successful writers. From the first dream, as if a floor in his unconscious had collapsed, he landed straight in the second, more horrifying of the two dreams, in which The Dog was trying to have sex with The Second Wife. The beast was slobbering as it pursued the young woman all through the house, its fluorescent glans flashing beneath its fur like an emergency light on a leather dashboard. The Writer and The Second Wife barricaded themselves in the bedroom, but the animal, which had been taught by its master to pull down door handles with its paws, managed to smash down even this final defence. And now they faced one another, The Dog, with its indecency on open display, The Writer, with his imperfect shield of honour, and The Second Wife, who was screaming like a virgin cornered by Saracens. It was then that a loud barking echoed through the room, making The Baby cry and jolting the couple awake, and they found The Dog standing at the foot of the bed, eager to play, or perhaps—who knows?—to communicate something.

If he had not already made his decision—but he had—after a dream like that, The Writer would have taken the stupid animal and abandoned it on the ring road. But it occurred to him that after The Great Moment, a bit of company, a bit of cheap warmth, would not come amiss for a future widow and a future orphan. That was the only reason he spared it. And he fell asleep again in the arms of his anxiety.

When he woke up, he could not find his shoes.

The shoes he had cleaned with care, nourished with water-proofing wax and worn all week to break them in for The Great Moment, were no longer there.

And yet he was sure he had left them in the bedroom, at the foot of the valet stand, where he always took care to place the clothes he would wear the following day. He asked The Second Wife, and she said she didn't know anything about them—in fact, she had no idea what he was talking about.

And that was how the morning passed. The Writer looked everywhere: he turned the wardrobes and the garage upside down, climbed up into the loft, rummaged under the beds, and generally searched in the unlikeliest places, finding things (a hat, an umbrella, the recharger for a mobile) he had been looking for for so long that he had convinced himself he could happily do without them.

"Tomorrow's going to be a long day for you."

The Writer, who was lifting the cushions on the sofa, turned abruptly and looked The Second Wife straight in the eyes.

"Forget about those shoes. The Filipino must have thrown them away."

"…"

"You have The Ceremony. Try to relax."

Maybe The Second Wife was right. Maybe The Filipino really had taken them. He could no longer quite remember if he had found the shoes before or after The Filipino had gone. He was starting to confuse the sequence of events. The last week had been like one of those festival films, the kind that plays around with chronology, which nobody understands and about which everybody coming out of the cinema says, "What a masterpiece!" Too many things had happened inside him. Things he couldn't talk about, things that were his business and nobody else's.

To assuage the pangs of anxiety, The Writer needed concrete facts, trivial acts, to reconnect him with reality. When it came to triviality, The Writer was a champion. In the afternoon he went to a medical supply shop and bought some clogs, those white openwork ones that nurses and dentists wore. He would go to The Great Moment looking very elegant, with those immaculate clogs on his feet: even death requires maximum cleanliness.

Then he spent the afternoon at home, playing on the carpet with The Baby, trying—without success—to make her say the title of his last novel. When The Baby had fallen asleep, he made love to The Second Wife, who wasn't really in the mood but, surprised by such boldness, yielded to him. Furtive and agitated, with a vague desire to finish quickly: that was how the last fuck of his life was. Afterwards they lay there on the dishevelled bed, panting.

"If you weren't with me who would you be with?"

The Writer had surprised the Second Wife as she was pulling her knickers up over her pale buttocks.

"What a thing to ask!"

"Answer me."

"But I'm with you."

"Who with?"

"Nobody."

"But if you really had to be with someone?"

"I'm going to make myself a herbal tea. Do you want one?"

The Writer stayed in bed a while longer, looking up at the ceiling. Then he dressed, went in the kitchen, ate a roll with the leftover omelette and knocked back a can of beer without pouring it into a glass. That was the best thing he had done all day. And so the afternoon also passed.

In the evening they called the best Japanese takeaway in Rome and ordered a sumptuous sushi and sashimi combo. Not long afterwards, there was a ring at the gate and The Writer saw a thin young man in trainers and baseball cap on the videophone screen. One of the many young people whose future had been stolen from them, as the media were always saying.

What if The Boy, the son he had had with The First Wife, the one he never saw except to shower him with video games, ended up doing that kind of work? Without The Writer there to provide for him, what would his future be like? Oh, come on! The judge had given his mother custody, so it was only right that his mother should take care of him.

The Writer opened the gate and, just to put the young man to the test, gave him instructions that would make it difficult for him to find their house. The young man materialized soon afterwards along with his polystyrene container and a vague smell of fish. The Writer had only large-denomination banknotes, yellow, green and pink, for which the young man had no change. So The Writer gave him an enormous tip, equal perhaps to what he earned in a month. The young man hesitated for a moment, but without losing his composure. The Writer watched him as he walked away to catch any sign of surrender or any manifestation of excitement. But there was nothing, unless it only happened when he was out of sight. He was on the ball, that young man. If his son did end up like that, well, when you came down to it maybe it wouldn't be so tragic after all.

They ate the sushi in the living room, watching cartoons on the satellite channels. That was how the evening passed.

Before going to bed, The Writer found a message on his answering machine. How about we read it and try to guess who it was from?

"Hi, big guy. How are you? How do you feel? I wanted to remind you it's one day to the great day... Go and see your mother tomorrow if you can... I'm sure she'd be pleased... See you at nine in the morning. We're really going to blow them away!"

The Publisher, of course. Who else could it have been? The following morning, he was going to drop by to pick up The Second Wife and The Baby and take them out of the city, maybe to the sea. Before the battle The Writer needed peace and quiet to concentrate on the task at hand. They had already talked it over and agreed on the plan. Yes, The Publisher was a real friend.

A long day is coming to its end. Surrounded by the darkness of the garden, the light is still on inside the house. In the bedroom, The Baby is sleeping. The Ukrainian Nanny has the day off and will be back at any moment. The Filipino isn't there, and we know he won't be coming back. The Second Wife is removing her make-up. As for The Writer, he is leafing through his last book. It's really terrible: hard to admit it, but even his mother has nothing more to say. He puts it down on the bedside table and turns off the light.

Now night has finally fallen, the night before The Ceremony, the last night of The Writer's life.

*The fear felt by a homing pigeon (*Columba livia*) flying over Rome at a cruise speed of about 70 kilometres per hour when it realizes that a peregrine falcon (*Falco peregrinus*) is plunging straight down towards it from the opposite direction at a speed of just under 200 kilometres per hour is the kind of fear that nobody will ever be able to describe.*

And it doesn't matter if at that speed the impact is so great that it causes the death of the falcon itself, even when it barely touches its prey with its talon. Nor does it matter if it wounds its prey first, then finishes it off by pecking it to death either in flight or on the ground.

What matters is that at the exact moment the falcon enters its field of vision, the pigeon's little heart starts beating so fast that it actually stops.

That's fear. The fear of not being there. Of not being there any more. It may last only a moment, but it seems like an eternity.

It is the fear that eats at us, the fear that stops us, the fear that drives us. The fear we have, the fear we will have.

PART FIVE

(The day of The Ceremony)

O N THE DAY OF THE CEREMONY, the sun rose at 5:29 and was due to set at 21:02. In the morning, the pressure at sea level was 1,014 millibars. A minimum temperature of 20°C and a maximum of 32°C was forecast, with an average humidity of 72 per cent. The maximum wind speed would be no greater than ten kilometres per hour, and no major phenomenon was forecast for Rome. That depends, of course, on the kind of phenomena we are concerned with. In short, it was a beautiful summer's day. Perfect for winning, or losing, a literary prize.

The Master and his bladder rose, as always, very early, in time to see a diffuse gleam rise behind the brown tops of Prince —'s pines and a young shepherd lead a flock of emaciated sheep across the uncultivated fields.

The Writer got up at seven-thirty and went straight into the shower. He soaped his feet, groin and armpits with particular care. Then he put on a tracksuit, went to the kitchen and made a pot of coffee, a jug of orange juice and some slices of toast with butter and organic quince jam. He put everything on a tray and took The Second Wife breakfast in bed. But she refused it, because she had never liked quinces, and because it was too early and she wanted to sleep a bit longer.

The same was true of The Beginner, who was still fast asleep, his arms around The Girlfriend, entertained by a dream of no particular importance.

The Master waited until day had properly risen for everyone, then walked down the road in slippers and vest as far as the café attached to the car wash, where he had breakfast every now and again. He ordered a cappuccino and a cream doughnut. He wanted to scrounge a newspaper to see what they said about The Prize, but as he put it down to take his breakfast to the table, a young boy with his hair gelled so that it stood up on end pinched it from him and there was no way to get it back. The cappuccino was lukewarm and the doughnut left a lingering aftertaste of fried food in his mouth. He walked back beneath a sun that had no pity on anyone, let alone the old.

The Beginner woke up just before midday, with the ill humour of someone who knows it is too late for breakfast and too early for lunch. The Girlfriend had gone to see her mother, who lived on the other side of the city, and had left a Post-it for him on the computer screen.

LOSE FOR ME ;−)
I'LL GIVE YOU THE BEST PRIZE EVER!
SEE YOU LATER
I LOVE YOU

The Beginner rolled the note into a ball, put on his dark glasses and his iPod headphones and went out onto the terrace in his pants to sunbathe.

At eight-thirty on the dot, The Publisher arrived at The Writer's house in his freshly washed and hand-waxed Porsche Cayenne. The Writer greeted him with a plain nod. Then they both loaded the pushchair and a bag full of nappies in the boot. The Writer did not deign to look at The Dog, which kept trying to jump into the wide-open boot, as if into the jaws of a shark, nor The Ukrainian Nanny, who caught the hem of her skirt in the door as she got into the Porsche. He kissed The Baby on the forehead. He hugged The Second Wife, moving aside her hair to reach the hollow at the back of her neck, a kind of inside-out oyster just below the hairline which he had always found very sensual, and kissed her, too. When all the women had got into the car, the two men embraced in a manly way, but without excessive camaraderie or, worse still, sentimentality. With the dexterity of a drug courier, The Publisher dropped an envelope into The Writer's jacket pocket.

"It's all there, you just have to copy it," The Publisher whispered.

The Writer nodded.

The Publisher looked at him just slightly too long behind his photochromic glasses and—a fraction of a second before he started to feel moved—got in the car. The six-cylinder 300-hp engine started up with a loud roar. The Writer pushed the button to open the automatic gate and the Porsche, as glossy as petrol, drove through. Through the squeaky-clean, almost invisible windows The Writer saw—for the last time—The Second Wife blow him a kiss and The Publisher make an unmistakable V for victory sign with the index and middle fingers of his right hand. The Writer did not have the strength to respond.

After breakfast, The Master returned home and looked for something decent to wear that evening, but couldn't find anything. He thought about what he would have for lunch. He looked in the fridge and cupboards. Only an already-started packet of penne. That was all right, though: you only win if you're hungry. He boiled the pasta, drained it and added oil, garlic juice, home-grown tomatoes given him by his neighbour, the wife of the caretaker of Prince —'s estate, and two leaves of basil he had grown on the window sill. As this was a recipe for cold pasta, he put it in the fridge to cool down.

When he was alone, The Writer walked through the empty spaces of his house as if floating in the light. He sat down at the computer. Using the home banking service, he transferred 200,000 euros into a savings account he had set up for the children he had with The First Wife (100,000 for The Boy,

100,000 for The Girl). If, when they were adults, they were ever interviewed for a documentary on The Writer's life—which was extremely likely—they wouldn't be able to say they hadn't had a generous father.

While cooking, The Master had built up an appetite. He was too hungry to wait. He took the pasta out of the fridge and ate it lukewarm, just as it was. He knocked back a bottle of chilled white wine from Torchio Wines, smoked a couple of cigarettes in his pants, closed the shutters because it was so hot that a fire might have been raging around the house, and switched on the fan, which made the fuse box blow for the umpteenth time. Cursing, The Master switched the circuit-breaker back on. He took off his pants and vest. With the fan not working and the heat more unbearable than ever, he got into bed naked. No sooner had his eyelids fallen like creaky shutters over dirty windows than the telephone rang. At the other end, a young woman's voice informing him that the courier would be coming that day to deliver the prize.

"What do you mean, the courier?" The Master said, confused. "Don't they give it at The Academy?"

"We have to deliver the prize from Torchio Wines."

"Oh, that prize."

"Yes."

"Not today. Bring it tomorrow."

"Tomorrow isn't possible. Our courier is only in Rome today."

"And I'm telling you I can't do it today, don't waste my time."

"There's no need to lose your temper. We'll find a solution."

"There's a perfectly simple solution. Keep your prize."

He uttered these words with a sense of satisfaction, as if he had thought up a beautiful line for a poem, but no sooner had he said them than he regretted it. Obviously the prize from Torchio Wines was nothing compared with The Prize, but it was still something. Could he afford to spit at a computer? After he won The Prize he would have time to learn, to take lessons, to spark the Copernican revolution of his writing. And besides, he really couldn't let all that hard work done by his liver go to waste.

"There must be a safe place to leave it. Isn't there a doorman?"

"No."

"A neighbour?"

"No."

"A bar, a shop, someone you can trust?"

"No. There's nobody here."

"How can that be? Are you sure?"

"There's a prostitute outside the gate, how about her?"

Meanwhile, The Beginner had gone down to get a kebab, without onion. Back upstairs, he put the air-conditioning full on because it was too hot on the terrace and switched on his PS3. A game of Pro Evolution Soccer 2011, which for the first time made it possible to play the Master League online, was the best way to relieve the tension, with so little time left before The Ceremony.

As it takes hours and hours of playing to complete the Master League, given that The Master has nodded off again after the phone call, and considering that between now and eight in the evening—the hour when finalists are expected in the grounds of Villa Naike, the evocative setting where the winner will be announced—the two do not have a great deal to do, it may be worth once again keeping the third finalist company: The Writer. Because dying alone isn't an easy matter.

After making the transfer, The Writer changed, putting on the outfit for The Great Moment: cream-coloured trousers, a white shirt with a mandarin collar, a blue jacket and white dentist's clogs. He looked at himself in the full-length mirror used by The Second Wife: he was still a handsome man. It really was a pity it had to end like this. How many women could he still seduce? But the decision had been made, he had a date, a date with the most demanding lover of all.

He left home, took a taxi and asked the driver to drop him at a florist's near the clinic. He bought a large quantity of flowers: orchids, gerberas, tulips, chrysanthemums. He entered the clinic, asked to be taken to see The Mother and gave the young nun a lot of money she didn't dare refuse in order to be left alone with her. He arranged the flowers around the bed and kissed The Mother on the forehead.

"Thank you for everything you gave me. I'm doing this for you, mother."

The Writer saw the switches and tubes thanks to which the life that had given rise to his life was still holding on. He was tempted to tear everything out, pull the plugs from the wall sockets, disconnect the tubes from the machines and take The Mother with him to writers' heaven. Then it struck him there wasn't room for everyone up there, and that if she wanted she could get there by her own efforts. He closed the door again and left.

By now it was lunchtime. The Writer had booked the best table in his favourite restaurant, where they knew and respected him, a place half hidden in the back alleys of medieval Rome. He ordered a pinot grigio, as a starter red crayfish from Ponza (almost impossible to find now in the overfished Tyrrhenian Sea), as a first main course spaghetti with fresh razor clams, and for the second a dentex he had seen buried in ice. A thin-hipped waiter took the order, clicking his heels, but then turned back to see if he had understood correctly. The fish weighed one kilo, 900 grams, he said: was the signore expecting guests? The Writer said he was alone and the waiter had indeed understood correctly: he wanted that dentex. Before taking the fish into the kitchen, the waiter showed it to him on a tray. It had black fins and a magnificent brownish-blue body, and in the light its scales looked like decorations on a silver shield. The Writer lifted its gills: they were red, suffused with blood. He felt the abdomen, still as hard and muscular as when it was escaping from fishermen's nets on the rocky seabed. This animal was more alive than he was. He looked at it with envy. He met its tired yellow eyes, and saw they were full of gratitude. The dentex was begging to be eaten by him, and by him alone. The Writer gave his verdict and the fish was led to the mouth of the oven.

To finish off the meal, he had pear and chocolate pie and a decaffeinated coffee. He did not even look at the bill. He held out his card, holding it between two fingers. The waiter brought him the receipt to sign. The Writer took his fountain pen from his pocket, and as he did so it struck him that one of the things he would miss terribly in a few hours was signing copies. The elegant gesture of the act of signing, as he had declared in a recent interview.

"What's your name?" he suddenly asked the waiter as he was about to walk away. The young man stopped dead.

"Stefano... Is something wrong?"

The Writer magnanimously shook his head to reassure him.

To Stefano, he wrote on the credit card receipt. He folded the paper in two, put it under the glass and left, with a nod to the owner and the cook, who had come out of the kitchen specially to shake his hand: he had read all his books.

Leaving the restaurant, he took a long walk, his eyes half closed in the blinding sunlight. It occurred to The Writer that if they performed a post-mortem on him they would find fish and wine in his stomach.

When he got home, it was after four. And he had planned everything for six. There was no time to waste. Death can wait, but only up to a point.

He called The Second Wife to find out how they were. She said they had had a wonderful day, they had eaten pasta with small clams and taken a walk on the windswept promenade with the pushchair to give The Baby a breath of sea air, and they would be back in an hour, in time for a shower before they went with him to The Ceremony. The Publisher wanted to talk to him for a moment, said The Second Wife. The Writer said no, he didn't want to talk to him. She told him not to worry, everything would work out as it was supposed to. Those were her exact words. Then she hung up. He went into his study and locked the door, even though he was alone in the house. He sat down at the desk, took a paperknife with an ivory handle and opened the envelope The Publisher had slipped into his pocket. There was a letter. The farewell letter prepared by The Publisher. All he had to do was copy it on the computer and e-mail it to a few selected contacts. He read it. Then he read it again. It was about corrupt prizes, mercenary critics, ignorant readers, mediocre writers, how point-less it all was—writing, reading—and what a relief it was to say farewell to such a world.

He sighed.

No, things weren't like that. In his long career he had met talented people, honest writers, shrewd critics, sincere readers. Not many, but he had met them. He hadn't got close to them, perhaps for fear of discovering that they were different, but he had met them. This letter was rubbish. A disgrace.

Surely he could do better? If there was a single cell, a single sequence of amino acids in his whole body that made him a writer, now was the moment to demonstrate it.

He cracked his fingers, lit a Cohiba which he kept for special occasions (and nobody could have objected that this wasn't one), poured himself a glass of whisky and sat down at the computer. It had been years since he had last faced that ski run, that wall of ice on which he had broken his collarbone when he was young: the blank page.

The Writer looked at the screen: the run was clear, the snow perfect. He took a deep breath, and flung himself down it.

*

256

There is no man who, a moment after switching off the light, isn't assailed by a question: Am I an impostor?

In other words: Do I really deserve what life has given me?

And there is no way to dismiss this question without turning the light back on. It is of little consequence if he is a writer, a carpenter or a horse thief. No human being can avoid the question without lying to himself.

We each of us have, deep in our soul, a fragile urn that contains the answer. But since we are convinced that the answer is even more painful than the question, we mostly prefer to ignore it.

That is how we lead our lives, either with studied caution or wild recklessness, either taking great care not to break the urn or knocking against everything and everyone and hoping that a glancing blow will smash it to pieces. Unfortunately—or fortunately—none of us knows if, how and when our urn will break. And in the case of most human beings, their secret goes to the grave with them.

The strongest or weakest among us manage to break the urn and peer inside. But after doing so, we can no longer look even at our dog with the same eyes, whatever the answer we have glimpsed there.

Now if we only stopped for a moment to think, it is quite obvious that there is no merit or design or logic in the way luck and talent are distributed and this world. For every man kissed by the sun there are millions in the shade, and there is no valid reason to rule out—or maintain—the possibility that the one is better than the other.

At the same time, it would be equally arrogant to deny it.

We see the result, but the process escapes us. In the dark, turbulent sea of doubt we glimpse lights every now and again, and we follow them, hoping they are the lights of the coast. Sometimes they are genuine landing places, sometimes only the reflection of the moon on the rocks. In both cases, the time that has been granted us to sail ends before the end of the journey, and there is no way to add a single second.

*But there also exists something immortal that cannot be grasped
or weighed in a balance, and that is the precious moment in which
we forget ourselves and become other. And the few times that happens
we stop the heartbeat of time and feel we belong to what surrounds
us, what has preceded us and what will follow us. It can happen
at any moment: listening to the background music while waiting
for a call centre to answer us, cooking for our friends, waiting for
our children at the school gate.*

*So there are countless reasons to remain on this Godforsaken planet
that was long considered the only world, if for no other reason than
to learn the end of our story: what the author of our lives has not
yet taken the trouble to finish.*

*But my urn is broken, and now that I know the answer, I can
remain no longer.*

Am I an impostor?

Excuse me, I have to turn on the light.

It had come all in one go. Without hesitation or correction. Never
in his entire career had he written such clean, precise sentences.
As he typed away at the keyboard, he had felt as though he were
carving the words on a wax tablet with a stylus. He read it again.
It was concise and effective. No need to change a single comma.
He wasn't so bad after all. What a pity he'd had writer's block all
these years. He sighed, and sent the letter as an e-mail attachment
to all the contacts in his address book (publishers, newspaper
editors, friends, whores, acquaintances and strangers). Then he
switched off the computer and his mobile and went out. The
Great Moment had come.

But were all those people passing him distractedly as he walked
towards the river, that bovine humanity dragging itself God knows
where, bustling through the streets to achieve its dubious plans, to
satisfy the vanity of its desires, aware of his greatness? Did that
human herd have even a vague idea of the privilege that had

been granted them in brushing against an artist of his calibre—
especially in the final moments of his vast, incomparable life?

Apparently not. One man even knocked him with his elbow
and didn't apologize.

The Writer had reached the centre of the city and was walking
now in the shade of the lime trees, alongside the ramparts beside
the Tiber. He looked at the people on the pavements, the cars
and mopeds speeding by just a few metres from him.

So was it for them that he had brought his books out over the
years? Were they his invisible readers, the silent enzymes that
swallowed his nonsense? The inscrutable sherpas who carried his
heavy books up to the top of the best-seller lists? In other words,
were they his employers?

The Writer descended the stone steps that led him to the banks
of the river. It was getting towards evening. At that hour, people
were coming out to get a bit of fresh air. In summer, they set
up an artificial seafront on the river bank, filled with stands and
stalls, a permanent *movida*. The Writer walked through it with a
touch of annoyance.

He walked until he was so far away that he no longer heard
the commotion.

At that hour, the sky of Rome turned a soft, hazy pink, the
kind you see in certain frescoes of the Neapolitan school; at
that hour the courier, after ringing in vain at the entryphone,
left the prize from Torchio Wines outside The Master's gate;
at that hour the staminate cells in The Girlfriend's uterus were
at work constructing organs and tissues; at that hour the lights
were being lit in the grounds of Villa Naike and the waiters
were getting their first reprimands from the maître d'; at that
hour The Writer's press officer was starting to get worried
because his mobile was switched off. At that hour The Second
Wife was looking for him in the house, at that hour a few
people had already read his e-mail. At that hour The Writer,

protected by the shadows of evening, stopped beneath the arches of a bridge.

He undressed solemnly and laid his clothes on the bench. Then, as naked as Adam, he looked at the sunset, and the yellow-brown river calling him to it. He put one foot in the water.

It was really cold...

Even dying has its disadvantages.

Victory by Suicide

Stunning gesture by the favourite. Motive still unknown. Nothing to suggest such a tragic outcome

FROM OUR CORRESPONDENT

This is a victory without victors. The party we would have preferred not to go to, the article we would never have wanted to write. For once, the world of letters is speechless.

It is a few hours to the proclamation of the winner. Everything is ready in Villa Naike. The lawn is like a billiard table, the grounds lit up as if in daylight, the tables allocated, the waiters lined up behind the buffet.

Politicians, journalists, writers and figures from the fashion world and from cinema and theatre are strolling about the grounds exchanging the usual wishes and predictions. It is an event like any other, a prize ceremony like any other.

And yet it isn't.

That something is not right is clear from the nervousness at the table of The Publishing Company that has won The Prize most often over the years. The Publisher, who is looking very elegant in his pinstripe suit, has not touched his food, nor has he issued any statements. The press officer's face is drawn as he paces the grounds nervously in search of a secluded corner to talk into his mobile phone. The dinner is served, but there is still no sign of The Writer. His plate is empty. He has not even appeared for the usual interviews. There is irritation among the organizers and the members of The Academy and disappointment among the photographers and cameramen, who in his absence have to make do with the other two finalists.

Visibly excited, The Beginner grants every interview he is asked for. "For me, getting this far is already a victory," he says. "But there are other things in life." He winks at his Girlfriend, who is half hidden behind the assembled journalists. "At my age," declares The Master, who is wearing a Panama hat and a creased linen suit, "I think I'm entitled to win. To be quite honest, I shouldn't even have to compete. They ought to give me The Prize as a matter of course." Someone teases him with the question: "Why isn't The Writer here yet?" "I don't know," says The Master with a laugh, "maybe he's afraid of losing."

But in fact it is much worse than that. The host takes his time as he recalls the names of past winners and thanks the sponsors. Then it is the turn of the Mayor, who says that The Prize "is part of the history of our country".

The final vote has not started yet. The audience are getting restless and noisy. The press officer is conferring with The Publisher, who finally stands up and goes to The President of The Academy. He whispers something in his ear. The President of The Academy shakes his head. He goes to the chairman of the jury. The chairman of the jury nods gravely. Then they call The President. There is a heated discussion at the back of the platform. The assistants come and go frantically. The audience want to know what is happening. By now it is obvious that something is wrong, but what?

In the end, after much consultation, the host gets up on the platform. This is going out live on the media. He looks ashen, and his voice breaks as he reads a brief statement: The Writer has taken his own life.

There is a murmur of dismay, incredulity, sadness. Then silence. A grim silence like that preceding a storm. Everyone freezes, like statues in a living Nativity. Mobile phones start ringing, all together, like crazed cicadas. The news is out, and people are calling. They have heard about it on television, they want confirmations or denials. Rumours are already circulating: it is said that there is a suicide note, although it has not yet been broadcast. After a while, the host returns to the platform. Yes, it is true, the note has arrived. It is more than a note, it is a long letter. The chairman gets up on the platform and reads it.

A few people weep. Others laugh. Others still remain silent.

The Prize committee gather. Something like this has never happened before. The rules do not even have any provision for it. After what seems an interminable time, The President of The Academy moves away from the group and gets up on the platform to make an announcement. After much consultation the jury has decided to award The Prize to The Writer, in his memory. It has been a difficult decision, and the controversy begins raging almost immediately. The other two finalists are besieged by the press.

"It's a real tragedy. I'm deeply shocked. I've lost a friend, and literature has lost one of its leading lights. I hope this sacrifice makes us stop and think. We are all responsible for what has happened..." These are The Publisher's first, spontaneous words. The Beginner weeps as he tries to brush off the TV cameras. "Leave me alone," he says. "I have nothing to say, I only want to go home." "Today, Justice died," says The Master. "This theoretical victory is a travesty."

It is almost midnight, and the journalists who are waiting to file their stories can wait no longer. From Police Headquarters comes the news that some clothes have been found on the banks of the Tiber and The Writer's Wife has identified them: they are her husband's. The search is beginning for his body. Villa Naike is emptying. The west wind is starting to blow. The sultry heat is fading. But not the grief.

F.B.

*Silent, like gloves fallen from the pockets of distracted pedestrians, an untold number of rooks (*Corvus frugilegus*) lie in the snow at the sides of the roads in Sweden.*

*In the Po Valley, hundreds of turtle doves (*Streptopelia turtur*) cover the fields and ditches with a carpet of coffee-coloured feathers.*

*Thousands of red-winged blackbirds (*Agelaius phoeniceus*) rain down like advertising leaflets from the oblivious sky of Arkansas.*

There's nothing unusual in this, says an expert. Hundreds of similar cases occur every year, some reported in the media, some not.

There are those who maintain that the blackbirds died because of a trauma suffered in flight, perhaps a sudden change in temperature between the different layers of the atmosphere, a patch of turbulence or a violent storm. Others claim that the birds flew too close to radar waves, or that they were electrocuted by high-tension cables.

Some ascribe the deaths of the rooks to a trauma caused by fireworks on New Year's Eve. Scientists are unconvinced by this theory.

There are those who hypothesize that the turtle doves were poisoned, or died of indigestion after eating sunflower seeds. The test results will soon be known, according to a veterinarian.

There are many who maintain that it is a bad omen, a threat of divine punishment, recalling the Old Testament and the ten plagues of Egypt (Exodus 7:14).

It could also be a variation in the Earth's magnetism.

If only men looked up at the sky, they would see the swallows turning acrobatically, the jackdaws returning at sunset with twigs in their beaks, the crows coming to rest on the lamp posts, the sparrows pecking at pots of basil on window sills, the egrets closing their wings like umbrellas with broken ribs, the bitterns drying their feathers in the cold morning wind, the water rails patrolling the banks of the river, the hungry kites flying up from ruined towers, the heavy-winged screech owls crossing the dream-laden night.

If only men looked up at the sky, they would see this and much more. But they don't.

We can die if no one looks at us.

EPILOGUE

(Four months after The Ceremony)

I N A MODEST CASKET in the middle of the nave lay the body of The Master.

A hurried ceremony, in a church on the outskirts of the city. Presided over by an elderly priest who couldn't wait to go home. On the coffin, carried by The Director of The Small Publishing Company along with the undertaker's assistants, a shabby wreath of flowers and a collection of poetry. When they left the church, the few mourners, instead of following the hearse to the cemetery, had drifted away.

In Rome it was late autumn. There was wind, and swollen clouds scurried across the sky. An oblique light hit the façade of the church and bounced off the roofs of the cars.

The Publisher descended the steps with his hands in his pockets. The Master had died alone, he thought, just as he had lived. A death as incomprehensible as it was absurd.

A short circuit. That was what he'd heard. The fuse had blown as he was inserting the plug of a robot vacuum cleaner, a kind of electronic broom The Master had won by gaining points from a mail-order wine company. The shock had been so great that, when the neighbour had found him, she hadn't managed to prise his hand away from the broom handle, as if they had been soldered together into one mass. Definitely far too prosaic for the death of a poet.

That was all the rumour The Publisher had managed to pick up. What he did not know is that days later, at Torchio Wines, they had realized that the number of stickers sent by The Master was definitely greater than they had counted, because he had stuck some on the back of the coupon. That changed everything. It wasn't the robot vacuum cleaner he was due, but the first prize: the laptop computer complete with scanner, printer and a distance-learning course in IT. Except that where The Master was now, the distance really was too far.

After ringing the bell in vain and checking the address again, the courier had deposited the package outside the closed gate. A prostitute whose pitch was outside the house had signed for The Master, maintaining she was a friend of his. Which was true.

Fortunately, there are also happy things to report: The Girlfriend has given birth to a lovely, healthy baby girl who weighed 3 kilos 200 grams at birth.

The Beginner isn't writing another novel, but has started work on a script for a not very good TV drama series. He is being well paid, but sometimes, before falling asleep, the thought hits him that he is wasting his time and ought to go back to literature. And there's no reason to suppose he won't, sooner or later.

The fauna of metropolitan areas is increasingly intelligent. Over the generations, the animals found in our cities have developed bigger brains and ever more sophisticated methods of adaptation. In a remarkably short time, the miracle of evolution has made them capable of adapting to an environment as rich in stimuli as the urban one. Among the many such animals, those that appear to be most comfortable in an urban environment are definitely the birds. And among the many species, the exotic ones have demonstrated a particularly surprising and unexpected ability to adapt. Along the avenues, in the heart of the city parks, or in the outlying districts, it is an increasingly frequent occurrence to come across multi-coloured specimens of parrots, like the ring-necked parakeet or the blue-fronted Amazon which—having escaped from their cages—have proliferated, driving away even the local bird life.

*

In nature, there are about 350 kinds of parrots. At least eighty-one have been recognized and studied. Some have never been domesticated. Only a few of these psittacines are birds that belong in aviaries or are raised as pets.

Outside the ring road, between uncultivated fields and abandoned warehouses, not far from an overpass, where the city comes together with the countryside without agreeing, is a house with a satellite dish on the roof. There are no other buildings in the immediate vicinity. Just a vineyard with withered grapes and a greenhouse with a shattered roof. The house is surrounded by a low wall of grey concrete ending in an iron gate. The plants have grown wild, the windows are closed. And to judge from the flyers heaped in the letter box, the occupants, assuming there are any, can't be very sociable people. If there were TV cameras at the entrance, it would be the perfect hideout for a fugitive. But there aren't any, there's only an entryphone. Without a name.

The one The Publisher has just rung. The automatic gate has opened, and The Publisher has driven his Porsche into the courtyard.

Now he opens the boot and takes out two plastic bags with the logo of a big supermarket chain. Swaying because of the weight, he drags the bags to the door. He puts them down on a doormat that stinks of cat's piss, sticks his hands in the pocket of his camel-hair coat, pulls out a bunch of keys, opens the door, picks up the bags again and, pushing the door with his shoulders, goes inside.

The light is off. There is no fire in the fireplace, of which all that can be seen is the blackened hood. The television, though, is on, tracing the outlines of things with its purple light. There is someone in the room. A man sitting in an armchair with his back to the door. He has an electric heater next to him. He is staring at the screen. Seen from behind, his motionless head looks like the head of a huge match.

"Why are all the lights off? What are you doing in the dark?"

The Publisher puts the bags down on the table, next to a typewriter and a ream of paper. He turns the light on. The room is untidy and smells musty. Everything is covered with a thin layer of dust, like morning frost. There are paintings on the walls, landscapes and still lifes. In a corner, an empty cage with the door open. It was the former tenant's. He had a magpie. Something is shining on the mantelpiece, an object rescued from oblivion, a brass plaque in a burnished frame. We are too far away to read what is on it.

"I got you a lot of shopping."

The Publisher takes the bags into the kitchen.

The man does not reply, he is motionless, watching the TV.

The popular evening quiz is on. Millions of Italians, at that precise moment, are seeing that same studio, with the chessboard floor, and a set that looks like a police station the way they are depicted in comic strips. On the stage, the usual mystery man with lights trained on him, standing on a platform. Just below him, the usual contestant. Obviously not the usual one, they change every evening, but you'd never know the difference. The usual presenter—he really is the usual one—is squinting and frowning in an effort to convey the pathos of the moment: everything is in the balance, nothing is yet lost.

"Pasta, tinned tomatoes, tuna, beans, peas, canned meat..." The Publisher fills the cupboards, making a great racket with the cans.

"Shhh!"

The man in the armchair wants to hear the programme. There are captions over the image on the screen. The contestant has to guess the identity of the mystery man just from his physical features.

The presenter reads from the outsize facsimile of an identity card that he has in his hand: "For 50,000 euros, this man *is a handwriting expert, makes Christmas cribs, tests mozzarella cheeses…*"

In the background, a choir of trumpets tries to increase the suspense, but it's so emphatic, so insistent, it sounds like a village band rehearsal.

The presenter continues: "*…is a local government councillor, took part in the 2000 Sydney Olympics…*"

"I've brought some newspapers and magazines. Shall I leave them here?"

"Wherever you like."

"I couldn't find the herbal teas you asked me for. They don't have them in the supermarket here. Maybe the next time I'll try in the centre…"

"Let me hear."

"I say… he makes Christmas cribs!" the competitor ventures.

"Is that your final answer?" the presenter asks.

"Imbecile."

"What?"

"It's obvious he doesn't have the hands for it."

"Who?"

"Him."

The man indicates the screen with his chin. The Publisher turns to look.

"For fifty thousand euros… do you make Christmas cribs?" asks the presenter.

The music draws out the sense of expectation.

"No, I don't make Christmas cribs," the mystery man replies.

"What a pity!" the presenter says, turning to the contestant. "You've just lost 50,000 euros!"

"What an idiot."

The man turns. We know him too well to introduce him again. He is a man who was afraid of dying.

"Were you at the funeral?"

"Yes."

"Was anybody there?"

"A few people, not many."

"What about mine? When are we doing it?"

"You can't have a funeral without a body."

"You promised."

"I'm working on it, give it time. There's a bishop we're publishing a book by, maybe he'll agree to—"

"I'm tired of staying here. When are the papers coming?"

"It's a matter of days. A month at the most."

"A month!"

"Weeks, I hope."

"I want to be on the island by Christmas. I saw the satellite weather report: slightly cloudy, 31°C."

"You'll be there, don't worry."

"..."

"..."

"And the book?"

"Still on top."

"How many copies so far?"

"Nine hundred thousand."

"..."

"..."

"How's your mother?"

"She's making progress. She can't talk. But she's started writing again. She's the ideal writer."

The Publisher smiles. The Writer doesn't.

"I'd like to see her before I leave."

"That's not a good idea. She's still quite poorly."

"How are my girls?"

"They're fine. I'm taking them to the mountains for a bit of skiing."

"…"

"…"

"What about The Baby?"

"We're taking The Nanny. But in a couple of years she'll be wearing skis herself. Children never fall. They have a low centre of gravity."

"Right… What are your sleeping arrangements at the hotel?"

"Shall I open the window just a little? It's stuffy in here."

"It's all the same to me."

The Publisher goes to the window and opens it. It's cold outside. The countryside is bare and bleak. The Writer also stands and looks outside. What he sees is a snow-white beach and a turquoise sea.

"I've started writing again."

"Oh."

"By typewriter. Like the old days."

"Will you let me read some of it?"

"Not for the moment."

"Can you tell me anything about it?"

"No. But it's coming along. It's coming along really well."

"I'm pleased. If there's nothing else, I should go."

"Go."

"I'll send you a postcard."

"If you like."

The Publisher goes towards the door, then stops.

"Shall I close the window for you?"

"I'll close it."

The Writer is still looking outside. In the distance, a dark stripe in the emerald green: the barrier reef.

"All right."

The Publisher leaves.

The quiz has finished. The Writer switches off the TV. There is a sudden loud noise, something falling. The Writer turns. It's a vase, which has fallen to the floor and smashed. On the window sill sits a bird.

A black parrot.

The parrot spreads its wings, flies cleanly, expertly and soundlessly across the room and into the empty cage, and lands on the perch.

The man and the bird exchange looks. They know each other.

Postscript

The Writer has written a good book: 230 pages, roughly 400 grams in weight, 300 short of the weight needed to break the floor at The Academy. He is unsure whether or not to send it to them. He would like to compete for The Prize. Under a pseudonym, obviously.

ACKNOWLEDGEMENTS

For many and various reasons, I would like to thank: Mario Desiati, Manuela Maddamma, Sandro and Manuela Veronesi, Edoardo and Carlotta Nesi, Edoardo Albinati, Domenico Procacci, Laura Paolucci, Alessia Polli, Francesca Comandini, Tiziana Triana, Giovanni Ferrara, Giovanni Veronesi, Ugo Chiti, Gianfranco Calligarich, Marco Vigevani, Marco Di Porto, Fabio Genovesi, Marco Bologna, Andrea Canepele, Vincenzo ed Elisabetta Bologna, Susanna Boscarelli, Gianna Bologna, Giuseppe Ragazzini, Federico Ferrone, Andrea and Francesca De Micheli. And Lisa Nur Sultan, who I forgot to thank in the first book, and all those I've forgotten to thank in the second.

Pushkin Press

Pushkin Press was founded in 1997. Having first rediscovered European classics of the twentieth century, Pushkin now publishes novels, essays, memoirs, children's books, and everything from timeless classics to the urgent and contemporary.

Pushkin Paper books, like this one, represent exciting, high-quality writing from around the world. Pushkin publishes widely acclaimed, brilliant authors such as Stefan Zweig, Marcel Aymé, Antal Szerb, Paul Morand and Yasushi Inoue, as well as some of the most exciting contemporary and often prize-winning writers, including Andrés Neuman, Edith Pearlman and Ryu Murakami.

Pushkin Press publishes the world's best stories, to be read and read again.

*